When her brother Robin disappeared somewhere in Burma, Isla was, naturally, frantically worried—and she was less than pleased with Woolfe Wieland's attitude. He seemed to be far less concerned with Robin than with the jade amulet that had disappeared with him! So, whether Woolfe liked it or not, Isla was going off to search for her brother in her own way!

Books you will enjoy
by SUE PETERS

MAN OF TEAK

Storm's whole future career depended on her getting back to England from the Far East immediately—yet here she was, stranded in the middle of the jungle, entirely dependent on the whims of Rann Moorcroft, who didn't seem to know or care how urgent was her need to get away. And then Storm realised she was getting emotionally dependent on him as well . . .

DANGEROUS RAPTURE

It had been very kind and generous of Roma's godfather to leave her a valuable racehorse—but had he known what he was doing when he also stipulated that the horse should be trained by Earl Paget? For, quite apart from his maddening, authoritative ways, he was, Roma was sure, not being honest about the situation. But what could she do about it?

TUG OF WAR

There was absolutely no reason why Dee Lawrence's and Nat Archer's paths should cross—but somehow they did, to Dee's dismay and fury. For every time they met the sparks flew—and what was far worse, Nat always got the better of her. Why didn't he just *go away*?

MARRIAGE IN HASTE

Trapped in a Far Eastern country on the brink of civil war, Netta could only manage to escape if she married Joss de Courcy—a man she knew only by his reputation as 'the Fox'. She didn't have much choice in the circumstances—but did he have to treat her as *quite* such a helpless idiot?

JADE

BY

SUE PETERS

MILLS & BOON LIMITED
15-16 BROOK'S MEWS
LONDON W1A 1DR

First published 1982
Australian copyright 1982
Philippine copyright 1982
This edition 1982

© Sue Peters 1982

ISBN 0 263 73901 5

Set in Monophoto Baskerville 9 on 10½ pt.
01 0882 58186

Made and printed in Great Britain by
Richard Clay (The Chaucer Press) Ltd,
Bungay, Suffolk

CHAPTER ONE

'This is *my* taxi. I hired it for my own use, not for public transport,' Isla hissed at him furiously. 'Get out!' she ordered imperiously, 'and hail yourself another. There are plenty of taxis about.'

Instead of getting out, he got in.

'The British Consulate, on the Queen's Walk.' He leaned forward on the seat, and instructed the driver coolly.

'How dare you!' Isla's temper erupted. 'First you invade my taxi, and then you have the effrontery to instruct the driver to take you to the Consulate, when I want to go to Barclays' showrooms.'

She assumed he knew her grandfather's firm had a branch in Kaul. 'If he doesn't, then he's just learned something,' she told herself hotly, and straightaway doubted if the arrogant, dark-haired creature who had just hijacked her transport—and herself at the same time, she realised with a faint prick of alarm—would ever acknowledge that he could learn anything from anyone.

'I should have hailed a tricar instead,' she realised, too late. There would have been no room for Woolfe Wieland to invade a tricar, the bicycle propelled sidecars that had taken over the duties of rickshaws in the narrow streets of Kaul, and wove in and out of the congested traffic with a dexterity that was at once a source of wonder and terror to the intrepid passenger.

'There's no point in you going to Barclays.' Authoritatively he signalled to the taxi driver to proceed, and leaned back comfortably in his seat as if that settled the argument. As if there *was* no argument against him taking over her transport, she thought indignantly. 'Huw Morgan isn't there.'

'Huw wrote to me. . . .' Her pansy-brown eyes flashed with a fire that the meek little flower could never know, ignited by the warning copper lights that glinted in the sun among her soft brown curls.

'It must have been the last letter he signed before he went down with appendicitis.'

'Huw? Appendicitis?' Isla stared at the unwelcome intruder, momentarily nonplussed.

'Huw. Appendicitis,' he confirmed gravely, and added, 'It happened over a week ago. He's out of hospital, so I'm told, and Bethan's carried him off to the coast to convalesce, and enjoy a well-earned holiday.'

His explanation removed the crease of concern from Isla's forehead as to Huw's wellbeing, but it did not remove her dilemma. She had relied on the bow-fronted little Welshman, and his cheerful and equally rotund wife, for accommodation while she was in Kaul, as well as on their help in her search for Robin. Now she would have neither. Their help was of more importance than the accommodation.

'I'll get a room in a hotel here.' She spoke more to herself than to her companion, but he answered her immediately, and with unnerving conviction.

'You won't be able to find a room in Kaul. There isn't any accommodation to be had anywhere within a twenty-mile radius of the town for the next three weeks at least. The place is full to overflowing with delegates to an international scientific conference being held here, and even the river boats are full until the gathering disperses at the end of this month. You'd have done better to have waited,' he informed her loftily, 'instead of rushing off impulsively like that.' His tone suggested that she was probably in the habit of rushing off impulsively, and she reacted to his criticism fierily, stung to her own defence.

'I couldn't wait. Robin's missing. I told you, when I came to see you at Herondale.' She wondered angrily if he had listened to a word she said, when she saw him at Herondale. She repeated her words now, with cutting emphasis, justifying what he so scornfully dismissed as an impulse. 'When I got back from South America I found a letter from Huw to say that he hadn't heard from Robin for over a month. The letter had lain on my desk at our London office for nearly a week, awaiting my return, and given the time it had taken in transit, that means Robin's been missing for six weeks. If you'd got a brother who'd been missing for six weeks, wouldn't you do something about trying to find him?' she demanded passionately.

'Since I haven't got a brother, the question doesn't arise.'

He was as cold as the steel grey coldness of his eyes. Isla decided. She regarded him with acute dislike, and realised that the taxi had drawn to a halt.

'The Consulate.'

Woolfe Wieland ducked out of the taxi door on to the pavement, and his upper half disappeared from Isla's view as he straightened his athletic frame to its full six feet plus, and held open the door for her, in the evident anticipation that she would follow meekly in his wake as he announced,

'The Consulate.'

'I know where we are,' she answered him shortly. She did not need him to tell her. She had been to Kaul before, on business with the branch showrooms there, so she was not totally ignorant of the layout of the town, but this time,

'I shan't be getting out,' she declared firmly. 'I've no need to visit the Consulate.' She sat stubbornly tight in her corner of the taxi seat. It was unsatisfactory, she decided with growing discontent, to defy a face she could not see. The top of the taxi door came to somewhere midway between the middle and the top button of the jacket of his faultlessly tailored tropical weight suit, and she could not judge the effect of her defiance, since she could not see the expression on his face.

'I'm going to Barclays' showrooms,' she stated determinedly. 'If Huw's not there, his relief manager will be, and he'll be able to find me somewhere to stay.' She wished she felt as confident as she sounded. Hotels in Kaul were scarce at the best of times, and a growing tourist trade made booking problematical at short notice. Isla had arrived without any notice at all, sure of her welcome in the Morgan household, and now, faced with a combination of Huw's burst appendix, and a town bursting with conference delegates on top of its usual influx of tourists at this time of the year, she looked like having to sleep on the highly polished floor of the Kaul branch of her grandfather's worldwide chain of antique and fine art emporia.

'If they've got an antique fourposter bed in stock, I could sleep on that.' It would be ironic if she put one of the highly prized artifacts to such mundane use. Perhaps it would help to sell it, she thought flippantly, and visualised the resulting placard.

'Isla Barclay, granddaughter of the founder, slept here. . . .'

A giggle rose inside her at the vision. Huw would have seen the joke; the relief manager might not. The giggle died, and Woolfe Wieland spoke with barely concealed impatience from somewhere above the level of the taxi roof.

'The man who stands in for Huw will be a relief manager, not a magician. He won't be able to produce a hotel room out of a hat. And besides,' he added casually, 'it won't be necessary. I've already arranged for a room to be made available for you at the Consulate.'

'You've . . . what?' His cool announcement slid her across the taxi seat, and cricked her neck at an angle that brought his face back into view.

'Do you still intend to throw yourself on the relief manager's mercy, and risk sleeping on the floor of the showroom?' He read her mind with disconcerting accuracy. 'Or are you going to get out of the taxi, and claim the room that's waiting for you here, and incidentally allow the driver to go on his way, instead of standing with his meter ticking over, and costing me about a pound a minute?' he reminded her with asperity.

'I'll pay my own fare,' she flared independently as the driver deposited her case on the pavement, and Woolfe Wieland deposited the requisite amount of currency in the man's other, outstretched hand. 'No, I won't. Why should I?' She instantly changed her mind. 'I didn't invite you to share my taxi.' More than ever she wished she had given in to Pat Kench's urging, to allow him to accompany her right to her destination, instead of simply dropping her at the airport on the outskirts of Kaul, and immediately taking off again to pick up her grandfather from his fishing holiday in Norway, and incidentally reporting her own whereabouts to the former without being too precise as to why she had come to Kaul.

'I'll telex Grandfather later,' she promised Pat to assuage his concern. 'Perhaps I'll have found out a little more about Robin's whereabouts, in the meantime.' She knew she could rely on the pilot's discretion. It was that invaluable attribute which had secured for him the position of Luke Barclay's personal pilot, when the head and founder of the House of Barclay first decided to take to the air to ease the growing pressure of travel demanded by his rapidly expanding chain, of which he now had a showroom in every major capital, and not a few second cities.

First Robin, and then later Isla, joined him in the business, each equally fascinated by what their grandfather, his enthusiasm undiminished in spite of his sixty-odd years, described as 'one long treasure hunt,' and each now took their share of the travelling, and relied equally as much as their elderly relative upon Pat Kench's services.

'I wish I'd allowed Pat to stay with me until I reached the showrooms. Woolfe Wieland wouldn't have been able to take over my taxi in this high-handed manner, if Pat had been with me.' Her eyes travelled wrathfully over the clean-cut face of the interloper, his square, determined jaw, and told her mind that even the Pat Kenches of this world, formidable though they might be, would in no whit deter the owner of such a jaw from following any course he chose to take, and that right to its conclusion.

And Pat was gone. Isla had stood at the airport and watched the sleek executive jet take to the air, and thrust aside the desolation that swept over her as it disappeared over the horizon, with the comforting thought that,

'There's Huw and Bethan. It isn't as if I shall be in Kaul completely on my own.'

And now, Huw and Bethan were gone too, and being on her own would be infinitely preferable, she decided with a hostile glare, to Woolfe Wieland's unwanted interference in her affairs. It was a replica of the glare she directed at him when they first met. His appearance was as unexpected then, as his presence in Kaul was to her now. 'And just as unwelcome,' she muttered sourly.

She knew his name, of course. Woolfe Wieland of Herondale Court was known to all the fine art world as a discerning collector, and a renowned expert on jade, but he was also known to shun publicity, and no photograph of him ever appeared in the popular press, as was usual with other wealthy collectors. When his name was mentioned in conversation between her brother and her grandfather, it was always in connection with their common interest, the antique under question at the moment, and Isla's mental picture of the collector remained a shadowy thing. If she thought of him at all, it was as an elderly, benign man, perhaps with a slight stoop, and a white beard.

The tall, athletic-looking, self-assured creature into whose presence she was ushered when she reached Herondale Court was the exact opposite of anything she had always imagined him to be. 'And not half so pleasant,' she told herself critically. Until that day, she had never crossed Woolfe Wieland's path. Even as the thought occurred to her, she wondered at the way in which her mind couched the words, but they so aptly described their first meeting, 'and the second one today,' she reminded herself tartly, that she let the description lie. Woolfe Wieland's interest in antiques lay in other than the ancient embroideries that were Isla's speciality, so when there was an article which he wished to dispose of, or to acquire, it was Robin's or her grandfather's expertise he sought, and there had previously been no reason for herself and the collector to meet.

In one brief afternoon, Robin's letter had changed all that. It gave her a reason, and an urgent one, to seek out the collector now. The envelope was waiting for Isla on her desk, along with the letter from Huw, when she returned from her business trip to South America, and went straight to the office to pick up her mail before going home. She had been away for nearly two months, and she slit open Robin's letter right away, eager for his news.

'The Kang amulet's been stolen,' her brother wrote baldly, and Isla gasped. The words seemed to leap up at her from the page, and dance before her disbelieving eyes. The Kang amulet. . . . Robin might as well have said, 'the Crown Jewels'. The drop-shaped pendant was of rare, carved white jade, inlaid with gold and precious stones, and opened like a locket. The space inside it contained an irreplaceable talisman, the tiny scroll brush written in minute detail in coloured Oriental characters, and intended to guard the wearer of the amulet against the ills and evils of the universe. Isla blinked, and read the words again to make sure that the fatigue of jet-lag was not making her imagine them.

'The Kang amulet!' she breathed, as if saying the words out loud might help them to sink in more clearly. Her grandfather's description of the piece came back to her. 'It's one of the oldest known pieces of jade of its kind, and together with the talisman, it's worth a king's ransom.' His ad lib valuation was to take on another, more frightening meaning later on, but now she hastily read on.

'In a way, I feel partly responsible for its loss,' Robin continued in a hurried scrawl. 'Some disagreement apparently arose as to which dynasty the scroll inside the amulet belongs. One school of thought put the amulet itself as being of the Shang dynasty, but the scroll it contains as being of a later period, probably late Chou, or even into the Han period. The argument's purely academic, of course.' Isla could imagine Robin's shrug. 'It doesn't alter the value of the whole, but I suggested to the Governors of the Oriental Museum that they might like to send the amulet to Wieland for him to form a judgment. There's no greater expert in the subject, and his opinion would settle the argument once and for all, before it becomes acrimonious.'

Isla knew how easily such arguments could flare up, and the often permanent estrangements that resulted. Each branch of the fine art world had its own devotees, and its own set of experts, firmly entrenched in their own opinions, and unwilling to concede an inch of jealously guarded ground to others who were equally knowledgeable, but who differed on what Isla regarded as unimportant detail. Robin had obviously attempted to pour oil on the troubled waters of one such conflict of opinions, and succeeded instead in starting a train of events that led to not only the Kang amulet going missing, but Robin himself as well.

'The amulet was stolen in transit to Herondale,' her brother's letter went on, 'you know how careless some of these people can be.'

'I know very well,' Isla thought wryly. She deplored the often casual way in which priceless objets d'art were sometimes transported, but had herself been equally guilty of slipping an antique ring on her finger, and her glove over the ring, and relying on the sheer everyday ordinariness of her method to protect the vaulable article she carried, believing, as did others in the trade, that over-assiduous precautions attracted rather than deterred the attentions of would-be thieves. With a growing crease between her eyes, Isla read on.

'By the most fantastic piece of luck, a whisper reached me through the Kaul branch as to where the amulet might be destined for, and I'm on my way now to talk to Huw Morgan. I can't say more on paper, but you'll understand when I tell you that I think it's on its way to a certain private collector. . . .'

'And once in that private collection, the Kang amulet will never see the light of day again,' Isla prophesied. Nearly all collectors enjoyed showing off their acquisitions, but there was a tiny minority of people in different parts of the world whose love of the items they collected turned into an obsession, and having the wherewithal to gratify their craving, they were prepared to employ any means to lay hands on the articles they coveted.

The Kang amulet was one such article.

'I'd be grateful if you'd let Woolfe Wieland know what's happening,' Robin ended his letter. 'I haven't time to write to you both. The trail seems to lead from Kaul to the north-east, and with luck I may be able to discover the whereabouts of the amulet, and invoke the aid of the authorities in its recovery, so long as it hasn't already been taken across the border. I'll keep in touch with Huw Morgan to report progress. Wish me luck!'

Isla did, most heartily. She saw no cause, then, to be alarmed by her brother's activities, until she learned what Huw had to say. Robin was more than capable of looking after himself, and was no doubt enjoying the added excitement of this particular treasure hunt. Unsuspecting, she started to read Huw's letter.

'Robin's following up several possible clues as to the whereabouts of the amulet,' the Welshman wrote. 'One particularly strong lead has taken him into the interior, and he promised to send word to me as to his whereabouts. For the first three weeks I heard from him regularly, through various sources.' They would be devious sources, Isla guessed. Robin would not want to advertise his journey, or its purpose. He had probably sent a runner back to Kaul with some innocuous message that would serve to tell Huw of his progress. 'For the last four weeks,' Huw wrote on, 'there's been no word at all from Robin, and I'm becoming concerned.'

To say that she felt the same would be an understatement. Isla's mind froze as she visualised the 'interior', as Huw called it. Wild, mountainous country, the lower slopes jungle-clad, the highest peaks towards the northern border almost permanently covered in snow, and all sparsely inhabited by only an occasional village, and the inevitable small monasteries that clung to the mountain ledges with the same precarious hold as the narrow mountain passes, across which only the most hardy would venture. Over the edges of which lay dizzy drops. . . . Isla shook her thoughts to an abrupt halt, and flicked the intercom to speak to her grandfather's secretary.

'Is Pat Kench in the country?'

Within the hour she was winging her way to Herondale Court. 'There's no problem, Miss Isla,' the pilot assured her cheerfully when she put her proposition to him, 'Mr Wieland's got a longer landing strip at Herondale than your grandfather has on the Downs.' Isla did not care how long the collector's landing strip was, provided its owner could help her.

'He might have a clue as to where Robin's heading.' She unburdened her worries to the pilot as they flew north. 'Woolfe Wieland knows the world of jade as well as we do. Better than I do.' She could have contacted Huw, or her grandfather, but Woolfe Wieland was in the country, and therefore closer. Besides, Robin had asked her specifically to contact him. 'Surely he'll be able to suggest something?' she worried. 'He *must* be able to suggest something,' she insisted tensely.

Woolfe Wieland's suggestion, when she was ushered into the high-ceilinged drawing room at Herondale, was as unpalatable as his appearance was unexpected to her, and before the double doors closed softly on the retreating manservant, Isla knew that her journey had been a complete waste of time. She had scarcely blurted out the reason for her presence at Herondale when he cut across her explanation with an incisive,

'Stay at home where you belong, and leave finding your brother to professionals.'

His suggestion was blunt, and to the point, and the tone in which he made it, turned it into an order. How dared he presume to order her? Isla stared at him, too taken aback by his totally unexpected refusal to help her, to think up an immediate reply. She felt as if her mouth dangled open, so great was her surprise at the collector's attitude. Indignation overcame her surprise, and she shut it again with a snap.

'You don't care that Robin's missing,' she accused him furiously. 'All you care about is the amulet.' When she obeyed Robin's instructions to go to Herondale she had felt so certain, so confident. . . . She followed the manservant to the drawing room doors with the feeling that her mission was already half accomplished. There was another man in the room with him, but the collector dominated his surroundings. Both the men rose as Isla was announced, but it was to the tall, black-haired man with the hatchet face and the keen grey eyes that she addressed herself, knowing him instinctively to be the owner of Herondale Court. A detached part of her mind jeered at her previously imagined picture of the well-known collector.

'How wrong can you get?' it laughed scornfully.

While her other, more immediate senses, reeled from the shock of the encounter. For some reason she felt suddenly breathless, as if she had been running, and became aware that her mouth and throat were dry, so dry that her tongue seemed to stick when she spoke. She swallowed, and her carefully rehearsed words deserted her.

'I'm Isla Barclay . . . Robin's written to say he's missing . . . I mean, Huw said . . . I mean, the Kang amulet. . . .'

He hadn't, and he didn't, and what she meant was. . . . Her tongue gave up trying, and Isla stammered to a halt, and all the time the cool grey eyes watched her, and their owner remained gravely silent, and made her confusion worse. She hated him for his aloof silence. She had come to Herondale Court intending to place the facts before him, and make a dignified plea for assistance, and instead she was stammering like a gauche schoolgirl, nailed to the spot by a pair of steel grey eyes that seemed to bore right through her, and pick the words out of her mind with consummate ease before they were even uttered. It had simply not occurred to her that he might refuse the assistance she sought. If only he would say something, exhibit some kind of concern, anything but this impenetrable barrier of silence. He broke it with a suddenness that made Isla jump.

'I think you'd better sit down,' he said.

Even the chair he offered to her was a surprise. 'You like it?' He noticed her instinctive appraisal of the piece of furniture as, she felt sure, his penetrating glance noticed every other single detail about her, from her short, slight figure, that obliged her to accept the indignity of a box to stand on when she was conducting an auction in the course of her work, to her fine-boned, mobile features that gave away more than she was aware of her inner feelings.

'It's elegant.' And modern, too, she saw with surprise. Somehow she had not expected to find modern furniture in Woolfe Wieland's ancestral home, but there the likeness to factory-made furniture ended. She ran her fingers across the beautifully shaped beech armrests, sank into the fine tweed upholstery, and relished the feel of both. This was modern furniture at its beautiful best, hand-crafted, and of inspired design. A prized antique of the future.

'I find the cost of much antique furniture is exceeded only by its extreme ugliness,' he read her thoughts with disconcerting accuracy, and a straight look that warmed Isla's cheeks with a sudden uprush of temper. It was an impertinence, she fumed, to attempt to read another person's thoughts. An unwarrantable intrusion on the last bastion of privacy. Her own thoughts became indignant, and bright flags of resentment hoisted banners under the attractive tan she had acquired during her stay in the deep South.

'This is beautiful.' She answered him shortly, unwilling to seem to praise the taste of the owner whom she most definitely did not like, but whose furniture, reluctantly, she did. Automatically she glanced about her. Nothing in the room could be deemed to be out of place, and yet antique was blended with hand-crafted modern in a perfectly chosen admixture that spoke volumes for the informed taste of the owner. Isla's eyes lighted on a lady's writing desk, near to the window. It was an antique, and the reverse of ugly, with dainty cabriole legs, and inlay work that bore the stamp of an artist.

'French, Louis XV,' she automatically dated the piece in her own mind, and wondered if the desk belonged to Woolfe Wieland's wife. And wondered still more at the sharp pang her own unanswered question sent through her.

'Your brother acquired that particular piece for me.' Once again, he knew what she was thinking.

'And now Robin's missing.' She felt sudden shame for even

such slight inattention that had caused her mind to wander away
from the purpose of her visit.

'I think you'd better sit down.'

He did not attempt to introduce the other man to her. Indeed,
he placed the chair in such a position that when she sat down,
she had her back to him. So silent was the other occupant of the
room that the only way Isla could tell he was still there was an
occasional sharp clicking sound as he thumped the top of a slim
gold ball point pen up and down. She wished irritably that he
would either desist, or go away. She found herself waiting for
the next click. It had the unnerving uncertainty of a dentist's
drill on her already overwrought nerves. It was not until afterwards she realised that, although she had noticed his ballpoint
pen was gold, she could not clearly remember what the man
himself looked like. He was acceptably dressed, but his features
were unremarkable, and would easily pass unnoticed in a crowd.
Isla sat down on the chair, and promptly forgot him.

'Robin's missing. He's not been heard of for six weeks.' She
had her tongue under better control now, even if her pulses still
hammered in the most disconcerting manner.

'So I understand.'

Her host did not say whether he understood from herself, or
from someone else. He evinced no surprise at the news, which
made her suspect that it was no longer news to him, and his
reply was as uncommittal as it was unhelpful. Isla's lips tightened, and she controlled her temper with an effort.

'Robin asked me to come to you, to let you know what he
was doing,' she persisted with a growing feeling of desperation,
which made her add sharply, 'so he must have thought you'd at
least be interested.' Her pansy brown eyes condemned him for
not being interested in her brother's plight. 'You collect jade,'
she reminded him forcibly, 'so you must have some idea as to
who might try to steal the Kang amulet, and where its eventual
destination might be.' Which meant, near enough, the possible
whereabouts of her brother.

'I study jade, I don't collect it,' Woolfe Wieland corrected
her. He paused for a moment, and then added deliberately, 'I
prefer to collect miniatures.'

He waved his hand towards a glass-fronted display cabinet as he spoke, on the polished shelves of which miniatures of all kinds were arranged to their best advantage; tiny portraits, snuffboxes, china. Minute replicas covering the whole spectrum of collectable works of art, each the finest of its kind, but while his hand indicated his treasures, his eyes, Isla realised with a distinct sense of shock, his eyes rested upon herself, and in them, the blood rose again to her cheeks with an angry rush, in them was an expression that made his underlying meaning crystal clear.

'*I'm* not a collectable item.' She gained her feet with one swift, furious jump, and wished too late that she had stopped to put on a pair of high-heeled shoes before she came. Her soft, flat pumps, so comfortable for travelling, did nothing to add to her oft-lamented lack of inches. She was herself miniature, and exquisitely formed, but her presence in his house gave its odious owner absolutely no right. . . . She faced him with blazing eyes, a tiny, outraged figure, whose rage was made the greater because she had to tilt her head back in order to fling her anger into his face.

'The man's an oaf! He's a . . . a. . . .' A gentle upbringing checked her thoughts to a shocked halt, and her cheeks warmed to an even deeper hue that they should cross her mind at all.

'If you won't help me to find Robin, I'll go on my own,' she blazed. 'Stay here among your miniatures!' she shouted at him contemptuously. In her eyes, the collector's image had shrunk to just about their size, and uncaringly she made plain her opinion of him. She was shouting at one of the most valued clients of the House of Barclay, and she did not care about that, either.

'The International Security Force has already been alerted to look for the Kang amulet,' Woolfe Wieland's voice hardened perceptibly. 'Any ill-judged action on your part might well jeopardise the results of their efforts.'

'What do I care about the Kang amulet?' Isla interrupted him passionately. 'It's Robin's safety I'm concerned about, not a piece of carved jade, no matter which dynasty, or whatever, it happens to belong to. And as for your International Security Force,' she dismissed that worthy body with a scornful toss of her head, 'so long as *they* don't jeopardise *my* efforts, I don't care what they do.'

'You little spitfire!'

The grey eyes fired, and unexpectedly the collector stepped forward, and grasped her by the wrist. Isla had no time to back away. Before she knew what he was about to do, steel fingers locked around her arm, and in spite of the armour of her own anger, a thrill that was not unlike fear pierced through her, and she flinched away from the rapier thrust of his steely glare. Fear, and something else she could not define, that sent tingles like electric shocks along her arm from where he held her, that had nothing to do with the force of his grip. She thrust the feeling aside, too impatient to try to define it, and opened her mouth to answer him back, but swiftly, he spoke first.

'I won't have you taking off on a hunt on your own, and probably snarling up any arrangements I've made with the Security Force.'

Arrangements that no doubt included the Kang amulet, and excluded Robin, Isla told herself bitterly, and defied him with the bitterness sharp on her tongue.

'I'll go where I please, when I please, and there's nothing you can do to stop me!' she cried shrilly, and added on an impulse, 'Perhaps if you'd condescend to share the details of your arrangements with me, I might be able to avoid my movements clashing with your so secret Security Force,' she suggested sarcastically.

'Mr Wieland. . . .'

The other man spoke, on a note of warning. Isla had completely forgotten his presence in the room, and surprise checked the angry words that tumbled from her tongue.

'He *has* got a voice, then,' she thought bitingly, and realised that Woolfe Wieland's grasp upon her arm had slackened. The other man's unexpected intervention had momentarily diverted his attention, and she took instant advantage of her opportunity.

'You can make whatever arrangements you please!' With a quick twist she freed her arm from the collector's grasp, and spinning away from him she ran towards the double doors of the big drawing room. 'I'm going to find Robin,' she flung her defiance over her shoulder, and fled. She passed the surprised-looking manservant who hovered in the hall, ran out of the house, and across the velvet-smooth lawns, to where Pat Kench waited patiently with the plane at the end of the landing strip which dissected the surrounding parkland in a ribbon of dark tarmac.

'Miss Barclay! Come back. . . .'

Isla ignored the shout. Although she did not look back, she felt certain it was not Woolfe Wieland who shouted, but the other, unknown man. She wrenched open the door of the light plane, and scrambled up beside Pat without waiting for him to help her.

'Take me to Kaul, Pat. Now!'

She slammed the door to behind her with unnecessary force, and leaned back in her seat, and discovered she was trembling, as if she had just evaded capture, and felt ashamed of the flood of relief that washed over her as the executive jet rose like a bird under the pilot's expert guidance, and circled to gain height over the trees before it set course on its journey.

Isla peered downwards through the window as they crossed low above the front of Herondale Court. The nondescript-looking man who had shouted, was standing on the gravel sweep in front of the house, looking up at the plane, and beckoning with both arms, as if he was trying to wave them down again. Isla saw something glint in the sun as he waved, as if he still held the thin gold ballpoint pen in his fingers. She wondered with a quirk of laughter if his thumb was still clicking the top of it up and down in his evident agitation, as he beckoned to them with fruitless urgency.

'Shall we drop down again, Miss Isla? It looks as if that chap's trying to call you back.' Pat peered downwards as well. 'Is that Mr Wieland?' he asked curiously.

'No, don't, and it isn't,' Isla replied decisively. 'I need to talk to Huw Morgan in person, and that without delay. Get me to Kaul, Pat, as quickly as you can,' she urged him. By sheer good fortune she had kept her luggage with her from her previous journey, which meant her passport as well, and she knew the pilot always carried his own papers with him, being accustomed to having to take off at a moment's notice to all points of the compass.

'That's Woolfe Wieland, standing on the top of the steps.' The owner of Herondale Court stood with his head upraised, framed by the stone canopy that rested on imposing pillars to shelter the entrance to his lovely old home. Isla caught her breath. The plane by now was too high for her to be able to distinguish the colour of the collector's eyes, but their height, and the closed cabin of the plane, were not sufficient, she discovered with a sudden shiver, to protect her from the steel of his stare, just as the rapidly increasing distance between them was not enough to allay the tingle in her arm that remained despite the fact that Woolfe Wieland's fingers had only held her captive for a brief moment or two, that seemed to her heightened nervousness to last for an aeon of time, and to brand his mark upon her arm for ever.

'That's Woolfe Wieland, standing on the top of the steps.' She responded automatically to Pat Kench's question.

The collector did not move. He did not wave, or gesticulate. He just stood there, watching the plane rise above him, and Isla stared down at him, transfixed, knowing that he saw her staring down, but unable for some reason to drag her eyes away.

Unwittingly, the pilot released her. He banked the plane in a steep turn, and the rising wing on Isla's side hid the house, and its owner, from her view. She collapsed limply back into her seat, and felt like a puppet that had suddenly had its strings released by its manipulator. The comparison acted like a goad on her independent spirit.

'He shan't manipulate me,' she vowed sturdily, and immediately felt better. 'He can remain behind in his olde ancestral home if he wants to,' she snorted scornfully. 'I'm going to find Robin.' With overnight stops for rest and refuelling, she calculated they would reach Kaul in about three days.

It took four days in all for them to reach their destination. For a frustrating twenty-four hours, Isla fumed and fretted while officials at a small border refuelling station hummed and haa'd over stamping perfectly straightforward clearance papers to enable them to start on the next leg of their journey, in one of those unpredictable, time-consuming delays that afflict all travellers from time to time, but,

'Why did it have to happen to *us, now*?' Isla asked the resigned pilot for the umpteenth time. Her only consolation was that the overbearing owner of Herondale Court had been left safely behind her, in England, where he was powerless to check on her movements, let alone to try to interfere.

'And good riddance!' she muttered vindictively.

Twenty-four hours later than she should have arrived, Isla extricated herself from the familiar bustle of Kaul airport, hailed a taxi, and discovered Woolfe Wieland was already there before her, waiting to pounce on herself and her transport, and carry her off to a destination that was quite the opposite to the one she had in mind.

CHAPTER TWO

'How did you get here?' Isla demanded, and without waiting for the collector to reply, fired another question after the first. 'How did you know I was coming to Kaul anyway?'

'It was quite simple, really,' he replied crisply.

Did he have to sound quite so patronising? Isla wondered angrily. She almost expected him to add, 'Elementary, my dear Watson.'

'Well, I don't intend to act as a Watson, simply to boost his ego,' she fumed, and immediately felt deflated when he added,

'You as good as told me your destination yourself,' he reminded her, and bent casually to annexe her luggage with one lean brown hand. With the other he took Isla firmly by the elbow, and steered her inexorably in the direction of the Consulate steps. 'You suggested your first step in trying to find your brother would be to get in touch with Huw Morgan, so it wasn't difficult to put two and two together, and work out your ultimate destination after you rushed away from Herondale with such speed,' he finished with maddening logic.

'You told me to leave finding Robin to professionals.' She tried to shrug herself free from his grasp, and discovered to her chagrin that although his hold upon her arm was light, she was unable to loosen it without engaging in an undignified struggle, which was patently impossible in the middle of Kaul's main thoroughfare, and which she felt uneasily certain she would lose anyway.

'And he knows it,' Isla fumed in helpless frustration, and

wished fervently she might free herself from his hold for another, and much more potent reason than a mere declaration of her independence from him. The feel of the collector's hand upon her arm was doing curious and unexpected things to her circulatory system, and her normally well behaved pulse throbbed with a force that made it sound like a drumbeat in her ears. A warning drumbeat?

The pavement was well sprinkled with strollers, and her unwelcome escort—or captor? she asked herself tartly—automatically drew her close against him to avoid them colliding with other pedestrians, which immediately exacerbated Isla's plight. When he held her at arm's length, it was bad enough, but close to, her breath became jerky and uneven to match her pulse, Woolfe Wieland projected a vibrant magnetism that she had been conscious of, but too angry to be much affected by, when she first met him at Herondale Court. Now, with his hand holding her elbow, and his arm brushing against her shoulder as he walked her beside him up the flight of steps to the Consulate, a strange sense of excitement gripped her that was unlike any other feeling she had ever known before, unlike anything she had ever felt, even while engaged on the exciting treasure hunts occasioned during the course of her work.

This feeling was something new, and strange, and frightening, and yet, she sensed through a growing haze of confusion, it was something that had always been there, biding its time deep down within her, and waiting to burst forth like sweet spring water from the dark earth, when the time was ripe for it to bubble up into the sunshine, yet dazzled by the light, at first not knowing in which direction it should run.

'Away—I must get away!' Panic-stricken, Isla only knew that she must run from Woolfe Wieland, as far and as fast as she could, until she had time to bring under control this strange new emotion that shattered her poise, undermined her confidence, and presented itself bewilderingly as both a promise and a threat.

'It's jet-lag. It's because I've flown west one day, and then straight back east again the next. It's unhinged something,' Isla told herself desperately. She suspected it might be her reason. Certainly it was her self-control. She loathed Woolfe Wieland

. . . didn't she? She caught her breath in a hard gasp, and her toe against the top step of the stone flight. The gasp turned to a cry of dismay, and she stumbled and would have fallen if the collector had not reacted with such speed. She did not see him move, but one minute he was walking calmly beside her, and the next her case rested on the top step, and she rested within the circle of his arms. He scooped her up and stood her on her feet, and held her tightly against him, and she raised enormous, startled eyes to his face.

'Let me go,' she pleaded with him urgently. The shock of catching her toe and stumbling swept away the excitement, but it left the fear behind, a growing tide of dread that threatened to engulf her, scattering her wits in panic flight, but leaving the rest of her still imprisoned in the circle of Woolfe Wieland's arms.

'Let me go!' Her voice rose on a note of desperation when he showed no sign of being willing to comply. 'What will people think?' She did not care, and from his lack of response, neither did he, she realised in dismay.

'If anyone saw what happened, they'll doubtless think I fielded you very neatly, and prevented you from falling flat on your face.' Infuriatingly he took her question at face value, and answered gravely in a tone that was in itself a mockery.

'How smug he sounds,' Isla thought grittily, and opened her mouth to tell him so, to deflate him as he had deflated her a moment ago, and then she caught the twin gleams of laughter lurking like imps in the cool grey eyes that looked down deep into her own. Laughing at her. . . . Bright flags of colour stained her cheeks, and a rising tide of wrath drove away the last vestige of her fear. She itched to smack him for mocking her, to extinguish the laughter from his eyes. Her own sparked with a fiery warning that lesser men might have heeded, but Woolfe Wieland did not.

'For those who didn't see what happened, we'll give them something to think about, shall we?' he murmured softly, and bent his head above her, and lightly, tantalisingly, brushed her lips with his own. Their first touch extinguished the fire, and brought back the fear and the excitement in an overwhelming flood. It captured her mind and drove out every other thought, even her fears for Robin, and brought with it the despairing conviction that no matter what the future might hold for her, she would never belong wholly to herself again. If Woolfe Wieland was to leave her at the Consulate now, and go out of her life for ever, one part of her would always follow him, like a shadow follows the sun, seeking a lost treasure that would never be her lot to find.

'Woolfe . . . darling!'

The girl had red hair, and green eyes. Cat's eyes, Isla saw critically. She must have been watching from one of the windows, to be able to time her arrival through the Consulate door with such exactitude, that left her in complete command of the situation, Isla realised wrathfully, and herself in total disarray.

'Loose me!' she hissed furiously, and pushed hard against him with both hands. This time, unexpectedly, he complied, and her push reacted against herself rather than against him. It rocked her feet as off balance as her poise, and from the gleam in the other girl's watching eyes, Isla felt convinced the timing had been arranged deliberately to put herself at a disadvantage. Even in these enlightened days, it is disconcerting to be disturbed in the middle of a kiss. Illogically Isla resented the intrusion as much as she tried to tell herself she resented the kiss.

'Zoe! It's good to see you.' Woolfe Wieland held out both his hands towards the girl, who grasped them with alacrity, and made a great display of standing on tiptoe to kiss him soundly on the point of the chin, which since the latter did not bend his own head was all she could reach, Isla noticed with vindictive satisfaction, her perception sharpened by the turmoil of her own disturbed feelings. 'How are you?' he asked, as if he really wanted to know. As if they might be old friends. Isla tried to subdue a stab of unexpected jealousy as the other girl replied effusively,

'I'm fine. What's more important, how are you?' She did not ask after his wife—if he had one. Isla noticed that, too, and the jealousy subsided a little under a surge of what she tried not to recognise as hope.

'Travel-stained, and hungry. We both are,' he replied meaningly.

'Then come along in.'

'I thought she'd never ask,' Isla criticised with silent lack of charity. It seemed like a lifetime since she first started to mount the Consulate steps. In terms of experience, it was a lifetime, she reflected bitterly. When she put her foot on the first step, she was heartwhole. Free. By the time she tripped over the last step her heart wore manacles, to which only Woolfe Wieland held the key.

'I've had your room made ready for you.' Zoe spoke to Woolfe, not to herself, as Isla expected.

'So Woolfe's staying here too. He isn't just going to leave me, and then go away himself. He isn't going out of my life. At least, not yet.' She knew just how a condemned prisoner must feel on learning that he was to be reprieved, and she lashed herself with scorn for a feeling she could neither help nor alter.

'I hope you managed to find a room for Isla, too?' Woolfe made the introduction casually, as if it did not really matter either way.

'Oh, yes.' The girl's green eyes flickered over Isla indifferently, and back again immediately to Woolfe. 'When you rang me from Herondale, I kept your usual room,' her smile was honey-sweet, 'and I reserved a room in the staff quarters for your— er—friend.' She left a question hovering in the air like a challenge, and Isla stiffened.

'So Woolfe's a welcome visitor at the Consulate. I wonder why?' That he was welcome to the redheaded Zoe was beyond doubt, but that would not be reason enough for him to stay regularly at the Consulate, often enough, it seemed, for him to have a 'usual room'. Doubtless it was fairly close to Zoe's own room, Isla deduced shrewdly, and a long way away from the staff quarters to which she herself had been relegated, deliberately she felt sure. Woolfe did not appear to have a wife. Perhaps Zoe aspired to that position? Whatever she was to the collector, or what she hoped to be, Isla did not know. 'Or care,' she told herself with staunch untruth, but with the same unquenchable spirit that had driven Luke Barclay to build up his now world-renowned chain of fine art showrooms, while at the same time bringing up singlehanded his two orphaned grandchildren, Isla made her own present position abundantly clear.

'We're not friends,' she declared in a clear voice, and felt rather than saw her companions stare. Woolfe, with a long, enigmatic look that she dared not meet. Zoe with open surprise, in which, Isla thought gleefully, she detected a flash of relief.

'I've come to Kaul to look for my brother,' she stated firmly. 'He's been missing for a number of weeks. Woolfe's come to look for a valuable jade antique that's been stolen.' Unforgivingly, she paraded his callous lack of interest in her missing relative.

'Could the two be connected, perhaps?' Zoe asked with saccharine sweetness, and Isla's face flamed.

'Yes, they are,' she snapped back, and had the satisfaction of seeing Zoe's eyes widen with startled surprise. It was clear the redhead had not expected her to reply, except perhaps to blurt out something in her brother's defence. She obviously did not expect Isla to retaliate. Isla pursued her advantage with unexpected relish. 'The two are connected, but not in the way you mean,' she said grimly, ruthlessly pulling aside the wraps, and exposing the other girl's spiteful insinuation for what it was. How dared Zoe imply that Robin might be the thief? She saw the green eyes narrow, and knew she had made an enemy, and she did not care about that, either. 'Robin was following a lead as to where the jade might be, but nothing's been heard from him now for several weeks.' She did not see any reason why she should give Zoe an explanation, but she gave it anyway. Jade might well be an apt description of the other girl, she decided waspishly, and felt thankful she had never succumbed to the temptation to wear make-up. Her own fine, clear skin, with the light dusting of freckles that aided her slight figure in taking several years off her acknowledged twenty-five, was infinitely easier to cope with in the humid Burmese heat than the heavy matt make-up, however skilfully applied, that still could not conceal Zoe's seniority of several years.

'Older than Woolfe, and trying to disguise the fact,' Isla guessed, intuitively putting the collector's age, correctly she learned later, at nearing thirty, and Zoe at past thirty-three.

'If your brother's been missing for several weeks, you took your time coming to find him,' the other girl suggested with a thinly veiled sneer. 'When Woolfe phoned me to say you were on your way, I assumed you'd come straight here. I expected you yesterday. When you failed to turn up I almost didn't bother to keep your room for you.'

'For two pins I'd tell her to keep it now. I'd rather sleep on the floor of the showrooms than be beholden. . . .'

'I'm afraid the delay was my fault,' Woolfe interrupted her furious thoughts, and sheer surprise kept Isla silent. He apologised to Zoe, not to herself. She stared at him, stunned.

'There was a hold-up at the border check point.' She found her voice, and put her bewilderment into words. How could such a happening be Woolfe's fault? She was prepared to blame him for many things, but. . . .

'A delay at a border checkpoint isn't difficult to manipulate when you've got a senior agent of the International Security Force with you at the crucial moment,' he grinned at her significantly.

'A senior agent . . .?' Her mind flashed back to the other man who had been with the collector in the drawing room at Herondale, and her face turned from scarlet to sheet white.

'The man with the gold ballpoint pen,' she breathed. The man whose appearance was so nondescript as to make him infinitely forgettable, a valuable trait in an agent of an international security force. He could melt into a crowd, and no one would even notice he had been there, let alone that he was gone. And at Woolfe's instigation, he had deliberately engineered twenty-four hours of sheer mind-bending frustration such as she had never experienced before, and hoped never to again, before the clearance papers were stamped, and they were able to resume their journey to Kaul.

'I needed time to catch up with you,' Woolfe grinned.

And to give himself time, he had manipulated her, like a puppet on a string. There was the connotation again, and it had the same inflammatory effect on Isla as before. She clenched her teeth until her jaws felt as if they would crack under the strain. Woolfe's face wavered in front of her eyes, and Zoe's light laugh reached her through a moving mist.

'I'm not a puppet, to be manipulated by you,' she gritted through stiff lips. 'You can't dictate my movements.' He already had, and the knowledge rubbed her pride raw. 'I won't. . . .'

'Did you signal me, Miss Rutherford?'

A man in the uniform of a Consulate guide appeared at Zoe's side, and a bell began to ring faintly in the background, and the other girl answered imperiously,

'Show Miss Barclay to Room Nine in the staff quarters.' She turned to Woolfe. 'We eat in half an hour.' She ignored Isla, and spoke directly to the collector. 'It'll just give you time to freshen up and join me for a drink before the meal.' Her turned back made it plain the invitation to a pre-dinner drink did not include Isla, and her temper rose at the direct snub.

'I won't be joining you for the meal.' She refused it decisively. She felt as if any food she might eat in the company of Woolfe and Zoe would choke her. 'The moment I've changed, I intend to go to the showrooms to have a word with the relief manager there. Robin might have been in touch within the last few days.' It was a forlorn hope, but it was better than nothing. Just as was the urgent wish that by some freak of good fortune the relief manager might be able, after all, to find for her other accommodation than her unwanted room at the Consulate. If he could, she told herself triumphantly, she could at a single stroke rid herself of both Woolfe Wieland and his redheaded girl-friend.

'It won't be of any use you going to the showroom tonight,' the former began, and Zoe interrupted him hastily.

'There's nothing to stop you, of course, if you really want to go.' Her concern was patently to be rid of Isla's company, rather than to aid her in her search, and Isla did not deign to answer. Instead, she turned hard eyes on Woolfe.

'I shall go where I please,' she began heatedly, but he interrupted her with a gesture of impatience.

'The showrooms will be closed by now,' he said curtly, and Isla's lips thinned.

'It's only just gone five o'clock.' She was aware that the showrooms did not close until six, if he was not. 'They're not far away from the Consulate, I can be there in under fifteen minutes.' Less if she could manage to hail a taxi.

'It's gone seven o'clock,' Woolfe contradicted her flatly. 'You can't have put your watch on the final two hours when you left the last border checkpoint.'

He was right, of course. Infuriatingly so. Isla bit her lip and glared helplessly from her innocent timepiece to the collector.

Kaul was seven hours ahead of G.M.T. She had adjusted her watch by the first five hours as their journey progressed, but the frustration of the unexpected hold-up at the border checkpoint had driven all thoughts of resetting it for the final necessary two hours, clean out of her head. Angry brown eyes met cool grey with a clash that seemed to ring through the silence, and Isla drew a deep, unsteady breath. Woolfe did not say out loud, 'if you hadn't rushed off in that impulsive manner.' He did not need to. His look said it for him.

'I'll simply *have* to shake him off my trail somehow. I must be free to look for Robin in my own way.' In the security of her room five minutes later she fumbled through her suitcase with hands that shook. She scarcely saw her clothes, and pulled out a dress at random. 'It's lucky I went to South America hunting for antiques, and not the Arctic Circle,' she thought with a wry attempt at humour. The clothes that were suitable for the sun of the far south would be equally adaptable for Burma.

'Every single move I make, Woolfe checkmates me. He's got no right!' she fumed as she dressed. It was intolerable on his part, and her independent spirit writhed under the restriction.

'I'll go and see the relief manager the moment the showrooms open in the morning. I'll get another room, somehow, away from the Consulate. Away from Woolfe,' she promised herself. The room at the Consulate was adequate. No, it was pleasant and comfortable. She could not denigrate her accommodation, although she could not remember how she reached it. She followed the guide in a daze along what seemed to be endless miles of corridors, and scarcely heard his promise as he left her at the door,

'I'll come back in about half an hour, Miss Barclay, and guide you to the dining room.'

Hurriedly Isla showered and changed, and tugged a comb through her curls, and winced as the teeth caught on a knot. The small, sharp pain steadied her, and she proceeded with her toilet with greater attention. If she was forced to spend the rest of the evening in Zoe's company, she wanted the confidence that came from knowing she looked her best. She refused to think that she also wanted to look her best for Woolfe.

'If you're ready, Miss Barclay?'

A discreet tap on her door heralded the reappearance of the guide, and Isla gathered up her handbag and followed him with reluctant relief. Her stomach, she discovered with scorn, was not so independent as her spirit. It was empty, and clamouring to be fed.

'It's a pleasure to see you in Kaul again, Miss Barclay.' The Consul was a tall, elderly, courtly man, whose manner reflected his calling. Isla had met him before, and she shook his hand with genuine pleasure.

'Why didn't I think of coming to him in the first place?' she regretted. 'He's the best person to help me to trace Robin. He may even have heard of his whereabouts, by now.' The thought was a comfort, and the only one available for the moment. The Consul had guests, she discovered, at least thirty of them. She viewed the assembly with a feeling of dull surprise. For some reason she had envisaged dinner as being a fraught meal, with only herself, Zoe and Woolfe at the table. It was at once a relief and a disconcertment to find others present, and in such numbers. They would armour her against Zoe's barbs, but they would also effectively prevent her from holding any sort of private discussion with the Consul, a course which had not previously occurred to her, and which now seemed so vitally, urgently necessary.

'If only I'd given myself time to think,' she berated herself bitterly, 'instead of rushing off impulsively. . . .'

Her lips tightened as her own thoughts echoed Woolfe's jibe. 'Hindsight's all very well,' her normal balanced thinking reasserted itself, 'I couldn't ignore Robin's request to go and see Woolfe.' But the regret remained. If she had not gone to Herondale, she need never have heard of the International Security Force, let alone been subjected to its machinations. She need never have met Woolfe, and he would have remained to her what he had been heretofore, a shadowy figure, bent, elderly, and bearded, and her feelings would not now be in such a turmoil, in the confusion of which a bewildering mixture of love and hate, longing and resentment, seemed to be warring together, and using her sorely tried heart as their battleground.

In a daze Isla felt the Consul take her arm and walk her with him towards the dining room. His courtesy exalted her position to that of an honoured guest, and under any other circumstances

she would have delighted in the subtle compliment, which con-
trasted sharply with Zoe's offer of a room in the staff quarters,
but the pleasure turned sour, and she walked beside her escort
with her ears listening to what he had to say, her mouth smiling
an automatic response, when all the time her mind and her
heart were agonisingly conscious that Woolfe walked immediately behind her, with Zoe clinging to his arm, looking up
into his face, talking to him in her soft, husky, deliberately pro-
vocative voice. Isla could see, without turning round, his dark
head bent above Zoe's, knew that his grey eyes looked down
into her green, knew that they did not look at herself immediately in front of him, because with her heightened sensitivity
she would know that he looked at her, would feel his grey
regard.

'It's a bad business, about the Kang amulet.'

Isla nearly choked on her soup as one of the Consul's guests
put into words the reason for her own presence at the table.

'What does he know about the Kang amulet?' She raised her
head sharply, and stared at the man in surprise. Her fellow
guests, apart from Woolfe, were without exception delegates to
the scientific conference being held in Kaul. 'What . . .?'

'Of course he knows. It's nonsense to suppose that only Woolfe
and I are aware that it's been stolen.' It had become such a
personal thing between them that she had forgotten until now
that the story had been in the London newspapers. Robin had
enclosed a cutting with his letter, and by the same token it had
probably been taken up by the media in other countries as well.
'Perhaps. . . .' She forgot her excellent soup as a possibility
occurred to her. 'Perhaps one of the delegates might have heard
of something, might know. . . .'

Almost as soon as the hope rose in her, it died away, and she
dug her spoon almost savagely back into her bowl of soup. The
dinner guests were internationals, it was true, but, 'They're
scientists,' Isla reminded herself firmly. 'They're only interested
in their own disciplines. The Kang amulet's just a topic of casual
dinner conversation to them, nothing more.' She dared not allow
herself to hope that it might be anything more. Even if they
were interested in the antique and fine art world, they were
unlikely to be serious collectors of pieces in the upper price

ranges, for were not scientists supposed to be like artists, dedicated to their calling, and popularly believed to live on a shoestring? The man who had spoken hardly fitted such a description. She studied him covertly. His dinner jacket was enviably tailored, but his balding, bespectacled appearance did not suggest that the rarer objets d'art might be within his reach financially, even if they were included in the scope of his interests.

'But if he is interested, and he can't afford to buy, might not that make the object even more desirable to him?' The Kang amulet was not for sale, it belonged to a state museum, but its very inaccessibility might enhance its value in the eyes of an unscrupulous collector. The thought persisted like an irritating mosquito, and on its heels, unbidden, came another.

'What if Woolfe finds the amulet desirable?' He was a collector. He was also a very wealthy man, and because his wealth could not purchase that which belonged to its country of origin, might not that make him covet the amulet even more? Even as her mind grappled with the idea, her heart rejected it, but. . . .

'It would explain why he's keeping me under surveillance.' It all slotted into place too neatly to be ignored. 'When Pat and I took off from the airstrip at Herondale, the International Security man tried to call us back.' Vividly she recalled his waving, gesticulating figure. But. . . The whole affair seemed to be littered in buts, she thought restlessly. But was the man a member of the International Security Force? Nobody had actually said so. Woolfe had implied so, but she had no proof that he was telling the truth. True, the border guards had been influenced to delay their plane for the time necessary to allow Woolfe to catch up with them, but a substantial bribe would have served the purpose just as easily. A bribe that Woolfe would be quite easily able to pay. And the collector had followed her, a stranger, half way across the world. Why? What reason could he possibly have? It could not have been impulse. Her lips twisted wryly at the thought, even as she rejected it. Even wealthy people did not embark on costly journeys from one side of the world to the other, for no good reason. He had even gone to the lengths of telephoning Zoe to obtain a room for her at the Consulate. Again, why? So that he might keep an even closer eye on her movements? The scientific conference being held in

Kaul made a plausible excuse for his action. 'For all I know, there might be dozens of rooms available in the town. We passed two brand new hotels on our way in from the airport.' Cold fury rose in Isla at the easy manner in which she had allowed herself to be duped.

'I've fallen for his plan just like a naïve schoolgirl.' Fallen for a hatchet face, and a pair of grey, grey eyes. . . . She thrust the thought from her, and heard the Consul speak from what sounded a long distance away.

'Come, Miss Barclay, you're not eating. Are you tired after your journey?' he asked her considerately, 'or, perhaps, worried about your brother?'

So he knew about Robin. Relief flooded over Isla that he knew, and redoubled her self-condemnation that she had not approached the Consul in the first place. It was such an obvious course to take. Anyone would have thought of it. Anyone but an impulsive. . . .

'I was miles away.' Hastily she pulled her thoughts back to her surroundings. Hardly, she wished she *was* miles away, from Woolfe.

'Everything possible is being done to locate the Kang amulet,' the Consul assured her, adding, 'and your brother too, of course.'

'Oh, of course,' Isla thought bitterly. 'Everyone puts the piece of carved jade first, and Robin comes only as an afterthought. Well, he doesn't come as an afterthought to me,' she told herself fiercely, and felt vindicated in her decision to come to Kaul to look for him herself. 'They can all go searching for their amulet.' She did not care if they scattered to the four winds to look for it, or indeed, if they did not find the jade at all.

'I'm glad I didn't have the opportunity to speak to the Consul, if that's the way he feels,' she told herself wrathfully. 'He'd simply join forces with Woolfe to prevent me from going in search of Robin.' She was possibly being unjust, but it was not a risk she was prepared to take. The shock of realising Woolfe's infamy made her feel she could not trust anyone, any more.

'I'll keep my own counsel and follow my own course,' she planned. And what better start to her search than a visit to Barclay's showrooms to discover from where Robin had sent his last communication to Huw? It was a pity the Welshman would not be there to talk to her personally, but. . . .

'It's a pity Huw Morgan was taken ill at this point in time,' the Consul continued, and Isla looked up at him swiftly, jolted out of her train of thought to discover that her host's mind was running on almost carbon copy lines to her own.

'There'll be a relief manager,' she began, and then stopped, and bit her lip, because she had vowed to keep her own counsel, and she must do so at all costs. If she discussed her plans, it was an open invitation to Woolfe or the Consul, or both, to foil them.

'Mmm, yes.' The latter did not look particularly impressed. 'Huw introduced me to the man who's standing in for him, before he went convalescent. He's a good lad, keen on his job, but he's young, and maybe a bit impulsive.'

Isla dared not turn to look at Woolfe. She could feel his eyes boring into her turned head, feel the accusation 'impulsive' vibrating in the air between them, almost hear his mockery. Her ear nearest to Woolfe burned with the force of his stare, and she almost put up her fingers to shield it, and checked herself with an effort.

'If the new manager's impulsive, that makes two of us,' she muttered rebelliously under her breath. Everyone else's impulse seemed to be to play down the whole affair. Only Huw and herself seemed to be in the least concerned about Robin, and since Huw was temporarily out of action, that only left herself to do something about it.

'It's possible Woolfe may pick up a whisper in Kaul,' the Consul went on. 'He has so many contacts.'

'Woolfe?' Isla voiced her surprise. 'What can he do?' she asked shortly. 'He's a collector, he's not even a dealer. What contacts has he got that Barclays haven't?' She could speak without danger of being overheard. The subject of their discussion was deep in conversation with his dinner neighbour. She noticed the collector seemed to be on easy terms with the delegates, one or two greeted him as if they might be old acquaintences. Zoe was talking animatedly to a young and extremely good-looking Canadian delegate. Isla noticed cynically that it was Zoe who did most of the talking.

'What can Woolfe do that Barclays haven't already done?' she asked repressively.

'Woolfe's contacts are very wide ranging.' It was the Consul's turn to look surprised. Surprised that Isla did not already know. 'He's done a great deal to promote the cause of international trade,' her host went on earnestly. 'This gathering here tonight was his brain-child, and a very successful one it's been so far. It was at his instigation that a society was set up for the interchange of scientific knowledge in all disciplines.' He seemed to take Isla's interest for granted, and she tried without success not to listen. This was a side to Woolfe that she had not suspected. This would explain why he was a regular guest at the Consulate.

'The Society is world-wide now, of course,' the Consul went on. 'It has students on sponsored overseas scholarships, learning their trade, and at the same time learning about other cultures.' He warmed to his theme with what Isla could see was genuine enthusiasm. 'The free interchange of all knowledge may sound idealistic,' he smiled, 'but men with ideals, like Woolfe Wieland, are making it work, and if young people of all nationalities can be brought up to work and study together, much will have been achieved in the cause of world peace. Woolfe was the prime mover behind the society, and he is its current President.'

'His aim might be world peace,' Isla decided wearily, but his immediate effect upon herself was the reverse of peaceful. Her emotions felt as if they had been trampled on by an invading army, and left her heart and mind engaged in a civil war within herself that bade fair to tear her apart.

'I only met Woolfe a few days ago,' she explained her ignorance, since the Consul's pause seemed to expect it. 'A few days,' she repeated to herself incredulously. 'A lifetime. . . .'

'My speciality is embroideries and fabrics,' she went on, since the good man still looked slightly puzzled. 'Woolfe isn't interested in collecting such things.' His interest lay in miniatures. Her pride still smarted at the memory of his jibe. 'So far, his contact has been only with my grandfather, and Robin.'

'Ah yes, of course, collecting is his hobby. But he has many interests, not the least of them his own estate at Herondale.'

'He appears to be a man of many parts,' Isla agreed drily,

and added with silent emphasis, 'and I don't like any single one of them.'

She would never forgive Woolfe for his deliberate manipulation of her actions, she told herself angrily, his cynical interference in her affairs, that blocked every move she had tried to make so far. 'He's well named,' she decided. Woolfe, the hunter. Cunning, wily. Only this man did not hunt in a pack, as did his namesakes. He hunted alone, and was the more dangerous because of it. He had penetrated her own defences with frightening ease, but she was aware of his treachery now, and wary. Anger, suspicion and mistrust strengthened the crumbling fortifications of her armour, and pride hoisted a flag above its reinforced walls. What went on behind those defences—the hopeless yearning, and the equally hopeless tears—need never be known to anyone but herself, so long as she did not allow any chink in her defences to betray her feelings, betray them to Woolfe, she could cope, she told herself valiantly, and rose from the table confident that what she told herself was true.

The rest of the evening passed in a blur. The delegates handed her from one to another, 'like a kind of animated parcel,' she thought amusedly, and supposed it was because she and Zoe were the only two women present. It did not occur to her that it might be her own delicate loveliness, fresh, as flowers are fresh, and unadorned except for a slender gold necklet loosely binding together the soft collar of her cream silk dress, in sharp contrast to Zoe's brittle sophistication, that appeared to frighten off the male contingent, rather than to encourage them.

Suddenly, the party was over. In that unsignalled moment that spells the end of all such gatherings, conversations languished, and one by one the delegates began to take their leave, and drift away. The uniformed guide who had brought her to the dining room became as six men, hailing taxis, sorting out macs and briefcases, and restoring them to their rightful owners, and in the midst of the flurry of farewells Isla realised with a feeling of panic that,

'If I don't go now, right away while some of the delegates are still here, I'll be left with Woolfe and Zoe,' and the threesome which she had dreaded earlier would become a reality. She was under no illusion that she would be even more unwelcome to share a goodnight drink with the pair than she was for the pre-dinner one, particularly if, as was likely, their elderly host took the opportunity and retired as soon as the last of his scientist guests departed.

'Goodnight! Goodnight!'

Isla threw out her farewells to the room at random, included the Consul, Woolfe, and the indifferent Zoe in her smile, and fled.

'I won't wait for the guide. I'll find my own way back to my room.' She had traversed two likely-looking corridors before she realised that her bump of direction was sadly awry. 'I'm sure I've passed that gargoyle twice before.' The ugly little figure graced, if that was the correct description, Isla thought doubtfully, the ornate plasterwork above the entrance to what appeared to be a banqueting chamber or a ballroom, the large double doors suggested elegant functions. The inelegant leer on the plaster face mocked her bewilderment, and on an impulse Isla grimaced back.

'I know I'm lost, but you needn't laugh about it,' she told the gargoyle crossly.

'I'm not laughing. And if you're lost, it's your own fault,' Woolfe told her sternly, and she spun round with a startled gasp. 'Why didn't you wait for the guide to take you to your room?' he demanded.

'He was busy,' Isla retorted defensively, 'and besides,' her chin came up and her eyes reflected the light of battle, 'I didn't need the guide. I can find my own way back to my room well enough by myself,' she lied independently.

'Yes?' Woolfe enquired silkily. 'Is that why you're heading in the direction of the passport office? Or perhaps you've decided to have a peep at the banqueting hall on the way?'

'I'm not ... I didn't....' Isla stammered to a halt. Infuriatingly, Woolfe appeared to be as familiar with the layout of the Consulate as was the official guide. And as she herself was not.

'The staff quarters are this way.' Woolfe took her firmly by the arm, executing a smart right turn past the next gargoyle....

'Why didn't I think to turn right, instead of walking straight on?' Isla asked herself with angry hindsight. 'I should have re-membered that potted palm.'

'Your room's number nine, isn't it?' Without waiting for her to answer, Woolfe strode towards a set of numbered doors, ignoring Isla's protest,

'There's no need to take me right into my room.' She tried ineffectually to shake her arm free from his hold. Really, the man was behaving as if he was her jailer! she told herself furiously. All her new-found suspicions of Woolfe rushed to the fore. 'He'll be locking me in my room next, to make sure I shan't escape his vigilance,' she told herself wrathfully, and said sharply, out loud,

'There's no need for you to see me inside, I don't need tucking up as well.'

'I hadn't exactly thought of doing that,' he murmured, and stood her to a halt in front of the door marked nine. 'But now you mention it. . . .' He met Isla's startled upwards stare with an expression in his eyes that she had begun to know, and to dread. 'Now you mention it,' he repeated softly.

'You wouldn't dare,' she breathed furiously. Would he? Her panic-stricken glance told her he most certainly would. Even white teeth gleamed in the mahogany tan of his face, matching the laughter that brimmed from his eyes. 'D-don't you d-dare! I'm not a ch-child,' she spluttered confusedly.

'Certainly you're not a child,' he agreed, and his voice held a curious note of satisfaction, though for what Isla could not imagine, and at that moment she was not inclined to try to discover. 'You're a very stubborn young woman,' he concluded with feeling.

'If Robin calls me stubborn, that doesn't give you the right. . . .' she flared, and checked herself too late. All too clearly the brightening gleam in his eyes told her he had caught the inference, and was about to retaliate.

'So Robin, too, says you're stubborn, does he?' he taunted, and Isla's temper snapped.

'That's a brother's privilege,' she threw back angrily, furious with herself for making the slip, even more furious with Woolfe for taking it up.

'I wouldn't dream of trespassing on a brother's privilege,' he assured her gravely, and immediately took one of his own. With a deceptive lack of haste that yet caught Isla unawares, his hand left her arm and slid round her waist. She could feel the wide span of it pressing her inexorably towards him. She tried to pull away, but she might as well have tried to pull against the wind, and he drew her to him and bent his head over her, and his lips silenced her panic-stricken, 'No, Woolfe! No!' And if the gargoyle had been able to see round corners, his grin must surely have ripened into a chuckle to see the rich tide of colour stain her throat and cheeks with burning confusion, as her wildly beating heart pulsed the blood through her veins at exhilarating speed, that robbed her of her breath, and her resolution, and left her helpless to resist the power of his caress.

With deadly skill, Woolfe explored the soft ripe fulness of her mouth. She began to tremble, succumbing to the overwhelming magnetism of his touch, the fierce, unrelenting demand of his mouth covering her own. Vaguely she could smell the fresh clean astringent tang of expensive aftershave lotion, and then her mind registered nothing except the quick upsurging of that dormant spring within her that had waited long years for this moment, and now burst forth in an eager response, flowing out to slake the thirst of his demand. Her lips moved softly under his, seeking to drink from the same lifegiving source, and she swayed in his arms, her senses reeling as if the spring contained not water, but potent, heady wine.

Woolfe's kiss wandered, seeking the delicate line of her jaw, and the dimple that was nature's tender fingerprint on her soft, flushed cheek, deserting her lips, but they no longer had the power to cry, 'No!' except in protest at their desertion, and to plead for his kiss to return to them. Instead they uttered a low moan of surrender, and her body ceased to strain away from his, and became pliant in the hard fastness of his arms.

'Woolfe. . . .' She murmured his name huskily, and lifted her pleading lips up to his, offering them. . . . 'Woolfe!'

The lone hunter, who tracked her across the width of the world, drove her with singleminded purpose into the very mouth of his lair, and even as she turned at bay, sprang with faultless timing to overwhelm her suspicions, scatter her resolutions to the wind, and leave her helplessly captive to a dark head, a lean, tanned, hatchet face, and a pair of grey, grey eyes.

CHAPTER THREE

'YOUR breakfast, miss.'

She might be housed in the staff quarters, but she was being given star treatment, Isla thought appreciatively, and wondered if Zoe knew she was being served breakfast in bed. She did not consider it politic to ask the neat maid who appeared with a smile and her tray. It could be that Zoe herself had been the instigator of this unlooked-for luxury, in order that she and Woolfe might breakfast alone.

'Highly unlikely,' Isla decided. Zoe was an interpreter at the Consulate, she had discovered that gem of information last night, and as such the other girl would be on duty during working hours. She did not look the type who would otherwise rise early, so her meeting with Woolfe this morning, if any, would be of brief duration, Isla thought with satisfaction. She topped her boiled egg, and mentally blessed the Consul for her unexpected treat, and discovered with some surprise that neither awakened love nor subsequent disillusion had seriously spoiled her appetite.

'It's just as well, I'll need all my energy to search for Robin,' she told herself, and bit into the crisp toast with fierceness as if she was biting at Woolfe.

'Fighting with the pack leader,' she quipped with a valiant attempt at humour that all of a sudden failed miserably, and succeeded in destroying her appetite where the collector himself had failed. She pushed aside the rest of her unwanted breakfast, and concentrated on the coffee in an attempt to swallow the mouthful she already had down a throat that was suddenly closed round a hard, immovable lump.

'It's high time I got up.' She swung her legs out of bed and swallowed the last of her cup of coffee at speed. It was so hot that it made her blink, but the strong, sweet liquid cleared the way down for the mouthful of toast, and concentrated her mind on immediate necessities.

'Like having a shower, and getting along to the showrooms to see the relief manager before his day gets too busy,' she rallied herself. Her travelling clock told her there was still plenty of time, but the pressure of activity was better than the pressure of her own thoughts. At least having breakfast in bed had saved her from meeting the object of them, she realised thankfully.

'I don't want to meet Woolfe, ever again,' she declared out loud, fiercely. 'Never, after last night.' Her cheeks burned at the humiliation of last night. At her eager response to Woolfe's kisses. At his careless,

'That's my payment for guiding you back to your room,' as he thrust her away from him, and added, as if he might be speaking to a wilful child, 'Now go to bed, and don't wander about the Consulate on your own, or you're likely to get lost again.'

He released her without any signs of regret, as if the ardour of her return kisses meant nothing to him beyond the satisfaction of a momentary whim, she thought furiously, like a child discarding a mechanical toy, bored with it once it had discovered how the plaything performed. And she had performed just as he wanted her to. Once again he had manipulated the strings, and she, like a puppet, had danced to his command.

'For the last time,' she vowed, and gasped as she pulled the shower lever, and a jet of icy water shocked her out of her train of thought. Deliberately she stood under it, steeling herself against the cold douche, and she tingled all over as she towelled herself dry, and searched among her luggage for something suitable to put on.

'This will do.' It reflected her mood, she thought wryly, and shook out the bright red dirndl skirt with its deep waistband of elastic shirring that held it into her own neat middle like a cummerbund, and frilled out the gay material in dainty fulness about her knees. A crisp white scoop-necked blouse with bright embroidery to match her skirt completed the outfit, and she regarded her reflection in the full-length mirror with renewed confidence.

'Woolfe had better beware,' she muttered darkly. She had bought the skirt for its gay colour, but she wore it as a flag of warning, to herself as much as to Woolfe.

'I should have known better than to trust him,' she berated herself bitterly. 'He'd got reasons of his own for following me to Kaul.' And for trying to prevent her from finding Robin, or the Kang amulet, or both. 'I should have known, and yet I still allowed him. . . .' Her colour rose at the memory of her weakness. In spite of her suspicions of him, she had still allowed him to kiss her. She ignored an even stronger suspicion that he would have kissed her anyway, whether she allowed it or not. At the first touch of his lips she had bared her heart in response, 'Like a teenager in the first throes of calf love,' she told herself disgustedly. How Woolfe must have gloated, to find her such an easy conquest! The memory of it rasped like sandpaper on her raw pride, and with an impatient hand she picked up her white leather bag and slung the strap over her shoulder, then left her room, slamming the door behind her as if she would shut her thoughts inside to prevent them from following her.

'Turn right at the potted palm, and left at the gargoyle.' The route she had taken with Woolfe last night was emblazoned on her memory like a map. She reversed it, and put it to good use now.

'I hope Woolfe's room isn't along this corridor,' she thought. She had no means of knowing in which direction his room lay. He might well have been on his way there last night when he discovered her addressing the gargoyle.

'I don't want to encounter him again this morning,' she muttered. The last thing she felt equal to was another confrontation with Woolfe. 'He'll want to know where I'm going, and then try to stop me.'

She stopped herself, with an angry, 'Don't be so spineless!' She was a free agent. She was not obliged to report every movement she made to Woolfe, even if he had obtained her room at the Consulate for her. 'If we meet, and he asks me where I'm going, I'll tell him it's none of his business,' she promised herself stoutly, but in spite of her brave attempt at independence, she could not quite stifle a sigh of relief as she peered cautiously to the right and left when she emerged into the main corridor that led to the banqueting hall, and discovered it was empty of life. With a thumping heart she gained the entrance hall, nodded a response to the commissionaire's cheerful, 'Good morning, Miss

Barclay,' and escaped thankfully out into the sunshine.

'I'll walk to the showrooms,' she decided. It was nearly nine o'clock, but she did not want to arrive there just as they were taking down the shutters. Even at this early hour the pavements were thronged with people, and the sheer everyday normality of the scene calmed Isla's strung up nerves. Sober Western dress mingled with gay sarongs, and everyone except the obvious tourists either wore wide-brimmed hats against the onslaught of sun and rain, or carried umbrellas which served a similar dual role.

'If there's a storm, I'll dodge into a shop doorway,' Isla promised herself, conscious of her own lack of protection, and the vagaries of the climate. Already it was stiflingly hot, and the high humidity drew prickles of perspiration from her, only minutes after she left the air-conditioned comfort of the Consulate, so that even though she slowed her walk to a dawdle, she welcomed the approach of the showrooms, remembering that it, too, boasted air-conditioning.

Two customers were already there, and Isla paused in the doorway, unwilling to interrupt the staff at their work. The one customer was in casual dress, but his back view looked vaguely familiar, she thought. He was examining some glass paper-weights, and Isla edged forward for a closer look, her professional interest aroused in his possible purchase.

'This one is a St Louis paperweight. Very lovely, of course,' the man who was assisting the customer unwittingly confirmed Isla's guess. 'And this one,' he held out another, reverently, 'this one is a Clichy.'

Glass baubles, worth about two thousand and nine thousand pounds respectively. 'I wonder which one he'll choose.' Isla watched as the customer studied the two weights thoughtfully. 'Or will the price put him off?'

'My wife collects these things,' the customer remarked chattily, 'I thought one might make a nice memento to take back with me from the Conference.'

Even before he mentioned his reason for being in Kaul, the man's voice gave away his identity.

'The man in glasses, who sat opposite to me at dinner last night,' Isla muttered in astonishment. 'The man who was discussing the Kang amulet.' Her attention sharpened, and her preconceived notion of scientists who lived on a shoestring vanished for ever as the man decided,

'I'll take the Clichy paperweight, I think. I find the patterns in it delightful, and in any case my wife already possesses one of the St Louis weights.'

'Will you take it with you, sir, or would you like me to send it on to your home address for you?' the salesman asked helpfully. 'We despatch goods abroad from here.'

'No, I'll take it with me,' the customer decided. 'I need something small because I'm travelling by air, but I want it with me as a present to give to my wife when I return home.'

When he described the paperweight as small, he must have meant its size, he could not possibly have meant the cost.

'So much for taking home the proverbial stick of rock!' Isla thought, and slid swiftly round a display of ceramics, and pretended an interest in a showcase against the farther wall, in the hope that the scientist would not recognise her. Her mind teemed with questions, one of which had just been answered in the most disturbing manner. Without doubt, the scientist was a collector of antiques, and a knowledgeable one, with the means to pay high prices for the articles he desired. Did he desire the Kang amulet? And what was his connection with Woolfe? It was too much of a coincidence, she thought disbelievingly, that their only mutual interest should be the scientific conference. But what a perfect excuse it made, for the two to meet without questions being asked. All Isla's half-formed suspicions crystallised into cold certainty as she watched the salesman wrap the paperweight in a carefully padded box, and offer accommodatingly,

'Would you like us to keep it in our strongroom for you, until you depart?'

'Indeed I would.' The paperweight's new owner accepted the offer gratefully. 'I'll call for it on my way to the plane. The Conference closes on the last day of the month, and I fly out the same evening.'

'I'll have it ready for you to take away,' the salesman promised, and with a further word of thanks, the customer turned to go. Hurriedly, Isla bent over the showcase full of miniatures, and hoped her own back view did not strike the same chord in the memory of her erstwhile dinner companion, as his had done with her. She watched the scientist's reflection through the glass door of the showcase, saw him disappear through the showroom door and gain the street, and frowned as he vanished from her sight.

'So he won't be flying out until the last day of the month,' she muttered reflectively. Presumably he would be returning home, which from his accent she assumed would be to England, although even that could not be taken for granted, she reminded herself. Scientists were, by the nature of their work, internationally minded, and cared little from where they pursued their chosen path so long as the facilities they required were provided for them. Or was that another misconception? she wondered uneasily. She would have to find out. Perhaps the airport would confirm what bookings had been made. She would have to be careful how she made her enquiries, it would not do to arouse suspicion by injudicious questioning. Suddenly the task she had embarked upon took on a new, and daunting, light. It was going to be more difficult than she had bargained for, but,

'I must find out. I've got to know.' When he returned home, the scientist would take his paperweight with him, legitimately, Isla conceded. Would he also take the Kang amulet?

'I must find out,' she repeated firmly. Where the man's flight was taking him to. Where the amulet was, and therefore Robin. And she had only got until the end of the month to do it, if her suspicions were correct. She counted backwards with a growing feeling of dismay. 'The first week's nearly gone already.' A sense of urgency took possession of her. 'The moment the other customer's gone, I'll demand to see the relief manager,' she comforted herself. The second customer had wandered away among a display of Oriental screens, she could just see his shoes and the bottoms of his trouser legs from where she stood. Nervily she hoped his business with the sales staff would not take long. When her turn came to see the manager, she did not want to be interrupted. Neither did she want to be overheard.

'If only Huw were here,' she muttered distractedly. Dear, understanding Huw, as concerned for Robin as she was herself. Huw would have listened to her suspicions and questions, and would not have dismissed them as figments of an over-active imagination. Huw would have told her what to do, and known how to deal with Woolfe.

'You're abroad early. I told the staff to send you your breakfast in bed, so that you'd have a long lie-in.'

'You!' Isla spun round with a gasp as Woolfe appeared in full view from behind the concealment of the screens, and greeted her presence in the showrooms with what could only be described as an ungallant lack of welcome, while at the same time brazenly admitting culpability for trying to detain her in her bedroom at the Consulate, by sending her breakfast in bed. Perhaps he thought she did not suspect his motives? She thrust down a pang that it had not been pure consideration for her wellbeing that had prompted his action, and told herself triumphantly,

'His ploy didn't work.' Now that her suspicions were aroused, she would be aware, and wary, of any such seeming consideration on the collector's part. Aloud she said ungratefully,

'I didn't need breakfast in bed, I'm not an invalid. I'm too accustomed to travelling for it to make me unduly tired, even on a journey from England to Kaul.'

'May you be forgiven!' her conscience reproached her for the lie. She had not felt merely tired when she dropped into bed the previous night, she had felt shattered, though how much of this was due to the difficulties of the journey from Herondale to Kaul, and how much of it was due to that much longer, but considerably swifter journey in time from being a carefree girl to a painfully love-awakened woman, she was not prepared to hazard a guess. Hurriedly, so that she should not even be tempted to try, she went on,

'In any case, I wasn't hungry.' That at least was partly true, her conscience conceded. The memory of Woolfe's last night kiss had effectively destroyed her appetite so that she could not have swallowed her breakfast if she had tried. She met his look with a level stare.

'I told you I intended to come to the showrooms this morning, and I've come,' she declared with dignity, and her stare told Woolfe that she saw through his attempt to detain her at the Consulate, despised him for it, and repudiated his right to try to restrain her movements. 'I had more than one matter to discuss with the relief manager here.' She had two, to be exact, she thought tartly. One, the most important one, was to discover from where Robin had sent his last message to Huw, and to try if she could to read between the lines of that message to probe her brother's possible move on from there.

Her second reason, which trod closely on the heels of the first—perhaps even temporarily eclipsed it, in view of the renewed suspicions awakened by her discovery of the scientist's unexpectedly extravagant purchase of a present for his wife—was her urgent need to find other accommodation in Kaul for herself, and by so doing, be freed from Woolfe's constant surveillance. 'I've got every right to come to my firm's showrooms if I choose to do so,' she defended her right hotly.

'There was no need for you to come to the showrooms at all, the relief manager here won't be able to help you,' Woolfe dismissed her right with an impatient wave of his hand. 'The Consul told you last night that everything possible is being done to locate your brother,' he reminded her with asperity. 'So why do you insist upon meddling in this business, when you've already been told twice, by me and by the Consul, that professionals are doing their utmost to locate. . . .'

'The Kang amulet, not Robin,' Isla finished for him with equal asperity. 'Everyone goes to great lengths to let me know they're doing all they can to find a useless piece of jade, and then they add, "and Robin, too, of course",' she mimicked bitterly, 'just like an unimportant p.s. on the end of a letter.'

'What good do you imagine you can do, against the efforts of professionals?' Woolfe questioned her harshly, and she bridled at his authoritative tone, but before she could retort he went on remorselessly, 'If you fancy yourself as an amateur sleuth, I suggest you go away and forget the idea. That sort of thing only works in detective novels. In real life, amateurs merely get in the way, and what's worse they usually hinder the efforts of people who know what they're doing,' he finished unflatteringly.

'If Woolfe's finished, I haven't. In fact, I've only just started,' Isla told herself grimly. She was tiny, but she was not insignificant, as another had discovered to his cost on the day she conducted her very first auction sale, and to the amusement of the assembled crowd had had to accept the indignity of a box to stand on, to counter her lack of inches. The man in question, there to bid for some pieces of antique furniture, refused to take a girl auctioneer seriously, and gave her a broad wink. She immediately punished his audacity, and neatly turned the joke on her tormenter, by taking his wink as a bid for a pair of particularly hideous china dogs, of doubtful origin and even more doubtful pedigree. The man took his defeat in good part and paid the frankly exorbitant price on which her vengeful gavel descended, and thereupon presented Isla with both the dogs as a souvenir of her first auction. She still treasured the unlovely pair, but she did not value Woolfe's advice nearly so highly. With her chin held high, she made her feelings plain.

'I don't intend to hinder anyone's efforts to try and find the *Kang amulet*,' she emphasised the last two words with biting force. 'By the same token, I don't intend to allow anyone to interfere with my efforts to find Robin.' Her tone, as well as her straight look at Woolfe added, 'and that includes you.'

'Good morning Mr Wieland—madam. I didn't know you were in Kaul, sir?' A man of about Isla's own age, obviously the relief manager, approached them across the expanse of polished floor, and, the civilities over, immediately turned back to Woolfe.

'Is there anything in which you're particularly interested, Mr Wieland? We've got a nice selection of miniatures in at the moment. Some trinket boxes of Indian origin, with particularly fine enamelwork.' Scenting a possible sale, the newcomer gave his whole attention to Woolfe.

'As if I'm a mere appendage!' Isla thought furiously, and for the first time felt herself in complete sympathy with Women's Lib. There was no reason why the relief manager should recognise her, she did not recognise him, but it rankled that in the showrooms of her grandfather's firm, Woolfe should take precedence. She ignored the obvious policy that as a valued customer, it was right that he should do so, and smarted at the unintentional slight.

'I'm not looking for that kind of miniature this morning,' Woolfe replied obliquely, to the manager's obvious puzzlement, but Isla had no trouble in recognising the implication, and her ready colour rose as Woolfe's eyes once more ignored the scaled-down antiques, and rested upon herself. Her lips set ominously, but she could not openly quarrel with the collector in front of a member of the staff, she realised helplessly, and fumed in silence as Woolfe went on urbanely,

'Miss Barclay needs to speak to you. She's anxious to discover the whereabouts of her brother.'

It was wrong that Woolfe should introduce her, a partner in the business, to a member of their own staff. It was wrong that he should tell the relief manager what her private business with him was, and thus render it no longer private. And by so doing, she realised angrily, must make the manager think Woolfe was in her confidence.. The collector had deliberately. and provocatively, implied an ascendancy over her that she could not even refute, she realised furiously, because if she tried to deny it, he would simply shrug and tell her she was imagining things, and the manager would assume she was being feminine and hysterical, and. . . . It was like trying to punch water, she realised in impotent fury. The moment the would-be blow landed, its target melted away from under it, completely unruffled. Which by now, Isla acknowledged wrathfully, her own temper certainly was not.

'I'm sorry, Miss Barclay . . . Miss Isla . . . I didn't realise. . . .'

The manager's obvious embarrassment should have acted as a balm to her sorely tried temper, but instead his stammered apologies merely inflamed her impatience to the point where she snapped,

'Don't try to apologise,' and instantly felt contrite as she witnessed his crestfallen look, so that she impulsively put out her hand, and made a strained attempt at a smile, and added in a kinder tone, 'There's no reason why we should recognise one another, we haven't met before. It's good of you to stand in for Huw Morgan while he's away.' She realised when she saw the man's mollified expression that she had made the right approach, and putting a tight rein on the almost overriding sense of urgency that made her want to fling questions at him, and demand instant answers, she smiled again—it was easier at the second attempt, she discovered—and said as casually as she could manage,

'I need to consult Robin on one or two matters, but I've been in South America for a number of weeks, and consequently out of touch. I understand from Huw that my brother was in contact with the showrooms here after he left Kaul. I wondered if you might know of his present whereabouts?' Even by exerting all her self-control, Isla could not quite eliminate the rising note of hope from her voice. 'Or if not, I'd like to see the last message he sent to Huw. It might give me some idea in which direction he was heading.'

'I'm afraid I haven't got anything I can actually show you, Miss Isla,' the manager replied regretfully. 'Mr Morgan told me before he left, Mr Robin didn't send any written messages, at least not back here to the showrooms. They were only word-of-mouth messages, sent by a runner. Mr Morgan was concerned that even these had ceased.'

'Oh. . . .' Isla's face fell, and she turned her back abruptly on Woolfe's straight glance that said, 'I told you the relief manager wouldn't be able to help you.'

'I thought . . . I'd hoped. . . .' With an effort she rallied herself. 'Did Robin's messenger say from whereabouts . . .?' she began without much hope.

'Oh yes, Miss Isla,' the manager instantly resurrected it for her, and showed himself to be delighted to help where his limited knowledge allowed. 'Mr Robin sent off his last message from half way along the road that leads on to the pass where the Tan Gwe monastery stands.'

She would remember the name of the monastery. It seemed to burn like fire on her mind. It should be easy enough to get hold of a map, that would mark the monastery and so tell her which road Robin had been travelling along when he sent off his last message to Huw. The road that leads on to the pass. . . . Perhaps there would be a map of the area she could borrow from the Consulate. No! She must not borrow anything, least of all a map, from the Consulate. The last thing she must do was to broadcast her intentions there, and by so doing, broadcast them to Woolfe. She gave what she hoped was an offhand gesture, and replied,

'It all sounds horribly exhausting, in this heat. Trust Robin to go tearing off up mountain slopes!' she said with sisterly scorn.

'He always was the energetic one.' She had always followed her brother on his climbing expeditions, with the same enthusiasm as he, and she intended to follow him this time, but it was vital that she should put Woolfe off the scent. She must somehow make him believe that she had temporarily abandoned the idea of seeking her brother herself. With assumed indifference she went on, 'If Robin's keeping to the roads and the mountain passes, I'm sure Huw's concern for him is quite unfounded, and if he does do a bit of climbing while he's in the hills, he's an expert mountaineer.'

'The road so far as the foot of the pass, is quite a passable one,' the manager offered, 'there are some villages along the route.'

It all sounded unexpectedly civilised, in fact rather urban, Isla thought, and her own fears for her brother began to subside a little. Where there were villages, even only occasional ones, there must be people, and where there were people there must be communication of some kind. It did not completely assuage her own concern for Robin's safety, but it began to make her search look slightly easier. At least she knew which road her brother had taken, and she could enquire from the villagers. There would not be all that many travellers along the road that they would not remember one. With a shrug she declared,

'My business with Robin can wait until he returns to Kaul. If he does get in touch with you, let him know I'm waiting to see him, will you? And I'll drop in here occasionally to find out if you've heard when he's likely to return.' Deliberately she changed the subject. It would not do to protest her disinterest too much, she decided. It was more essential for Woolfe to believe she would remain in Kaul, than it was for the manager to do so, and if she made too emphatic a point of it, he might begin to suspect her words were merely a smoke screen to cover her activities. She thickened the smoke by a not altogether spurious show of interest in the antiques on display.

'The showrooms look very attractive,' she complimented the manager. 'I see you've got a good selection of small items, as well as the larger stuff, in stock.' There was no fourposter bed in evidence, she noticed, not even a couch on which she could have rested the previous night.

'We've got a lot of small items in the hope of attracting the visitors,' the manager preened himself under her praise. 'There's a scientific conference running in Kaul at the moment. Perhaps Mr Wieland has told you?' Mr Wieland had, Isla thought tartly, but she was unwilling to tell her informant in what context she received the news. 'We've already attracted quite a lot of custom from the delegates, who want to take home something a little out of the ordinary from the usual run of souvenirs. The gentle-man who just left, was one.'

'A Clichy paperweight is certainly out of the ordinary as a souvenir,' Isla agreed drily, and the manager laughed.

'That was a bit of luck for us, to have a genuine collector drop in,' he said happily, and urged Isla, 'While you're here, do stay and have a look at some of the stock.'

'I'd love to.' She wanted to rush off and find a map and trace the road Robin had taken, but she restrained herself with an effort, and made believe that she had all the time in the world to study antiques instead of modern maps. She smiled sweetly at the manager and suggested,

'I'd like to see the enamelled miniatures, and I noticed a sandalwood and ivory workbox in the window that looked attractive.' She turned to Woolfe as if on an afterthought, and added in a voice from which she could not quite manage to eliminate the bite, 'Don't let me detain you.' There were still two things she wanted to ask the manager, and she much preferred Woolfe to be out of earshot when she asked them.

'I'm not in any hurry. I'm interested in miniatures, too.' His eyes mocked her transparent attempt to get rid of him, and the underlying steel in his glance warned her he was not willing to be disposed of so easily. Isla bit her lip, and felt her colour rise.

'The man's the absolute limit!' she fumed. No one else she had ever met before had the ability to make her personal thermometer rise to such a disastrous level, so that within minutes of being in Woolfe's company, her temper and her patience both were in imminent danger of boiling over. Anyone else would have made an excuse, and taken her hint and their departure, but not Woolfe. As the manager turned to escort Isla towards the showcases, Woolfe turned too, and walked with them, purposely she felt sure taking up position on her other side, 'Like a jailer, making sure I can't escape. . . .'

'I know just how someone in custody must feel,' she told herself wildly. Trapped, desperate—and oddly frightened. It was going to be as easy to get rid of a leech as to get rid of Woolfe, she realised, and shivered. Suddenly she longed to hit out, trip him up, and run from the showrooms and along the street, anywhere, in any direction, so long as she could shake off his persistent surveillance. Trappers in the far North must share her feelings when they knew themselves to be shadowed by a wolf pack. But this was a lone wolf, persistent, tireless, and unshakeable. The pleasant coolness of the air-conditioned showrooms suddenly seemed to drop by several degrees, and Isla shivered again.

'I'll join you at the case of miniatures in a moment, Mr Wieland. I'll just take Miss Isla to see the sandalwood workbox.' Unwittingly the manager gave her an avenue of escape, and it was all Isla could do not to throw a triumphant glance up at Woolfe as the man drew her away towards the window display. With a reluctant effort she desisted, denying herself the satisfaction in case Woolfe should take her look as a challenge, and pick up the gauntlet, and accompany them just the same. She could not help a quick, fearful peep over her shoulder that he might come in any case, and gave an inaudible sigh of relief to see that he had turned without demur to the showcase full of miniatures, and bent to study the contents with every appearance of being absorbed by what he was looking at.

Isla was not deceived by his seeming acquiescence. 'He's still within earshot,' she realised worriedly. And Woolfe, like his namesake, had exceptionally keen hearing.

'This is lovely.' She took the sandalwood and ivory workbox from the manager's hands with genuine pleasure. 'The inlay work is superb.' The intricate delicacy of it gave her an idea. 'I'd like to study it more closely, but those Oriental screens cast a shadow here. May I take it back to the door, in the sunlight, and you can tell me what you know of its history?' She needed the manager to accompany her in order that she might question him, but not about the sandalwood workbox. To her intense relief he accepted her reason without question, and turned willingly back with her towards the door. She did not look at Woolfe as she moved away, she did not need to, his sharp glance bored a hole in her back as she walked past him, but again the manager innocently came to her aid.

'The box is well preserved, as you can see,' the manager paid her the compliment of assuming she could date and place the antique for herself.

'It looks to be Indian in origin, like the miniatures.' Isla raised her voice to answer him, making sure that Woolfe should hear, and know that they were discussing nothing more important than the sandalwood box. 'I'd love to possess it myself, if it isn't too expensive?' Her suite of rooms in her grandfather's house on the downs held a carefully chosen selection of antiques, and she had been looking for a workbox that was beautiful as well as functional, for some time. This one just fitted her requirements.

'I'll debit your account in London for you.' The manager mentioned a figure which gained Isla's approving nod, and helpfully repeated his earlier offer to the scientist, to have it sent on for her.

'I think I'd rather take the box with me.' Isla refused to risk her new-found treasure to the post. 'In fact, I could use it while I'm at the Consulate.' An inspiration struck her. 'While I'm in Kaul this time I'd like to have a look round. I've never had time for much sightseeing when I've been here before. I suppose you haven't a map of the area you could lend me, while I'm here?' she asked craftily, and dropped her voice to a conspiratorial murmur. 'I don't like to ask Mr Wieland and the people at the Consulate,' she connected the two unrepentantly, 'they've been so kind in offering me accommodation at short notice, that I don't want to trouble them further. I'd much rather ask a colleague.' Deliberately she raised the manager's status to that of her own, and he replied in an equally low voice, with obvious gratification,

'I'll put a selection of maps and brochures inside the box, and send it to you at the Consulate,' he complied eagerly. 'I quite understand how you feel.'

He did not, but Isla declined to enlighten him. 'Could anything have been simpler?' she asked herself gleefully, and tried her luck again.

'I suppose you couldn't include a list of likely hotels, as well?' she asked hopefully. 'I do feel I'm imposing on the Consul's hospitality.' She paused and unobtrusively crossed her fingers, out of sight in the generous folds of her dirndl skirt.

'Whatever you do, don't give up your room at the Consulate, Miss Isla,' the manager begged her anxiously. 'There isn't a room to be had in Kaul until the Conference finishes at the end of the month. Why, some overnight visitors have even had to sleep in the departure lounge at the airport, hotel rooms are that hard to come by until the Conference ends.'

Isla began to feel heartily weary of the Conference. She uncrossed her fingers and to the manager's obvious relief agreed resignedly,

'In that case, I'll have to remain where I am,' the while she railed inwardly at the unkind quirk of fate that had thus loaded the dice against her, and in favour of Woolfe. To hide her expression, she opened the lid of the workbox and sniffed appreciatively.

'Mmm, it's lovely. The smell of sandalwood never fades, does it?' The opened lid released the spicy, aromatic odour, and made her wish wistfully that the box could talk, and reveal the secrets of its previous owners. She inhaled deeply.

'It'll make you sneeze.'

'Aa'tchoo!'

Woolfe's warning came too late, and he grinned at her glare— an, 'I told you so,' grin that made her snap the lid of the workbox shut, and snap back at him,

'You were too late . . . aa'tchoo!' The second sneeze completely spoiled the effect of her jibe, and she groped frantically for her handkerchief. 'Bother!' she exclaimed vexedly, 'where's the beastly thing got to?' Her fumbling fingers failed to locate the missing cambric square in any of its usual hiding places.

'Perhaps you put it down your—er—thingummy, and it slipped out at the—er—bottom?' Woolfe regarded her pretty ensemble with an appreciative gleam in his eyes, and typical male non-comprehension of its component parts.

'I didn't put it down the neck of my blouse,' Isla retorted irately. 'How like a man, to suggest such a thing,' she thought scornfully. With his own suit abounding in capacious pockets, to assume she would spoil the line of her blouse with a lumpy handkerchief. . . . Besides, it would show up through the gauzy material. But if it was not in her 'thingummy', as Woolfe so disrespectfully described it, where on earth had her handkerchief got to? Her nose tickled an urgent warning. 'Where on earth can it be?' she muttered crossly.

'It *must* have slipped through, and dropped to the floor,' Woolfe insisted as Isla continued to fumble without success. 'Perhaps on your way here . . .?' Isla could cheerfully have slapped him for his derisive grin.

'It couldn't slip straight through,' she hissed back at him furiously. 'I'm wearing a dirndl skirt.' She saw from his blank expression that her description bypassed him, and proceeded to explain with heavy sarcasm, and fast vanishing patience, 'I don't suppose you've noticed, but the waistband of my skirt is made up of elastic gathering several inches deep. Nothing, but nothing,' she repeated cuttingly, 'could possibly fall through. If my hanky had lodged there, I should feel the bump.'

Automatically she continued to run her fingers round the waistband of her skirt. They stopped when they got to the one side, and she felt herself go pink. Too late, she remembered tucking her errant handkerchief inside the short puffed sleeve of her blouse when she dressed. She put it there so that she should not forget it, and fully intended to transfer it to her bag before she came out, but she had been so concerned to escape the Consulate without encountering Woolfe, that it had slipped her mind, and slipped down the inside of her blouse and lodged at the waistband of her skirt, just above her left hip.

'I . . . it. . . .' She could not, *would* not, admit to Woolfe where it was. 'I'll wipe my nose on my skirt first,' she vowed, and wondered what excuse she could make to vanish from sight for a few minutes, and rescue her handkerchief, before such a disastrous course of action became necessary. She searched the showrooms with a desperate glance. It was a choice of either the Oriental screens, or the 'ladies', she decided. The screens were the nearest. Instinctively she made a turn towards them, and caught Woolfe's eye as she moved. Twin imps of laughter lit up the grey, taunting her, challenging her to admit she had found her handkerchief where he said it would be. She countered his glance balefully, locking swords in a long, defiant stare.

'Help yourself to a handful of these tissues, Miss Isla.' The manager returned and held a box of paper handkerchiefs towards her, breaking the deadlock, and saving both Isla's face and her dignity.

'Bless you!' She accepted his offer with alacrity, and hid her burning cheeks in a welter of soft white paper.

'I'll send your workbox on for you,' her benefactor promised, when she eventually emerged, with her colour more or less back to normal.

'Why not take it with you now?' Woolfe asked, and held out his hand for it. 'I'll carry it for you.'

'No!' With gritted teeth Isla instantly rejected his offer, and added hastily, less he should infer more than she wanted him to from the very force of her refusal, 'I don't want to be encumbered with it now. I'm going for a stroll round Kaul, to do some sightseeing.'

'The market's a colourful sight,' the manager suggested helpfully, 'and it's got the advantage of being traffic-free. There'll be lots of people there, of course, but they add to the colour if you're looking for atmosphere.'

'That's a wonderful idea,' Isla enthused, and the young manager beamed.

'I'll hail a taxi for you. The market's only a short walk from here, but if you're feeling the heat, it's best not to miss your way,' he said considerately. 'As for your workbox,' he held on to it tightly, and pretended not to see Woolfe's outstretched hand, 'I'll have it sent on for you *exactly* as you requested.' His meaning glance at Isla rewarded her by entering wholeheartedly into her conspiracy, relegating Woolfe firmly into the sidelines as 'Consulate', and placing himself and Isla pointedly side by side, as 'colleagues'.

'I win the first round,' Isla told herself gleefully, considerably cheered by the knowledge that she had acquired an ally in the young manager.

'Since you're not being encumbered by your workbox,' with a grave face Woolfe repeated her childhood abbreviation, 'you won't need a taxi. I know a short cut to the market, which makes it only five minutes' walk away from here.' And a patent waste of time, as well as money, to hail a taxi. With a single deft stroke, Woolfe won a decisive second round. He gave a cool nod to the manager, took Isla firmly by the arm, and propelled her towards the door.

'It's a draw.' Isla could not release herself without doing battle, and she could not do battle in front of the manager. If she had been thinking in tennis terms, it would have been 'love all'. She winced away from the inappropriateness of the tennis terms. Her relationship with Woolfe could only be likened to a perpetual sparring match, she acknowledged wearily. A match in which Woolfe seemed to have most of the advantages, and if by sheer good fortune she had so far managed to hold her own against his superior skill, what, she asked herself with growing apprehension, what would be the outcome of all the further bouts between them, that she knew with a sinking heart were still to come?

CHAPTER FOUR

IT was a different world.

Isla lost her anger in wonderment as Woolfe steered her round a side turning away from the main street of the town. Away from the rows of elegant shops that bore internationally famous names, like their own showrooms, and turned the main shopping area into a replica of all main shopping areas in all large towns throughout the world, so that except for the climate, and perhaps the architecture, it would be difficult to tell whether you were in Berlin or Bangkok, Isla thought.

'It's a different world,' she murmured, and ceased to try to pull away, angrily, from Woolfe's hold, her attention caught and held by the narrow, twisting byway into which they turned. Woolfe seemed to be perfectly at home with his surroundings, she noticed observantly, familiar with them as a local is familiar, and Isla found herself wondering about him, and regretting that she had never joined in conversation about him with her grandfather, or Robin, who both knew him well. He had walked into her life, tracked her across the world, and taken her heart by storm, and she knew nothing about him, not even if he took sugar in his tea, she realised with a half hysterical surge of laughter that held no amusement, only a bleak emptiness that drained her heart of its life within her.

'We seem to be the only ones in European dress.' She fixed her eyes on the colourful, crowded little street in the hope that Woolfe would not notice their sudden brightness.

'This is the real Burma, the one that lies behind the façade,' Woolfe replied. 'The main street,' he shrugged, 'is any main street, anywhere in the world.' He latched on to her own train of thought without difficulty, and Isla hurriedly switched off her inner feelings in case he should latch on to those as well, and cap her unhappiness with humiliation because he did not feel the same way in return.

His hand left her arm, and she looked up at him quickly, bereft by his unexpected release that she would have fought to gain only a few minutes before, but he smiled, and took her by the hand instead with an unselfconscious movement that made her wonder wistfully if he was even aware of what he did.

'Slow down,' he checked their steps to a dawdle, 'there's no haste to go back to the Consulate, we might as well enjoy this while we can.'

And suddenly, there was no haste, and she *was* enjoying it, treacherously enjoying the warm, firm clasp of his hand, that set bells ringing in her heart to match the sweetness of the chimes that wafted down to them through the hot air from the top of a nearby pagoda, tantalisingly out of sight except for the bright gold top of it shining in the sun above the cluster of surrounding buildings, Dangerously enjoying Woolfe's closeness as he drew her to him in the crowded, narrow street, walking shoulder to shoulder, hands linked in a touch that tingled through her veins and brought all her senses vividly alive to match the golden sunshine and the gay sarongs of the men and women, and the hot spicy smell from the shadows of a nearby eating house, spicing the danger, so that she threw aside her sense of caution, and forgot her resolution to be wary of this man and told herself recklessly,

'It won't matter if I allow myself to feel this way just for an hour or two. Afterwards, everything will revert to the way it was before.' And she knew that afterwards it would not, and she would have to pay for her rashness with suffering and tears, as the price for the bright, gilded moments that matched the top of the pagoda, and like the latter would lose their shine as soon as the sun went down, and left only darkness in its wake. Woolfe had become her sun, but he did not shine for her. If for anyone, Isla thought unhappily, he shone for Zoe, and left herself grappling with the shadow that grew darker and colder with each hour that went by.

She knew a moment's swift envy as they passed a calmly smiling figure of the Buddha, gazing out at them from a corner niche, endlessly serene, as if the secret of the universe was happiness. A jar of fresh flowers stood at the base of the small shrine, a simple offering that Isla knew would be renewed the moment they faded. Perhaps if life was simpler, it, too, might be happy. . . . Perhaps the life of the young man coming towards them was a simple one. His face looked happy, Isla saw enviously, elated, even.

'He's just had his palm read,' Woolfe noticed Isla watching the man. 'From the expression on his face, he must have found the reading to his liking. I hope it comes true for him. They're keen on horoscopes here,' he smiled, and added teasingly, 'Would you like your palm read?' They strolled abreast of the palmist, squatting on the pavement, trading in dreams, but Isla shook her head and urged Woolfe past.

'Another day, perhaps,' she demurred. Today she only wanted to live in the present, to savour every sunny moment of it while she could, because the future, the dark, cold, empty future, did not bear thinking about.

'Everyone seems to be going in the same direction.' She grasped at the obvious, changing the subject to check thoughts that had become too painful to bear.

'They're all going to the market.'

'Of course.' She should have known. She should have cared, but of a sudden her enjoyment in the bright scene faded, and her heart was heavy as the brightly dressed throng crowded about them, and carried them with it out of the narrow street and into the hot and dusty, and even brighter market square.

'The relief manager said there'd be lots of people.' There seemed to be hundreds, crowding round the wares for sale.

Baskets of vegetables, glistening fresh; golden corn cobs; green and orange peppers; fruit of every colour and description, which made Isla's mouth water just to look at it.

'Let's have a peach to eat.' Woolfe drew her to a halt beside a trader with baskets of the largest, most luscious peaches Isla had ever seen. 'You like peaches, don't you?' he asked. He did not know anything about her tastes, either. The knowledge brought a pang of desolation with it, and a small comfort,

'We each know the other likes peaches, now.'

'Mmm.' She accepted his offering, and bit into it gratefully. 'They're gorgeous!' It was drink as well as food, sweet, and ripe, and heavy with juice. 'Nectar,' Isla breathed happily, all the sweeter because Woolfe had given it to her, and shared her enjoyment in his own.

'The juice is running down your chin,' he teased. They laughed into one another's faces, sticky with juice, and eyes merry with shared enjoyment.

'I put the paper tissues in my bag, I think.'

Once more she searched for her handkerchief, paper or otherwise, grappling with the zip of her shoulder bag with juice-stained fingers that slipped and fumbled with the fastening.

'Keep your tissues for your hands afterwards.' Woolfe shook out a clean lawn square from his top pocket, but instead of handing it to her, disconcertingly he cupped her chin with firm fingers and tipped her face up towards him, and began to mop it clean himself.

Across the soft handful of white lawn her eyes flew upwards, wide, startled, and with the laughter fled from them as they met a lurking something deep in his that flushed her cheeks to the delicate colour of the forgotten peach in her hand. She quivered under his touch, as a violin string quivers under the bow of a maestro, echoing notes from its heart full of longing, and edged with pain. The handkerchief ceased its busy ministrations, its duty done, but still Woolfe held her face up to his, gazing down into its flushed confusion with eyes that read all her secrets, and gave away nothing of his own.

'Is he going to kiss me?' Isla felt herself go deathly still. Woolfe's face hovered close, so close, above her own. He would only have to bend a little lower ... an inch, half an inch. Her palpitating heart cried the question, 'Will he kiss me again? Even here, in the middle of the busy market place, among the crush of people?' and was answered by an unarguable certainty within her,

'What cares wolf the hunter, for people?'

She held her face still, waiting for his kiss, while her breath fluttered in and out through her softly parted lips like a small white bird, beating its wings to be free, longing to fly, and yet caged by a longing that was far stronger than any bars, or any desire for freedom.

'Finish your peach, and let's go and get a straw hat for you, before your nose gets sunburned.'

He loosed her chin and pocketed his handkerchief, then tore aside the bars, and Isla quivered again, her eyes mutely beseeching him, as an instrument that is laid aside by the musician beseeches the touch of the bow to bring it back to life again.

'Finish your peach.'

She finished it, then threw away the stone, the precious seed of future life that, untended, would wither, as her love for Woolfe must wither, unrequited, in the years to come. She wiped her fingers herself, using the tissues the manager gave to her, and the busy, noisy bustle of the market place reasserted itself once more around her, though to her dull eyes the colour and the brightness and the gaiety were gone.

'Didn't you bring a hat with you?' Had he mistaken her flushed cheeks to be the result of the sun? she asked herself hopefully.

'I didn't pack one. I didn't think.' She had rushed off from Herondale impulsively, without pausing to consider that she might need anything other than the luggage she already had with her.

'You need an umbrella hat out here, the storms can be as fierce as the sun.'

The storm that raged inside her was fiercer than anything nature could produce, Isla told herself wearily, bruised and bewildered by the conflict wrought between an errant heart that loved, and a mind that cried, 'Beware!'

'Would you rather have an umbrella, perhaps? It'll serve the same purpose.'

'Not an umbrella. I should put it down and forget it.'
Somehow she managed to make her voice sound normal as she
answered him. She did not want an umbrella. It would not
shelter her suddenly white cheeks from eyes that were too keen,
and must even now make their owner wonder at her change of
colour. She prayed he did not guess its real cause. A hat brim
would shade them. She chose a hat at random, heedless of its
shape or colour, conscious only of its wide and kindly sheltering
brim. She tugged at the zip of her bag, but Woolfe was before
her, and paid for her choice before she could get her purse out.

'I'll pay for my own hat.' Pride reasserted itself. If she could
not have his love, she did not want his patronage, she told herself
fiercely.

'Keep it as a souvenir,' he replied carelessly, and handed coins
from his own pocket to the hat seller, and the hat to herself,
much as he had given her the peach.

'Mind you don't slip on the rubbish,' he added, before she
could protest further, and steered her round a clutter of orange
peel, banana skins and assorted debris that littered the surrounds
of a nearby fruit stall, pointing to a busy trade, and untidy-
minded customers.

'Why doesn't the trader sweep it up?' Isla began critically,
and paused as a sudden outburst of shouting sounded from
somewhere among the crowd behind them.

'It sounds as if someone's having an argument.' She looked
back over her shoulder to try to see the cause of the affray.

'It looks as if someone's in trouble,' Woolfe responded drily,
as the loinclothed figure of a youth burst from the crowd and
raced towards them along the aisle between the stalls, hotly
pursued by a stout man who looked as if he might be a market
trader, and a similarly portly individual in the uniform of the
local police.

'They haven't got a chance of catching up with him.' Isla
viewed the chase with interest, and mentally laid her shirt on
the shirtless figure of the youth. His slender brown body sped
towards them with the speed of a gazelle, his bare brown feet
and legs easily outdistancing the less athletic ones of his pursuers.
Isla automatically stepped back to Woolfe's side to give the
youth room to pass, instinctive sympathy for the underdog,

rather than reason, guiding her action.

'He's only a boy.'

Whether the youth saw her move and guessed her intention, or whether he heard the quick compassion in her voice, Isla could not tell, and she had no time to think, as the boy suddenly veered and ran straight towards her. Her sympathy gave way to alarm as the runner reached out his hand, and before she could back away she felt her arm grasped by urgent brown fingers. She had a quick impression of a thin, frightened face, felt something small and hard and knobbly downpressed into the palm of her hand, the brown fingers swiftly closed her own over whatever it was, and with a muttered word or two in a language she was unable to understand, the boy sped on, twisting and turning among the market stalls until he finally disappeared from sight among the crowd.

'What . . .?' Isla started to ask Woolfe, 'What did he say?' but he gave her no time to finish her question. With a hard hand he grabbed her round the waist and spun her to face him. With his other he snatched from her hand whatever it was the youth had put there, and reached for the top of her blouse. Isla went rigid as his fingers slid inside the material of the deep, scooped neckline.

'Take your hand away—this minute!' she cried, shrill with outrage. Had he gone completely mad? How dare he! How da. . . .'

His mouth closed over her own with a force that cut off her cry, and drove her lips back against her teeth, and the furious words back into her throat, unuttered. She tried to struggle, but she was as helpless as an infant against his superior strength. He pulled her against him with a pressure that pinioned her one arm to her side, but her other arm was still free. She raised it frantically, and swung it back to strike a blow to his head with the last ounce of her remaining strength.

'I must stop him! I must. . . .' His fingers fumbled with the top of her blouse. She felt them gain entrance and slide down inside the gauzy material. She half expected to hear it tear, so urgent was his seeking hand. Her senses began to reel, and with a last desperate surge of energy she swung her arm.

Something small and hard and knobbly slid down inside her

blouse. She felt its unyielding shape against the softness of her skin, and then it was gone, slipping right down inside to join her fugitive handkerchief at her waistline, a small lumpy pain between them as Woolfe pressed her body relentlessly against his own. Instantly his fingers disentangled themselves from the neck of her blouse, and his hand flashed upwards and caught her own a second before her vengeful blow could fall. With a quick twist he turned her arm behind her back and held it against her waist, not painfully, but with a strength that denied her the freedom to move, since the movement brought both his arms right round her, arching her body so that her face was upturned to his.

'Don't speak. Whatever happens, stay silent.' With his lips hovering only a fraction of an inch above her own, he hissed a low, urgent warning. It seemed to reach her disbelieving ears from a long distance away.

'Stay silent. . . .'

She was in no condition to do anything else, she realised hysterically. Her lips felt numb from the brutal force of Woolfe's attack—it could be described as little else, she thought furiously—but even anger could not dispel the daze of shock that closed over her mind like an impenetrable mist, and she swayed, half fainting in his arms, her breath coming in gasping sobs so that she was unable to speak even if she wanted to. Unable to answer the voluble trader who panted to a relieved halt beside them, or the sweating policeman who, when he managed to get his breath back, demanded,

'What did the thief give to this woman? We saw him run towards her.'

'He gave her nothing, except the fright of her life.' Woolfe brushed aside the questions angrily, and the policeman paused, nonplussed by the unexpected authority in his manner, an authority that his slackly open mouth recognised as being of a much higher rank than his own.

'If I'd known the market abounded in thieves and rubbish,' Woolfe roundly condemned the area and its security, 'I'd never have brought Miss Barclay to see it.' He warmed to his theme as the policeman repeated hesitatingly,

'Miss. . . .?'

'Barclay, from Barclays showrooms, the fine art dealers in the main shopping area,' Woolfe pursued his advantage relentlessly. 'Like his namesake,' Isla thought bemusedly, 'cornering his quarry ready for the final spring.'

'What Miss Barclay's firm will have to say about such happenings, I cannot imagine. It's infamous that one cannot bring a lady,' the glint in Woolfe's eye punished the policeman for calling her, 'this woman', 'bring a lady sightseeing without having her subjected to such distress.'

Her distress was not occasioned by the youth, but by Woolfe's behaviour, but Isla let it pass. The daze was clearing from her mind a little now, and she listened amazed to Woolfe's harangue, while his warning echoed sharp in her ears.

'Stay silent. . . .'

Numbly, she obeyed him. She would demand her own explanation from him later. 'It had better be a good one,' she told herself grimly, but the small, hard something that rested underneath her blouse and against her midriff suggested that it might hold at least part of the explanation, so she remained silent, and played up to Woolfe's description of her as a damsel in distress. She nearly made the mistake of smiling at the description, and for fear that she might unwittingly spoil Woolfe's ascendancy over the arm of the local law she turned her face against his shoulder and clung to him with both hands, and closed her eyes as if she was still feeling faint. It was easy to cling to him, dangerously easy, and with her eyes closed she could shut away reality, and dream.

'I saw the youth reach out.' The policeman made a final attempt to regain his lost authority.

'He did,' Woolfe snapped. 'He slipped on the appalling mess of rubbish lying round this stall.' The collector's disgusted gesture made the rubbish twice as deep as it really was. 'The lad grabbed at Miss Barclay for support to save himself from falling, with the result as you can see,' his curt nod indicated Isla's limp form in his arms, and his condemnation was as harsh as it was unforgiving.

'Never mind, love,' his arms cradled her, and his voice crooned above her, and Isla's heart wept because it was only play-acting, for the policeman's benefit, and not for real.

'Don't! Don't!' she longed to cry, but her numb lips could not speak, and her closed eyes could not plead for her.

'It's all over now,' Woolfe reassured her. It *was* all over, she thought, before it had even begun, for her, and the knowledge and the anguish contracted her heart until her faintness became real again, and she clung to Woolfe, this time with a genuine need of support.

'If the lady . . . if Miss Barclay could give me a description of the youth,' the policeman caught Woolfe's glare, and hurriedly remembered her name.

'It all happened so quickly, I doubt if the youth's appearance even registered with her,' Woolfe replied briefly. 'I know it didn't with me.'

He maligned himself, Isla guessed shrewdly. His eyes were as keen as those of his namesake, his observation as unerring, and his reactions as swift, so that she had no doubt that the boy's face, figure, and any identifying features were at this moment clearly imprinted upon his mind.

'Do you think you'd recognise the youth again, love?' Did he *have* to use that particular endearment? Isla asked herself chokingly, and shook her head without attempting to open her eyes.

'I thought not.' With a swift, decisive movement Woolfe swung her up high into his arms, and she stifled a gasp as the move brought her face once more, agonisingly, close to his own, the top of her head just touching the tip of his chin as he bent to look down into her face.

'Miss Barclay's staying at the British Consulate. If you want to ask her anything else, you must contact her there through me.' He ensured that she would not be personally pestered by questions, she thought with unwilling gratitude, and winced as he added for good measure, 'Miss Barclay's travelling under my protection.'

She did not need protection *by* Woolfe, she needed protection *from* him, Isla thought raggedly, but she felt too limp to argue, and lay quiescent in his arms as he gave his own identity offhandedly, 'My name's Wieland—Woolfe Wieland.'

'Mr Wieland . . . of course . . . the Conference. . . .' Comprehension, dismay and awe struggled for supremacy across the policeman's shiny face, and he galvanised into helpful activity.

'Clear a space—give the lady air. Somebody call a taxi!'

Somebody must have done, Isla realised dimly, because a taxi appeared as if by magic, although she did not see it come. It stopped beside them, and the driver opened the door, and the policeman and the trader stood respectfully aside as Woolfe gently placed her on the back seat, then got in himself beside her. The door slammed shut and the vehicle started away, and from under lifting lids Isla saw the policeman draw himself to attention, and salute smartly. The market trader looked as if he felt undecided whether to follow suit, and as the taxi gathered speed, and left his dilemma still unresolved, Isla opened her eyes fully, and let out a weak giggle.

She felt rather than saw Woolfe turn swiftly to look at her, and the giggle died, and tears blocked her throat as reaction set in and she began to tremble. He did not speak. The taxi drew up at the Consulate steps, and without waiting for the driver to open the door Woolfe ducked out of the cab, and his upper half disappeared from view as he straightened his athletic frame to its full six feet plus, and Isla thought wildly,

'All this has happened before.' But this time she did not remain stubbornly sitting in her corner of the taxi seat. She slid towards the door after Woolfe without any prompting from him. Her legs did not feel capable of carrying her up the Consulate steps unaided, and as if he sensed this Woolfe paid off the taxi driver, then bent in through the opened door and reached in to draw her from the taxi with surprisingly gentle hands. They did not release their hold when she gained the pavement, but adjusted themselves round her waist so that she felt herself half helped and half lifted up the steps. And at the top of the steps, exactly as she had done before, Zoe stood waiting for them.

'It's like the playback of an old film.' Isla gave herself a mental shake to make sure which day she was in. 'There's one piece of the playback missing—the best piece.' When they gained the top of the steps on the first occasion, Woolfe put down her suitcase, and kissed her. This time, there was no suitcase—and no kiss. Her heart mourned the omission, and nearly made the tears overflow. Zoe's figure wavered in front of her blurred vision, and she heard Woolfe say,

'Isla's not feeling too good. I'll see her to her room.'

'Too much sun, I expect. Tourists never learn,' Zoe answered contemptuously, and gave Isla a look that would have cooled any temperature as she suggested indifferently, 'why don't you turn her over to the first aid room? They'll look after her.' The look she turned upon Woolfe patently invited, 'And come with me. . . .'

'Too much jet-lag, not too much sun.' To Isla's surprise, Woolfe contradicted Zoe, and made no move to follow her suggestion. His own diagnosis was wide of the mark as well, she thought tartly. You did not suffer from jet-lag after you had been kept kicking your heels at a border post for a frustrating twenty-four hours, you suffered from mounting fury, resentment, impatience, and all sorts of other things, but definitely not jet-lag. The memory of the delay, and its cause, revived her flagging spirits, and she assumed cynically,

'I suppose Woolfe doesn't want to give Zoe the true reason for my being upset. Perhaps he's afraid she might make a scene.' She would have made a scene herself if she had been able to, she told herself wrathfully, and as for the reason, she intended to demand one from Woolfe the very moment they were alone. If he saw her to her room, that would be an excellent opportunity, she decided determinedly.

'Miss Rutherford? Your help's needed with a visitor, miss.'

Zoe gave the uniformed page a glare indicative of her feelings at being so interrupted.

'I'll come in a minute,' she snapped.

'The Consul said to come right away, miss, the visitor's got a plane to catch.'

There was nothing Zoe could do about it. She was on duty, and the Consul was her ultimate authority.

'Duty calls,' Isla murmured sweetly, and blinked at the look of blazing hostility in the other girl's green eyes, but she was beyond caring any longer. She shrugged as Zoe flounced away after the page. Any tantrums the redheaded interpreter could produce would be an anticlimax, she felt, after the events of the morning, first in the showrooms, and then in the market place. Without speaking, Isla turned to walk beside Woolfe in the direction of her room, and silence lay pregnant between them.

Zoe's image walked through the silence, and so did Woolfe's kiss, and the still unexplained reason for his behaviour.

'Now perhaps you'll explain your outrageous behaviour!' Isla spun round inside the doorway of her room, and faced him with a hostile stare, but instead of trying to apologise he compounded the outrage by pushing into the room after her.

'You can't come in here,' she protested indignantly. 'It isn't allowed.' She did not know what rules pertained at the Consulate, but she was sure there must be one against male visitors invading the female staff quarters.

'I'm already in,' Woolfe retorted uncaringly, and to emphasise his in-ness he kicked the door closed behind him. Wood met wood with a resounding thump, isolating them from the world outside, and Isla swallowed hard. She had not anticipated this, and his move took her completely unawares. Her heart began to pound with quick, uneven beats, and the trembling that had plagued her in the taxi returned to plague her again. She groped behind her for support, and leaned back against the dressing table, and mourned that it was hard wood that supported her, and not Woolfe's arms. . . .

'I could scream for help,' she told herself without conviction. If Woolfe kissed her again in the same way he had done in the market place, she would not have the opportunity to scream. Her hand rose shakily to her throat. Woolfe towered over her, watching her, judging her reaction, she realised, probably guessing her thoughts.

'You owe me an explanation—an apology,' she stammered, dragging words out of a dry throat, because words were the only weapon she had to keep him at bay. While they were talking he could not. . . .

'Never mind explanations now.' He thrust aside her demand, and made no attempt to apologise, and indignation at such casual dismissal of his infamous behaviour brought her courage back with a rush.

'I do mind,' she flung back at him furiously, 'and I want. . . .'

'I want to have a look at the thing that boy thrust into your hand in the market place,' he interrupted her tirade impatiently.

'And which you instantly snatched from me,' she reminded

him angrily, 'and stuffed down the neck of my blouse!' She choked into silence at the memory.

'I relied on the elastic in the waistband of your skirt to hold it safe until we could get back here and see what it was the boy was in such a hurry to get rid of.' He made no attempt to apologise, even now. He spoke as if stuffing whatever it was down the neck of her blouse was the most obvious place to put it. Like rubbish in a dustbin, Isla thought, speechless with indignation. 'Did you imagine,' he stared down at her in silence for what seemed an endless minute, and meeting his gaze she quailed before the expression in his eyes. 'Did you imagine for one moment that I'd any other reason for behaving in such a manner?' he asked her at last, icily, and his tone held all the cold and all the fury of a midwinter blizzard across the Polar ice-cap.

'Yes . . . no . . . I. . . .' She ground to a halt, unable to meet his look, unable to go on.

'I'm not in the habit of assaulting women.' His proud repudiation of such behaviour was the biting wind that rode the blizzard. His words, his look, sliced through her like a knife, and she shivered under their cutting blast.

'I want to see what it was the boy gave to you,' he demanded, when she did not answer.

'It's under the waistband of my skirt.' The ice numbed her brain so that she was incapable of coherent thought, and his demand did not immediately register.

'Then get it out,' he shouted at her impatiently, 'or do you want me to do it for you?' His demeanour was a promise rather than a threat.

'You wouldn't . . .?' She decided he would. His eyes were gimlet-hard, and in them was a look of implacable resolve that sent her cheeks first scarlet and then white, and she capitulated with a hurried,

'I'll go into the shower cubicle.' Each bedroom boasted one. 'I shan't be a minute.'

'Don't be.' His tone was curt, and warned her that any delay would bring him into the cubicle after her. Uneasily she remembered that, as part of the bedroom suite, the cubicle had no lock. 'And don't let whatever it is drop on to the tiled floor,'

Woolfe warned her urgently. 'Jade's brittle.'

'I won't.' She smarted under his authoritarian directions. '*What* did you say is brittle?' She spun round half way across the room, and stared at him, the import of his words striking her like a blow.

'I said, jade is brittle,' he repeated his words deliberately, seeing the rush of understanding, and doubt, and hope flash across her mobile face.

'I didn't have time to look at it properly, everything happened so suddenly in the market place, but if the lad gave you what I think he did, you'll be as interested in it as I am,' he reminded her significantly. 'And in case my assumption's correct,' the stunned look on Isla's face prompted him to repeat his previous warning, 'don't let it drop on to the tiles.'

'I'll get it out in here, where there's a carpet. Turn your back.' As if in a dream Isla met his long, level regard. 'I'm not going to escape through the door,' she snapped when he remained watching her. 'If what you suspect is true, the fewer people who know about it the better.'

'I entirely agree,' he answered drily, and Isla stared. Woolfe was actually agreeing with her! Wonders would never cease. Another wonder happened. He did as she asked him to, and turned away, strolling over to the window, where he remained looking out with his back ostentatiously turned towards the room, and Isla.

'It went down here, next to my hanky.' With fingers that shook so much she could scarcely control them, Isla slid her hand under her waistband. It encountered her handkerchief.

'The thing isn't here.' She gulped. 'It must have slipped through. Perhaps in the taxi. . . .' A wave of panic gripped her, and she fumbled frantically round the elastic shirring on the top of her skirt. 'No, here it is. It had slid round, that's all.' She went limp with relief, and sat down hurriedly on the side of the bed.

'Give it to me. Let me see it.' With two long strides Woolfe moved away from the window and crossed the room to her side. The bed sagged as he sat down beside her.

'Wait a minute, it's got tangled up in the material of my blouse.' Fear that impatience might drive him to repeat his performance in the market place galvanised Isla's fingers with new life, and she untangled the small, knobbly thing from her waist-band and produced it triumphantly. There was a moment's tense silence, and then, quick as light, Woolfe grabbed it from her.

'The Kang amulet,' he breathed, and cupped it reverently in his palm.

'The Kang amulet?' Without thinking, Isla found herself whispering, too. A heady sensation gripped her as she stared at the amulet, a strange mixture of excitement and awe, mingled in no small measure with fear. This was the thing that had dominated her thoughts and dreams and actions since she returned from South America. This bauble of human vanity, that lay looking up at her from the palm of Woolfe's hand, had brought her across the world, and Woolfe in her train. Originally fashioned as a love gift for a queen, the amulet had suffered many vicissitudes in its long history, and aroused many passions; wonder at its beauty, greed, avarice, and desire. Men had lied for it, and died for it.

Isla stared fascinated at the drop-shaped pendant, the colour of pale putty, and not much larger than a large cameo brooch. It was deeply carved in a floral pattern, the centre of each tiny flower bejewelled, and the edges of the petals picked out in gold. Intricate, delicate work, performed by a master craftsman using the primitive tools of three thousand or more years ago.

'How can you be sure it's the genuine amulet?' Isla found her voice at last, a dry, reedy travesty of her normal voice that faded into silence as she looked up and caught the expression on Woolfe's face. He stared down at the amulet, his eyes devouring it, seemingly oblivious to all else except the globule of white jade in the middle of his palm. With one finger he traced the outline of it, gently as if he was afraid that even that light touch might somehow damage the brittle material. Isla caught her breath, and a cold finger traced its way along her spine, and all her half-formed suspicions of Woolfe returned with renewed force.

The Kang amulet. Over the centuries, men had lied for it, and died for it. Was Woolfe the latest of that band?

'It could be a copy, a fake,' she insisted. Suddenly she found herself wishing it was a copy, that the real amulet no longer existed. She felt she hated the amulet, and all that it stood for. She felt the desire to cry, return with renewed force.

'The carving could be copied,' Woolfe spoke abstractedly, as if he was hardly aware of her presence at his side, 'but no one could copy the ageing of the jade, nor the signs of wear, where the edges of the carving have been rubbed smooth by use and handling over the centuries. See here, and here.' His long, slim index finger, with the short-cut filbert nail, pointed to the signs of wear. 'The carving on a copy would have sharper edges.'

'I wish we'd found Robin, instead of the amulet.' Isla stirred uneasily. The jewels set into the jade seemed to wink at her mockingly, as Woolfe turned it this way and that in his hand, catching the light. 'I wish I knew what it was the boy said to me, when he pushed it into my hand.'

'Roughly translated, he said, "Take it, missie," ' Woolfe replied casually. Too casually? Isla searched his face, trying to see any sign of concealment, but his lean features were inscrutable, giving nothing away. But now he had the amulet, was actually holding it in his hand, what possible reason could he have to lie to her? Unless—she felt suddenly sick at the possibility—unless Robin, too, suspected Woolfe, and the collector had become aware of his suspicions, and meant to silence them. . . .

'If only I understood the language,' Isla wished helplessly. There was no one else she could ask. No one but herself and Woolfe had been close enough to hear the boy's panted words, and the boy himself, like Robin, had disappeared. If she could somehow manage to find him. . . . In spite of her denial, she felt convinced she would recognise the youth if she saw him again.

'The amulet doesn't appear to be damaged in any way.'

Isla became aware that Woolfe was speaking, and she hastily switched off her thoughts. He had an uncanny ability to read her mind, and it was imperative that he should remain in ignorance of the half-formed plans that were racing through it now.

'I hope the talisman it contains is in similar good condition. The scroll isn't made of such durable material as the amulet.' Carefully Woolfe turned the jade over in his hand, and using a light pressure with the tip of one finger, he slid the back of it upwards to reveal a hollow space inside.

'It's empty!'

They both spoke at once, and their eyes met above the drop-shaped pendant.

'The scroll's gone.'

'I haven't taken it.' Isla denied the charge before it was even made.

'I know.' Woolfe answered her flatly. 'I saw you take the amulet out of your skirt top, just now.'

Implying that he believed her only because he knew she had not had the opportunity to remove the scroll? Isla's eyes flashed angrily, but before she could give voice to the indignant denial that trembled on the tip of her tongue, Woolfe spoke again, harshly, and with a look on his face, she shivered, that boded ill for the one who had removed the precious, painted scroll.

'Whoever's taken the talisman has removed the most valuable, as well as the most vulnerable part of the pendant. If the scroll's been damaged in any way,' Woolfe declared grimly, 'the person responsible will answer to me.'

CHAPTER FIVE

DID he believe the person responsible for removing the talisman from the amulet might be Robin?

'You'll have to find the culprit first,' she countered.

'I'll find him, if it takes for ever,' Woolfe assured her grimly, and Isla believed him. He possessed the timeless patience of his namesake, and if it took the rest of his life, she knew he would not rest until he traced the talisman, if it was still in existence.

'Unless someone's destroyed it, I'll find the scroll and return it to the amulet. And in the meantime,' his tone altered, and became brisk, 'I'll lodge the jade in the Consulate safe.'

'No, it must be placed in our own strongroom, at Barclays,' Isla objected instantly. 'Woolfe's got no right to dispose of the amulet. The boy gave it to me, not to him,' she told herself angrily. It should be her decision where it was to be lodged. If she had thought Woolfe would take this proprietorial attitude towards it, she would not have handed it over to him in the first place.

'The Consulate safe is perfectly adequate.'

'And I say it's not. The strongroom at Barclays is specially built to hold priceless objects.' She faced him defiantly, with the glint of battle in her eyes.

'The safe at the Consulate is specially built to hold State secrets.' He broke off as a sharp knock sounded on the bedroom door.

'Just a moment,' Isla called out hastily, and then in a worried undertone, 'Who on earth can it be?'

'We're caught in the classic compromising situation,' Woolfe taunted her wickedly, accurately reading the expressions of concern and dismay that flitted across her mobile face, and she stared at him, amazed. He was actually laughing at her, enjoying her confusion, and making absolutely no effort to help her out of the latter, she realised with mounting fury.

'It's all very well for you!' she lashed out at him hotly. Even in this so-called enlightened age, men were excused many things that would damn a woman. 'If you're seen here, in my room, what will people think?' Too late she wished her words unsaid. Too late she remembered asking him the same question at the top of the Consulate steps, and his lightning response. Was it only yesterday? Since then, she seemed to have travelled in time for as long as the Kang amulet itself.

'They'll probably think all sorts of things they shouldn't,' Woolfe grinned at her unsympathetically, and her face flamed. Did he think she remembered yesterday, and was deliberately trying to repeat it? 'So long as they don't suspect the real reason I'm here,' he added casually, 'there's no need to worry.'

For Woolfe, maybe there was not. For herself. . . . Isla gasped as he leaned down and lightly, tantalisingly, brushed her lips with his own. Repeating the sequence of events that told her he remembered yesterday. Gone was the glacial cold of the Polar blizzard, his kiss seared her lips with a bolt of lightning, burning its impression upon her mouth like a brand. Woolfe's brand.

So he did think. . . . Shame and humiliation darkened her colour still further, and his grin widened as he surveyed her scarlet cheeks.

'Keep on blushing,' he told her approvingly, 'then whoever it is who's just knocked on the door for the third time will think the very worst, and our secret,' he tapped the amulet significantly, 'our secret will be safe.' Twin devils of mischief lit his eyes, and Isla felt as if she could cheerfully slay him as he raised his voice and invited the knocker loudly to, 'Come in!'

'How could you!' But he already had, and there was nothing she could do but face whoever it was who was trying to gain admittance, who even now pushed open the door and said, with an interested glance towards Woolfe, and a too carefully impassive face turned towards herself,

'A parcel for you, Miss Barclay. It's just been delivered.'

Even as she reached out to take the carefully wrapped parcel from the hands of the Consulate messenger, Woolfe made his expedient escape through the door. Isla opened her mouth to call him back, to demand her right to a say in the disposal of the jade, but she might as well have tried to capture quicksilver. She just had time to notice that Woolfe kept one hand deep in his pocket, the hand that held the Kang amulet, and then he was gone, and she was left to face the messenger alone.

With a visible effort Isla collected her scattered wits sufficiently to thank the man, and reward him for his trouble. She hoped the size of the reward would ensure his silence on the subject of her room visitor, and knew fatalistically that it would not. People who were marooned by their work among fellow countrymen in a foreign city inevitably formed small cliques, and Isla could imagine that in such a gathering, gossip would be rife. Sooner or later it was bound to reach Zoe's ears, and then. . . .

'Woolfe's got no right!' she stormed distractedly as the door closed behind the departing messenger and his latest titbit, no doubt to be regaled larger than life to the first colleague he encountered when he got outside into the corridor. Probably the commissionaire. Isla's face burned again at the snide remarks and unpleasant insinuations that would attach to her name.

'It's my room, not Woolfe's. He'd got no right to invite anybody in.'

He had invited himself in, without questioning his right. And then he had taken himself out again, with the amulet still in his possession, and used her good name as a smokescreen to cover his departure, ostensibly to put the amulet in the Consulate safe. But what proof had she that he intended to do just that? By his act of calling the messenger into her room, Woolfe had neatly trapped her for just long enough to ensure she had no check on his movements. It was of no use her trying to ask the Consul, she knew. No doubt Woolfe would present a package of some kind into the safe keeping of the custodian of the Consulate safe, and the Consul's discretion was absolute. He was as unlikely to ask Woolfe what were the contents of the package as he was to discuss one guest's valuables entrusted to his safe keeping with another guest. And who was to know whether it was the amulet that was in the package, or a worthless trinket? Tears of frustration blinded Isla's eyes, and she sank limply down again on to her bed as the door closed behind the messenger.

'If only I hadn't given him the amulet! Woolfe's got no right. . . .' And suddenly rights ceased to matter, and with a strangled sob Isla flung herself face downwards on to the pillows. 'He shouldn't have used me so,' she wept bitterly. But he had used her, shamefully used her good name to cover his escape, and left her to cope as best she could with an impossible situation, that she felt despairingly certain would lead to endless embarrassment later on when it became known among the Consulate staff.

The storm broke, and the tears flowed, and agonisingly Isla paid the price for the bright, gilded moments of reckless emotion that the chiming of the pagoda bells had warned her was to come, and like a basking butterfly spreading its wings in the fickle sunshine, that in its innocence it believed would last for ever, she had given no heed to the warning, until the sun went down, and the darkness came, and hurtled her heart into an abyss of despair from which the only arm long enough to rescue her must belong to,

'Woolfe! Woolfe. . . .'

Her own voice woke her, calling his name. Bewilderedly she sat up and pressed her hands to her throbbing head. Her cheeks felt wet against her palms, and her breath still caught in small, sobbing gasps. Listlessly she swung her legs off the bed, and her one knee knocked sharply against something hard and oblong.

'Ouch!' She rubbed her fingers across her eyes to clear her vision, and discovered the parcel the messenger had left. She tested it experimentally in one hand. It was remarkably heavy for its size. She fingered it for a moment or two before the clouds of sleep dispersed sufficiently to allow memory to return.

'Of course,' she exclaimed, 'the sandalwood workbox! And the maps. The manager must have put the maps inside, as he promised.' That would account for the weight. She tore at the wrapping with eager fingers. It did not come apart easily, she discovered. It was securely taped, as befitted the value of the workbox, and, she noted approvingly, it had been carefully sealed at each end with the House of Barclay seal, as befitted what she anticipated the contents to be.

'A diplomatic seal of a different kind,' she gave the relief manager full marks for his diplomacy, and thrust the last of the wrapping aside. Without vouchsafing even a glance at the beautiful ivory inlay work on the box lid, she flung it open, and gave an exclamation of satisfaction as she viewed the contents.

'Thank goodness he's been able to send some maps!'

The aroma of sandalwood wafted upwards from the opened lid, but Isla had no time to appreciate it now. With quick hands she turned the box upside down, and shook the contents on to her lap.

'He's done me proud!' she thought. A total of three maps, and one guide book fell out of the box, to be followed by a pen and ink sketch. It was crudely drawn on Barclays headed note-paper, and Isla picked it up curiously. It depicted a line leading out of a circle marked 'Kaul'. Half way along the line there was an asterisk, and beyond that, another line across the paper, intersecting the first. The second line led off at a tangent towards a series of humps that Isla presumed represented a mountain range. The line carried on across these—a mountain pass?—and at the highest point was scripted another name: Tan Gwe monastery. At the bottom of the page was another asterisk, and a brief handwritten note bore a cryptic message. Isla caught her breath, wide awake now, and a tingle of excitement coursed through her as she read it.

'It was from about here, where I've marked the asterisk, along the road leading away from Kaul, that your brother sent his last message to Huw Morgan.' That, and a scribbled signature, was all.

Bless the relief manager! Bless, too, the impulse that had prompted her to invite him to conspire with herself against the people at the Consulate, and Woolfe. It was a childish, spur-of-the-moment 'ganging up', and it had paid handsome dividends, Isla thought with satisfaction.

What if Woolfe came back? Thoughts of him galvanised her into hurried action. Quickly she stuffed the maps back under the brown paper wrapping. If Woolfe did return, he might simply knock on the door and walk straight in. Or even not bother to knock at all. 'Whatever happens, he mustn't discover me studying maps. He mustn't even know I've got them,' she told herself. It was imperative she should guard her very thoughts from him until she had formulated her plans, and was free to carry them out undetected. She hurried over to the door. The stout wood boasted an equally stout bolt, even if the shower cubicle did not. Hastily she slid the steel bar home as far as it would go.

'He'll have to burst the door down to get through that,' she muttered maliciously, and hurried back to the maps. All three, she saw thankfully, were large-scale detail prints, and she shook them out flat on the counterpane the better to study them. One she pushed aside for the moment. It was of Kaul itself, and obviously went hand in hand with the guide book, since it marked all the places of possible interest to an ordinary tourist.

The other two maps were complementary to one another. The one followed the main road out of Kaul to the north. Main road was a euphemism, she saw, since there was only one road marked on that side of the town, which would make her task easier because she could compare it with the ink sketch, confident that they each followed the same route. The other map was of the mountain pass from where it snaked down the slopes to join the road running out of the town.

'Miss Barclay?'

A sharp knock sounded on the door, and Isla froze, as a wild creature freezes when danger threatens. Her eyes, wide and startled, fixed themselves on the door.

'Miss Barclay? Are you there, miss?'

'Yes . . . yes, I'm here. What is it?'

'Don't be silly!' she scolded herself vigorously. She was as nervous as if she was engaged in some criminal activity, instead of merely studying maps. And since the door was firmly bolted, no one, not even Woolfe, could get in unless she opened it for them. But it was not Woolfe's voice calling her from outside the door.

'Only to tell you, miss, that lunch is being served in the small dining room today, not the large one, because we haven't got many visitors.'

'Thanks for the warning,' Isla called back, and her voice sounded almost gay with relief. 'I know the room you mean, the one next to the banqueting hall.'

'That's the one, miss,' her informant confirmed cheerfully. 'Now I'm sure you know where it is, I won't wait, I'll go on and warn the others.'

'The small dining room,' Isla murmured dubiously. The one presided over by the second gargoyle. Not a small room by normal standards, only by comparison, but small enough to make the meal uncomfortable if only a few people were present, and the messenger who brought the parcel had broadcast his discovery that he had seen Woolfe in her room. Small enough to be untenable, she owned uneasily, if the messenger's version of the incident had already reached Zoe's ears, and the interpreter decided to be spiteful. Isla shook herself mentally, and squared her shoulders.

'I might as well brazen it out now, as later,' she told herself resolutely. 'I've got to eat some time.' Breakfast had been a non-event, and the peach Woolfe had given to her in the market place was a long-forgotten dream. She was, she discovered with surprise, ravenously hungry.

Cloak and dagger activities evidently suited her digestion. But in spite of her attempt at levity, she could not shrug off the qualms of trepidation that accelerated her heart beat as she reached the door of the small dining room, and paused with her hand on the knob.

'It isn't Zoe I'm afraid to face, it's Woolfe,' she admitted with ruthless honesty. The gargoyle's plaster grin seemed almost friendly, she decided ruefully, in comparison with the reception she expected to get when she stepped into the room. With a faint moue upwards at the ugly little character, Isla braced herself and turned the knob.

Zoe had heard. The moment she set eyes on the interpreter, Isla knew The other girl flashed her a look of pure venom as she walked through the door, but to Isla's surprise, instead of the shrill denunciation which she half expected, the redheaded girl remained silent on the subject of her room visitor, and contented herself with a critical,

'You're only just in time. Another five minutes and we'd have started without you.'

Since it was only a buffet lunch anyway, Isla could not see that it mattered. She made no answer to Zoe, and turned away to collect a mixed plateful of food from the buffet table, and the necessary cutlery, and used her movements as a cover to look round the room to discover if Woolfe was already present. His tall figure made her task simple. He stood out among the twenty or so people grouped about the room, distinguished by his appearance as much as by his height, she saw with a quick pang that vanished in a wave of suspicious conjecture when she saw to whom he was talking.

'The scientist who bought the Clichy paperweight,' she muttered, and wished fervently, 'I'd give a good deal to know what the connection is between the two.' She frowned. Could it be the Kang amulet? She forgot Zoe and her spiteful remarks. Dimly it dawned upon her consciousness that the interpreter could not openly embarrass her without at the same time implicating Woolfe, which she was hardly likely to do. Suddenly it did not seem important beside the far greater urgency of learning what it was the scientist and Woolfe were talking about.

Isla eyed the small groups of people who stood between them, busily eating and talking. If she could unobtrusively edge through the crowd and get somewhere within earshot. . . . There were one or two people in a loosely knit group standing by the buffet table not too far away from the scientist and the collector. If she could edge along the table and attach herself inconspicuously to the outskirts of the group, she might be able to hear what the two were talking about, without either of them noticing she was there. Slowly she began to move across the room, using the subterfuge of collecting another helping of food in order to cover her movements.

'An extra inch or two round my waistline will be worth it,' she told herself unrepentantly, and haphazardly spooned unknown things on to her plate, with the whole of her attention concentrated on the conversing pair, and none on her digestion.

'Ah, Miss Barclay, I'm glad to see you've regained your appetite.'

'Oh ... er ... Consul. ...' Isla suddenly became aware of her host and her heaped plate, and regarded both of them with equal dismay.

'I notice Wieland and Armstrong are talking shop again.' The diplomat did not seem to notice her disconcertment, and went on genially, 'Those two have a great deal in common.'

They had a lot more in common than the Consul imagined, Isla thought grittily, and made a mental note of the scientist's surname. The knowledge would come in useful when the opportunity arose for her to check the destination of the man's flight home at the end of the month.

'These collectors!' the diplomat exclaimed indulgently. 'But I expect you're accustomed to their enthusiasms?' he smiled down at Isla. 'Indeed, you must share them, being in the fine art business yourself, so why not let's join them, and find out what it is they're discussing so earnestly? It might be of interest to you, too.'

It was of paramount interest to her, but not in the way the Consul meant. Always the perfect host, her kindly escort ushered her across the remaining space between themselves and the two men, his intention being to ensure that Isla was not left to lunch alone, which she wanted to, and to join her with Woolfe and his companion, which she did not. She most urgently desired to be left on her own, to hover within earshot of the talking pair without disturbing them, in order to learn what it was they were talking so earnestly about, while remaining undetected herself. The Consul's kindly intervention effectively broke up any conversation that might have been of interest to her, and completely foiled her attempt to discover what was the link between Woolfe and the scientist.

'I probably wouldn't have been able to get close enough to

hear what it was they were saying, anyhow,' she consoled herself resignedly. Woolfe had already seen them coming, his alert eyes caught their movement in his direction while the sound of his voice was still an indistinct murmur to Isla's straining ears. She saw him look up as they approached, his glance taking in the room and all that was happening in it, in one comprehensive, sweeping look, and then he glanced back and said something to his companion—warning him of the imminent arrival of the Consul and herself?—and the scientist instantly stopped whatever it was he was about to say, and turned as well to greet them.

'You've already met Miss Barclay at dinner last night, Armstrong.' Tactfully their host ensured each remembered the other. 'Two collectors and a fine art dealer should have a great deal in common,' the diplomat smiled, and with his duty done he gave Isla a kindly nod, and left her with the two men.

'Thrown to the wolves,' she told herself bitterly. Or rather, to Woolfe. She caught his eyes above her loaded plate. They glinted at her derisively, telling her that he had watched her efforts to get within earshot, and mocking her lack of success. Taunting herself with having burdened herself with an unseemly second helping of food that she did not either need or want, simply in order to further those efforts, and daring her to leave the plateful now she had acquired it.

'I can't leave it,' she realised with growing panic, and, 'I can't possibly eat all this! What on earth shall I do?'

'Eat up,' Woolfe encouraged her heartily, and his eyes laughed down into her face, acutely observant of the doubt and uncertainty, the frustration and dismay that flitted across her telltale features, allowing him to read her thoughts as clearly as a book.

'That lot should keep the wolf from the door,' he misquoted with a meaning look at her plate, and Isla knew with impotent fury that her hot cheeks betrayed to him all too clearly that his double meaning was not lost upon her. She stabbed at a piece of cucumber with a vicious fork, and hated him for goading her when he must know she was powerless to retaliate. Hated the conventions that demanded she listened to polite small talk from the scientist, when all the time she longed to scream at Woolfe, to denounce him for taking the Kang amulet from her, demand that he produce proof that he had put it in the Consulate safe, and, almost irresistible temptation, hurl her plate of buffet delicacies at his grinning face, the look on which warned her clearly that its owner intended to detain her until she had eaten every last morsel, as a punishment for trying to eavesdrop on his conversation.

'I can't possibly eat another mouthful. If I do, I'll be sick.' Ten minutes of gastronomic desperation later, Isla's eyes met Woolfe's in a silent plea for mercy over the mound of unwanted food, that in spite of her valiant efforts still seemed enough to feed a good sized regiment.

'It'll serve you right if you are,' his remorseless glance replied.

'If only someone would shout, "Fire!" Or even just come across and join us, and take Woolfe's attention for a few minutes, while I dispose of the plate.' Isla glanced round her with a hunted look.

'I really must rush.'

Unexpectedly the scientist Armstrong rescued her. He gave an urgent glance at his watch. 'It's being in such charming company,' he blamed Isla gallantly. 'I'd completely forgotten the time.' He held out his hand, and she grasped it with fervent gratitude, and with her other quickly grasped the opportunity and slid her plate on to the end of the buffet table. 'It's been most interesting to talk to you, Miss Barclay.'

'You must visit our showrooms again, some time.' She tried to instil some enthusiasm into her voice, guiltily conscious that she had scarcely heard a word the man said. If his conversation had been interesting to him, it had completely passed over her head. Her whole attention had been on Woolfe, desperately trying to resist the mental pressure that forced her to eat the unwanted food, steeling herself to withstand him and bitterly aware that her efforts were to little avail.

'You've left your lunch,' Woolfe said evenly, and reached out to retrieve her plate.

'Eat it yourself!' Isla hissed back at him furiously, and turned her back quickly to cover a disconcerting burp, too late, she felt irritably certain, to avoid him hearing. Crossly she held her breath, trying to stop the threatened attack of hiccups, and trying at the same time to ignore his low chuckle of amusement that rang maddeningly in her ears as she turned beside the scientist towards the door.

'Do you really have to go so soon, Professor Armstrong?' She did not want the man's company, but she urgently needed him as a buffer between her self and Woolfe.

'Indeed I do, my dear young lady. I happen to be speaking at this afternoon's meeting of the Conference, and it begins in half an hour.'

'I'll see you to the door.' As a temporary resident at the Consulate, Isla felt it gave her the excuse to act as a sort of hostess. She did not care whether the scientist was a speaker, or a member of the audience at the afternoon session of the Conference, but seeing him off would provide her with an excellent excuse to remove herself from the room at the same time, without exciting Woolfe's curiosity. She glanced over her shoulder. One of the other guests had detained him, she saw with relief, and hoped he would be kept talking for long enough to enable her to make good her escape. There were things she needed to do with the afternoon that she did not want Woolfe to know about. The moment she had waved Professor Armstrong goodbye, she would go straight to her room and collect the maps and. . . .

A thought stopped Isla in her tracks. The maps! She had left the maps and the guide book strewn across the top of her bed, where they would be clearly visible if she opened the door to her room. If Woolfe came with her as far as her room, and she opened the door to let herself in, he would see them. It was no use hoping he would not notice, his eyes missed nothing, she thought uneasily. And if she stood at her door and waited for him to walk on before she opened it, he would be instantly suspicious. He might even—she blanched—he might even insist on coming inside to discover what it was she was trying to hide.

'Perhaps Zoe will annexe him,' she thought hopefully. The other girl had tried hard enough to extricate herself from the group she was with, and cross the room to join Woolfe during the lunch session. Isla had seen her make several unsuccessful attempts, and had been conscious of the other girl's barbed glance in her direction when the Consul steered her across the room towards Woolfe and the scientist.

'No doubt she thinks I talked the Consul into taking me

across to them, just to annoy her. Well, she can have Woolfe's company if she wants it. They're welcome to one another,' Isla told herself vindictively.

'I thought Wieland was coming along as well.' Professor Armstrong paused and looked back vaguely. 'I really ought to say goodbye to him. . . .'

'I'll say it for you,' Isla promised hurriedly, and tried to steer her companion back towards the door again. 'He simply mustn't turn back now,' she breathed frantically, and relaxed as he said gratefully,

'Thank you, my dear, that's very kind . . . oh, it won't be necessary, after all.' Her companion beamed, and Isla's heart descended into her sandals as Woolfe broke off his conversation with the other guest, and looked up to see the two of them about to disappear through the door.

'It only needs another two steps,' Isla thought despairingly. 'If only Zoe would grab him!' She looked towards the interpreter, and her hopes rose again as she saw that the redhead was aware that Woolfe was now free, as she had probably been aware of his every movement the whole of the way through lunch, Isla thought uncharitably. Zoe even took a step in Woolfe's direction, only to be foiled in her attempt by the Consul himself. The diplomat saw her move away from the group she was with, and instantly signalled her to join the one of which he was a member. For a moment Isla thought the other girl was going to ignore the signal. Zoe hesitated, and Isla held her breath, but training, and doubtless the need to keep her job until she was certain she had snared Woolfe, Isla surmised drily, combined to enforce her obedience, and Zoe turned back as she was bidden, while Woolfe strode towards herself and the scientist, and it seemed to Isla as if some malign fate was conspiring against her when he remarked casually,

'Perhaps Isla would like to hear your lecture this afternoon, Armstrong.' Woolfe turned to Isla. 'The Professor is lecturing on. . . .'

'No!' Isla refused him explosively. She did not want to hear what it was the Professor was lecturing about. Through a darkening mist of rage she was aware of the scientist's surprised expression, but she could not help herself. The Professor might think Woolfe's invitation was hospitably meant, 'But I know better,' she told herself wrathfully. The lecture might go on for hours, and once in the lecture theatre Woolfe knew she would be obliged to remain there until the talk ended. No doubt he was au fait with the times of the lectures, and their probable length. 'It would suit his purpose admirably to trap me in one place, so that he knows where I am, and for how long, and he can go about and do just what he pleases in the meantime,' Isla thought angrily. It was neatly done, as neatly as the way he had trapped her by calling the messenger into her room. Woolfe was a master of expediency.

'The deceit of the man!' she fumed. 'The conniving, devious, scheming. . . .' Her mind ran out of adjectives for the second time. But this time his manipulations had failed. 'This time, I won't dance to his tune,' she vowed.

'I'd love to listen to one of your lectures, but some other time,' she dredged up a smile for the scientist, remembering in time that he was also a customer of her firm, and one, moreover, with whom it would be politic to remain on good terms if she was to discover what was his connection with Woolfe. 'I spent most of the morning sightseeing, and I'm afraid the heat. . . .' She trailed off languidly, and hoped the man had not noticed her loaded lunch plate, and taken it as an indication of an unaffected appetite.

'Ah yes, the heat. It's the humidity that does it, of course,' the scientist sympathised. 'I thrive on it myself, but it does affect a lot of people. Rest's the best course,' he advised Isla kindly. 'Take it easy until you're accustomed to it.' He turned to Woolfe. 'I'll see you about three o'clock, Wieland. It's good of you to offer to chair the question-and-answer session after the lecture's over.'

So that was why Woolfe wanted her to go to the lecture. Isla fixed the collector with baleful eyes. He would be incarcerated in the lecture theatre himself, and his invitation had been a means of ensuring that he would be able to keep an eye on her during the period when he himself would be tied up on Conference business.

'I'll doubt every word he speaks, from now on,' she vowed. 'I won't trust a thing that he either says, or does.' Even such an innocuous invitation, issued on the spur of the moment, had a double purpose, or rather one main purpose that dictated every move Woolfe made so far as she was concerned, Isla thought bleakly, and that purpose was to prevent her from making any attempt to discover the whereabouts of her brother. Perhaps, the thought occurred to her uneasily, perhaps Woolfe already knew of Robin's whereabouts?

'I'll be there.' Woolfe's tone betrayed no disappointment that she had escaped his trap.

'It's good of you to give up your valuable time,' the scientist told Woolfe gratefully. 'You see,' he smiled at Isla, 'he's in great demand.' His nod took leave of them both, and indicated a man who was even now following the commissionaire's pointing hand in their direction.

'The policeman from the market place.' Isla swallowed on a suddenly dry throat as the uniformed lawman recognised them, and turned in their direction. 'What does he want with us again.'

'Don't panic,' Woolfe murmured sotto voce, 'leave him to me to deal with.'

'With pleasure,' Isla murmured, and lapsed into silence as the policeman reached them.

'Miss Barclay.' He remembered her name this time. 'Mr Wieland.' The man held out an envelope towards Woolfe. 'Two members of the British delegation to the Conference applied for passes to travel into the interior,' he explained the contents of the envelope. 'These papers will allow them a week's travel, but if they need an extension, you have only to contact me.' He puffed himself up importantly.

'Ah yes, thank you.' Woolfe took the envelope from him, apparently familiar with the reason behind it. 'The two delegates are botanists. They want to study the flora and the various soil conditions. I'll see they get their permits,' he promised, and Isla pricked her ears.

So permits had to be obtained to get into the interior. This was news to her. Unwelcome news, since it meant another, and totally unexpected difficulty to overcome. She sighed. Just when the maps had begun to make her search seem a little easier, this had to crop up. But it was better to learn about it beforehand than to run into difficulties with the authorities later on, she told herself philosophically. It would have been the last straw if she had tried to travel into the interior to look for Robin, and been ignominiously escorted back to Kaul by the local representative of the law, simply because she did not have a permit. She frowned. How Woolfe would have laughed!

'I hope you're recovered from this morning's unpleasant experience, Miss Barclay?' She became aware that the policeman was addressing her, and hastily eradicated her frown.

'She is, more or less,' Woolfe replied easily, and a flash of irritation brought Isla's frown back. She was quite capable of answering for herself, she thought crossly, and asked a question instead, quickly, before Woolfe could intervene, or the policeman take his departure.

'What were you chasing the boy for, anyway?' she asked casually. Even a disinterested tourist could be excused curiosity on that score, she told herself defensively, and forbore to look at Woolfe, and meet the disapproval she knew she would find in his face for detaining the policeman unnecessarily. 'What had the boy done?'

'He stole a peach,' the policeman began self-righteously, and Isla nearly laughed. A peach. 'Only a peach?' With an effort, she kept her face straight, and said, 'It seemed a lot of fuss to make, over one peach.' The entire market place had been reduced to uproar, and yet when Robin went missing, everyone concerned had seemed to ignore it, and carry on as if nothing had happened. She hated the crazy, mixed-up sense of values that made a peach more important than a person.

'The trader gave chase,' the policeman began pompously.

'And you chased the trader,' Isla remembered, with what gravity she could muster. 'Did you catch the culprit, in the end?' she asked sweetly. She was no longer interested in whether the youth had been caught or not. If anything, her sympathies lay with the taker of the peach. She felt an acute dislike of the policeman, and unutterably weary of the whole business. Heartily she wished herself, and Robin, safely back at home where they could put it behind them, and forget the whole unfortunate episode. Except that she knew, hopelessly, she could never forget Woolfe. With an effort she shook her thoughts back to immediate necessities. What she had started, unlike her lunch, she must finish, so she asked quickly,

'Did you catch the culprit?'

'He escaped into the crowd,' the policeman shrugged expressively. 'If he had fallen on the rubbish. . . .'

Isla nearly asked him, 'What rubbish?' and felt rather than saw Woolfe's warning glance slice through her, cutting off the question before she could utter it.

'They run like deer, these Tamils,' the policeman excused his own inability to keep pace with the fugitive.

'So you know who he is?' Isla could not help regret sounding in her voice.

'Only that people said he was a Tamil.' Presumably he meant onlookers among the crowd. 'They work mostly at tea picking, but who is to know on which plantation?' Again the resigned shrug, that told Isla the policeman had given up the taker of peaches as a lost cause.

'It was good of you to bring the passes to me here.' Woolfe's tone was dismissive, his glance at his watch even more so, and Isla remembered with satisfaction that he was due to present himself in the lecture room by three o'clock.

'It was nothing, my office is but a step along the street.' The officer gave the information unthinkingly, and Isla stored it in her memory against the time when she would have to apply for a pass to travel into the interior. But the time was not yet. Not until Woolfe was safely occupied in the lecture room. She nodded casually in answer to the policeman's salute as the latter took Woolfe's hint and his departure, while a dozen unasked questions and as many half formulated plans buzzed like a swarm of bees through Isla's mind. The policeman had scarcely turned his back when she demanded the answer to the first of her questions, quickly, before Woolfe should disappear after him, and leave her to wonder for the rest of the afternoon,

'What have you done with . . .?'

She spoke in a low voice that only Woolfe could hear, because the scientist and the policeman were still both in sight, but his reaction was as swift and decisive as it had been in the market place that morning, and it took the same heart-stopping form. He raised his voice so that it must have carried clearly to the departing men, and with the admonition to, 'Rest in your room until I come back from the Conference,' he bent his head above her, like a solicitous husband, Isla thought furiously, and could have cried out at the vile deception of it, but before she could utter a sound his lips descended full upon her mouth, and silenced the cry as effectively as they shut off the rest of her question, and posed instead a thousand more in her confused mind.

She tried to fight him, to pull away from his hold, but she might as well have tried to defy gravity as to escape the inexorable pull of his arms. Her lips parted and her breath deserted her under the fierce onslaught of his kiss, and her resistance vanished with it, drowned by the wild, responsive clamour of her heart as his lips plundered her own, the hard pressure of his kiss subtly changing, deepening, making her senses reel with its heady intoxication that drugged her mind, and undermined her will. The desire to fight him left her, and she felt herself go pliant in his arms.

'Walls have ears.' He raised his lips free for a moment, just sufficiently to enable them to utter the warning, not sufficiently for a casual observer to see that they were not still locked in a lovers' kiss. The irony of it twisted Isla's heart with a searing agony that stilled the clamour, and shocked her mind clear of the intoxication, and her clinging hands stiffened with new resolve, and pushed hard against him.

'I want to know,' she insisted angrily.

'. . . plenty of time to get to the lecture. The commissionaire will call a taxi for you.'

A babble of voices checked Isla's furious demand, and Woolfe's arms dropped to his sides as the doors of the small dining room opened on an eruption of people, and Zoe's voice, brisk and competent, ushered out a group of the Consul's guests. Her eyes sped straight to Woolfe and Isla, standing in the entrance hall.

Isla felt her cheeks go hot. Had Zoe seen the kiss? If she had not, it was plain from her look that she had drawn her own conclusions, and her green eyes hated Isla for them. 'She should hate Woolfe, not me,' she thought. But men and women being what they are, she knew that she was hoping for too much. Zoe

came towards them, drawing two of the Consul's guests with
her.

'Perhaps you'd share a taxi with Woolfe, since you're all going
to the same place?' she suggested, and looked at Isla as she said
it, a single, comprehensive, challenge of a look that said she
guessed about the kiss, and intended to break up whatever was
going on between them.

'There's nothing going on. At least, nothing of that kind,' Isla
thought drearily, and tried unsuccessfully to stifle her heart's
mournful plaint,

'If only there were. . . .'

'There isn't,' she told it fiercely, 'Zoe's arming herself for a
battle that isn't even being fought.'

The interpreter deployed her forces with the slickness of a
military manoeuvre. She sent the commissionaire to obtain a
taxi, 'For three people.' Then, as if on an afterthought, 'No,
make it for four. I might as well come along myself to collect the
write-up of last week's lectures. The Consul's interested in reading them.' She brushed aside one delegate's helpful, 'I'll bring a
copy back for you if you like, Miss Rutherford,' and declaimed
with a wave of her beringed hand, 'I wouldn't dream of putting
you to the trouble, when you'll have all your own notes of this
afternoon's lecture to write up.'

'And Zoe will have Woolfe to herself until the question-and-
answer session begins at three o'clock,' Isla muttered with reluctant admiration. Zoe was an excellent tactician. She was as
formidable an adversary in her way as was Woolfe, and Isla felt
the pressure of antagonistic forces stacking against her as the
taxi drew to a halt at the foot of the Consulate steps, and Zoe
ushered Woolfe and the delegates towards it, 'Like a well trained
sheepdog,' Isla thought sarcastically, meeting the other girl's triumphant glance in her direction as Zoe slid into the taxi next to
Woolfe, and the door slammed behind them both, leaving Isla
standing alone in the entrance hall.

'Alone, but not forlorn,' she told herself staunchly, 'and definitely not lamenting!' Sternly she subdued her heart's wail of
denial, and turned away towards her room. By going along with
Woolfe, the other girl had unwittingly played right into her
hands. Zoe had ensured that Woolfe had no opportunity to

accompany Isla to her room, and thus risk him seeing her precious maps, and, an added bonus, Isla realised with satisfaction, now that Zoe herself was safely away from the Consulate, and likely to remain at the hotel where the Conference was being held until at least three o'clock, when Woolfe had to chair the question-and-answer session, there was no one to note her own movements, and report them to Woolfe when he returned to the Consulate.

The knowledge that she had a clear field in which to operate, at least for a few hours, recharged her vigour, and Isla hurried to her room. With eager hands she picked up the maps and the guide book and carried them to a table in the window the better to study them in more detail, and enable her to crystallise the plans that were seething through her mind. Carefully she spread the papers flat on the table and drew up a chair, and only then did she remember that Woolfe had still not given her an answer to her question as to what he had done with the Kang amulet.

CHAPTER SIX

'I'LL take the guide book with me,' Isla decided, and tucked it carefully out of sight in her shoulder bag. The book told her all sorts of useful things, like where she could hire a car, for instance.

'What a blessing I can drive,' she thought. She would not need to ask anybody's help to take her on her journey. No one except herself need know that she was going, or where. The relief manager at the showrooms had said the road out of Kaul was passable, she remembered thankfully. The guide book said nothing about the procedure for obtaining permits to travel into the interior of the country, but magnanimously Isla forgave the author. Ordinary tourists would be unlikely to require such a facility, and in any case she already knew where to go to apply for a pass. Unsuspecting, the policeman had told her himself.

'I hope he's not on duty when I call,' she thought uneasily. She was not enamoured of that particular representative of local law and order. 'Oh well, he can't be on duty all the time,' she comforted herself. 'Someone else is bound to take over at some time.'

She studied her limited wardrobe, wondering what to wear. 'Perhaps I'd better stay as I am,' she decided thoughtfully. The germ of an idea that had been at the back of her mind ever since Woolfe had put her into a taxi and brought her away from the market place that morning now presented itself to her as a possible starting place in her search for Robin, feasible only because Woolfe was safely out of her way for a few hours, and unable to follow her.

'I'll try the local authority offices for my pass first, and then go on to the market,' she decided. 'It's just possible the boy who gave me the amulet might still be there.' As a hope it was a forlorn one, but not more so than some of the hopes that had buoyed her since she first read Robin's letter. 'If I'm wearing the same clothes, the boy's more likely to recognise me.' The sense of remaining in her dirndl skirt and blouse outweighed her desire to change. The boy was more likely to catch sight of her than she was of him. As a European she would stick out like a sore thumb among the locals, and there would probably not be so many tourists among the market crowd that the Tamil boy would not be easily able to pick her out again if she wore the same clothes, and if he recognised her there was just a chance he might approach her again. It was a chance she must take, for Robin's sake. She picked up her hat that Woolfe had bought for her, and told it jauntily,

'Come on, we'll go hunting on our own account!' The odds were heavy against her finding the boy, she acknowledged ruefully, but, 'I've got to start looking somewhere, and sitting down studying maps won't find Robin.' Swinging her hat in her hand, she put the maps safely out of sight, and left her room.

'Would you like me to get you a taxi, miss?' The commissionaire rose from his seat as she entered the hall.

'No, thank you,' Isla refused decisively. Calling a taxi meant giving the driver directions, which she did not want the commissionaire to hear. 'I'd rather walk,' she said.

'Well, if you say so, miss. . . .' The man regarded her doubtfully.

'I do say so,' Isla muttered under her breath, and wondered with a frown, 'why does everyone try to push me into taxis?' First it was Woolfe, and now the commissionaire. It was like being hedged in with a bodyguard, she thought restlessly, and with a quick nod she made good her escape before the man could argue, and ran down the Consulate steps.

'Phew, the heat!' She gasped to a dismayed halt at the bottom of the stone flight. No wonder the commissionaire had looked doubtful, when she refused his offer of a taxi. Coming out of the comfort of the air-conditioned Consulate building, it was like stepping straight into a blast furnace. A solid wall of simmering, shimmering, breath-destroying heat stopped her in her tracks.

'Perhaps I'd better let him call me a taxi, after all.' All the doubts expressed in the uniformed man's face surfaced in her own mind with double force, and automatically her hand rose to fan herself with her straw hat.

'How silly!' She looked at her headgear with new affection. 'If I wear this instead of carrying it, the brim will shelter me, and I shan't be affected by the heat.'

The brim sheltered her from the direct rays of the sun, but nothing could shelter her from the midday heat. It pressed down upon her like a leaden weight, until soon she prickled all over with perspiration; it struck back at her through the surface of the pavement until her feet, even in open sandals, felt as if they were on fire. She hesitated before a water-seller, crouched dozing beside his container and drinking vessels. His basic stock in trade looked cool and clear. But was it? What if the water was doubtful, and she drank, and went down with a tummy bug? She could imagine Woolfe's wrath if he should discover the cause. And Zoe's contemptuous scorn. 'Tourists never learn. . . .'

'I won't give them the satisfaction,' she scolded herself for even being tempted to drink in the street. She could not afford to be ill, there was too much for her to do, and only until the end of the month in which to do it, she reminded herself. It would simply play into Woolfe's hands if she landed herself in bed for a couple of days. Her resentment of Woolfe's interferences burned even hotter than the sun's rays, and made her raging thirst a little more bearable, and stoically she walked on until the grateful sight of the local authority building offered sanctuary from the glare. By contrast, it seemed cool inside. The lower temperature struck at her perspiration-damp clothing, and she shivered.

'I'm likely to go down with a chill as well, if I'm not careful.' The danger was a real one, and as unwelcome as the prospect of a tummy upset from doubtful water. For the first time Isla began to question her wisdom in coming out during the worst heat of the day, whose hazards seemed to multiply by the minute.

'I couldn't afford to wait until it gets cooler, Woolfe will be back later on,' she defended her own impulsiveness, and cast about her for the pigeonhole from which to obtain her pass into the interior. There were only three counter spaces altogether, each with a stout wire mesh screen in front of it. Taking a chance, Isla chose the centre space. She glanced at it with some apprehension as she approached. What if the policeman from the market place was presiding over it? It would be just her luck if he was, she decided, and stopped.

The policeman was not behind the grille, and neither was anybody else. For the first time since she had entered the building, she became aware of the silence. It was almost as oppressive as the heat outside, a void of soundlessness that declared itself as empty of life as it was of noise. Public authority offices should have a stir and bustle of busy activity about them, no matter what the time of day.

Perhaps there was someone at the other pigeonholes. She knew even before she checked that there was not. Where on earth *was* everybody? Pens, pencils and official-looking forms littered the counter behind the grille, but of the people who wielded the pens, there was no sign.

'Coo-ee!'

Her call echoed eerily through what she sensed was an empty building. She shivered again, not entirely this time from the contrast in temperature.

'Surely even if they're changing shifts, there should be somebody around? Or perhaps,' a possibility struck her, 'perhaps they're having a local crime wave, and the staff have been called out to attend to it.' She followed her train of thought with sudden amusement. 'Maybe there's been an epidemic of peach stealing,' remembering the peach offered her the solution to her present difficulty. 'I'll go on to the market place, there's bound to be a police officer there, and I can ask him to send me a pass to the Consulate. No, not to the Consulate, that would be too risky,' she changed her mind instantly. If she was not around when the messenger called, the commissionaire might be tempted to hand the envelope to Woolfe instead, he might even tell him what it contained. 'Better to ask for it to be sent to Barclays showroom instead. When I've been to the market, I'll carry on there and have a word with the manager, and warn him to expect it.' She knew she could rely on the relief manager's discretion.

Reinvigorated by such an easy solution, and the temporary respite from the heat, Isla left the silent building and turned for the market place. She had not gone ten yards before her new-found energy flagged.

'This heat's appalling!' Her steps lagged, and her head began to throb, and even the wide brim of her hat could not prevent her eyes from aching in the pitiless glare. 'I should have brought my sunglasses as well.' She remembered them too late, and tried to ignore the complaints from her sorely tried frame, that told her she should not have come out at all in the midday heat. 'You've got to put up with it,' she told it firmly, 'there won't be such another splendid chance, if I let this afternoon slip by. After today, the Tamil boy may be gone.' And tomorrow, Woolfe might not be safely engaged on Conference business. She tried unsuccessfully to quell the uneasy question,

'What will Woolfe say, when he knows I've come out in the midday heat? He won't know,' she declared aloud. 'If I hurry, I'll be back at the Consulate long before he returns.'

The resolve to hurry was easier to make than it was to accomplish, she discovered. Her legs and feet felt leaden, and her head heavy with the intensity of the heat. Her mouth and throat were sandpaper-dry, and she bitterly regretted refusing a second cup of coffee at lunch time. She licked her lips, and tasted salt from the rivulets of perspiration that trickled down her cheeks.

Thank goodness the market place wasn't far away. It could not have been more than a quarter of a mile, and the streets were practically deserted, which should have made walking the normally crowded pavements easier, but the distance seemed more like a hundred miles to Isla, and she felt as drained as if she had just run a marathon when she finally limped to an exhausted halt at the edge of the market square.

'Where *is* everybody?' She repeated her previous question in bewilderment. The market square was as empty as the police offices. The stalls were there, all, she saw, now sporting a small strip of tarpaulin over the top of the wares to shade them from the sun. But where were the stallholders? And where the customers? And more important—she swallowed drily, sick with sudden disappointment—where was the Tamil youth whom she had come to try to find? There was not even a stray dog wandering in the aisles between the stalls. Nothing except the rubbish, lying as limp as she felt herself under the scorching sun. The heat beat down with an energy-destroying force, and the silent market place mocked the hope that had enticed her to challenge the fierce rays.

'Where . . .?' She swallowed again, gulping down an urgent desire to cry. A sound like a snore came from under the nearest tarpaulin, and was her only answer. It came again, and told her heat-dazed mind where, and why.

'Siesta time! Or whatever they call it in Burmese. Why on earth didn't I think of it before I came rushing out in the midday heat?' she wailed. What was it the song writer said, about mad dogs and Englishmen? 'He can add Englishwomen now, as well,' she told herself disgustedly. With the exception of herself, the entire population, behaving in the only sensible-manner, had settled itself to sleep until the temperature cooled later on, and her dual need to obtain a pass to travel into the interior of the country, and to find the Tamil boy, would have to wait until the world woke up again. And by that time Woolfe would be back at the Consulate, and her opportunity would be gone.

Bitter disappointment and frustration rolled two tears to join the rivulets of perspiration coursing down Isla's cheeks. She let them roll, too exhausted to trouble to reach up and brush them away. There was no one to see them anyway, so why bother? she asked herself dully, surveying the empty market place.

'It's no use my waiting here, I might as well go on to the showrooms.' They at least would be open for business, and cool. She turned listlessly away, and a wave of dizziness assailed her, and she wondered, panic-stricken, how she would ever manage to reach the showrooms unaided. The sickness of disappointment was already threatening to change to real sickness, from the heat.

'I daren't get sunstroke,' she told herself. Could one get sunstroke, even when wearing a wide-brimmed hat? Her throbbing head warned her that it was more than possible, and hard on the heels of the warning her weary mind gave her another.

'Woolfe will be furious if he finds out.' Which he surely would if she succumbed to the heat. She should not care, she told herself miserably. It should not matter to her whether Woolfe was furious or not, but the sun seemed to have melted her resistance as well as her energy, and she did care, very much. Her pride, already raw from self-chastisement for her own foolishness, winced away from what she knew would be his harsh condemnation. He had already accused her of being rash, stubborn and impulsive. She shrank from giving him the opportunity to accuse her, with justification, of being crazy as well.

'I must get to the showrooms, while I can still walk.' The heat made each step an effort. She turned into the twisting byway along which she had walked so joyfully with Woolfe only that morning. The bells still tinkled from the top of the pagoda, and the figure of the Buddha still smiled, assuring her that she was going in the right direction. For the showrooms, perhaps, but not, she thought bitterly, in the direction she really wanted to go. Not in the direction of Woolfe's arms.

Her mind registered that there was another pot of flowers at the feet of the little shrine. Flowers meant water, something to drink. If she could only reach the showrooms, she could have a drink there. A cup of tea, perhaps, or a glass of water. Liquid of any kind. Her body felt dehydrated by the heat.

'A cup of tea. . . .' Visions of it gave her flagging feet the impetus they needed, and Isla stumbled round the corner at the end of the byway, and on to the main thoroughfare, and from there into the blessed coolness of the showrooms, at last. She gasped thankfully. She pushed at the heavy glass door with the last of her strength, and collapsed into an antique chair that had been blessedly placed just inside the entrance. With a weary hand she swept her hat on to the floor, and leaned back and closed her eyes.

'Miss Isla? Whatever's the matter?'

She had to blink hard, twice, before the relief manager's face came into focus. Three separate outlines of his head and shoulders swam before her vision, and the middle one said, in tones of concern,

'Would you like something to drink? A cup of tea, perhaps?'

'Tea?' The magical word put the other two outlines to flight, and she nodded, and forced her parched tongue to speak.

'Don't tell Woolfe,' it said. She had meant to declaim, airily, 'I've been sightseeing, and I feel a little tired.' But her errant tongue took over, and croaked instead, 'Don't tell Woolfe.'

She wanted to sink through the floor at the humiliation of it, at the craven admission that she was afraid of facing Woolfe's wrath. She wished she had gone back to the Consulate instead of coming on to the showrooms. She wished, how fervently she wished, she had lain on her bed and rested, as Woolfe told her to do, and had not attempted to come out at all in the burning heat.

'Come into the office with me, Miss Isla, it's more private there.'

The relief manager was a man of considerable perspicacity, and an understanding beyond his years. He helped her to her feet, rescued her hat, and steered her through a door at the back of the showroom, where he put her into a modern, and infinitely more comfortable chair, and produced an ice cold drink that laved her lips and tongue with lifegiving coolness, brought the ability to swallow back to her throat, and the need to think, back to her heat-bludgeoned mind.

'That was a life-saver,' she acknowledged gratefully as she held out the empty glass. 'I suppose there isn't another?' she asked hopefully.

'Have a cup of tea instead,' he advised sagely. 'Too many iced drinks and you'll risk tourist's tummy.'

She accepted the cup of tea, which revived her sufficiently to remember to thank the manager for sending her the maps.

'I thought you'd be studying them in the cool of the Consulate,' he probed her reason for appearing at the showrooms at such an hour. 'What was so urgent that you had to come out in the heat of the middle day?'

'I wanted to get a pass to go into the interior. I simply didn't give the heat a thought.' She did not mind the manager knowing she wanted a pass, she had already told him on her previous visit she intended to see something of the country while she was here. She carefully refrained from mentioning her search for the youth in the market place. That information, she decided, was best kept to herself.

'A pass into the interior?' The manager looked suitably impressed. 'Are you intending to go along with the botanists from the Conference?' he asked her interestedly. 'I hear they're mounting quite an expedition. A week's supplies for themselves and half a dozen porters will take quite a bit of organising.'

'I'm not going with the botanists, and I don't want either porters or supplies,' Isla shook her head. 'I simply want to go a little way along the road out of Kaul, to follow in my brother's tracks.' She made it sound as if she was actuated by casual curiosity, and nothing more.

'You won't need a pass to do that, Miss Isla.' To her amazement the manager laughed outright at her suggestion.

'Do you mean I've endured this appalling heat, all for nothing?' Isla exclaimed aghast. 'What a fool I've been,' she derided herself bitterly. 'If only I'd asked first!' But there was nobody she *could* ask. Nobody on whom she could rely, not to mention her questioning to Woolfe.

'Passes for the interior are only needed for expeditions that go right off the beaten track, into the forest regions,' the manager explained. 'Naturally, if non-nationals are mounting an expedition of that nature, the authorities here want to know what it's for, and where they intend to go. You won't need a pass if you are going to stick to the road. Your visa will be all that's necessary for ordinary travelling.'

Her bid to find Robin hardly came under the heading of ordinary travelling, Isla thought drily, but the manager was not to know that. 'I certainly don't need porters or supplies.' She joined in his laughter, as if the whole thing was a huge joke. She almost added, 'All I need is a car to drive,' and stopped herself just in time. The manager was almost too helpful. After her expedition in the midday heat, and her arrival at the showrooms in a state of obvious physical distress, he might regard her as a helpless female not fit to be trusted out on her own—an opinion, she thought tartly, which was already held by Woolfe—and want to accompany her on her journey, and whatever happened she must make that journey alone.

'I certainly don't intend to hack my way through jungle,' she assured him, 'simply looking at all that mass of trees from the air is quite enough for me.' She paused as a thought struck her, reminding her sharply of her third reason for braving the heat. 'By the way, while I'm here do you think I might use your telephone? I need to ring the airport and enquire about flight times. I'm not thinking of returning home just yet,' she answered the manager's look of enquiry, 'I think I told you I intended to do some sightseeing while I'm here.' The only sights she wanted to see was her brother's face, and the Kang amulet and its attendant talisman, in that order, she thought wearily, and finished out loud, 'I need flight times to give me a base to think on, say, in a couple of weeks' time.' She hoped the information vouchsafed by the airport would give her some answers, as well as thought starters, and anything after a fortnight from now would be too late to be of any use to her.

'Shall I . . .?' the manager offered instantly.

'I'd better do the telephoning myself, then if there are any alternative flights on offer it might help me to decide my route home,' Isla demurred. 'I've got the telephone number of the airport in the guide book you sent to me.' What an excellent disguise was a guide book! To a casual observer it would appear that she was genuinely interested in sightseeing, and nothing else. She pulled the book out of her bag and flicked over the pages.

'I'll leave you to your phoning,' the manager said tactfully. Isla waited until the door closed behind him and his footsteps receded across the floor of the showroom before she reached for the receiver, and dialled.

'Yes, madam, Professor Armstrong's booked out on the thirty-first.' Isla held her breath and hoped, and got her wish when the disembodied voice added, 'he's on the eighteen-twenty plane. It's a straight through flight with only two intermediate stops,' he named them briskly. 'There are still three seats available. Yes, the Professor's booking is straight through to London.'

'I'll let you know if the other seats are required.' Isla made herself sound like a busy secretary trying to organise block return bookings at the end of the Conference, and digested the information with a frown as she replaced the receiver.

'It sounds straightforward enough, and yet. . . .' There was nothing to prevent the Professor from leaving the plane at one of the intermediate stops, and making his way overland to some prearranged meeting place. 'It'll bear thinking about,' Isla muttered reflectively, 'but while I'm here I'll phone round and see if I can hire a car.' She put the scientist and his activities to the back of her mind for future cogitation, and concentrated on her more immediate need of personal transport.

'Yes, tomorrow at nine-thirty. No, I don't want it delivered, I'd rather come and collect it from your premises.' It would be disastrous if a car were delivered to her at the Consulate. The entire staff, including Woolfe, would know within minutes of its arrival, and Woolfe, if not the entire staff, would demand an explanation of where she intended to go in the car, and why, and would not rest, she felt uneasily certain, until he was satisfied she had told him the truth.

'I must get back to the Consulate before Woolfe returns, or he'll want chapter and verse on where I've been this afternoon.' She felt in no condition to parry questions, and it only needed one slip of the tongue to inflame Woolfe's already smouldering suspicions. 'Perhaps on the way back I'll slip into the market for a minute or two, just in case. . . .' She stood up, and frowned. Her legs felt distinctly rubbery. Her recuperative powers were slower to act than she had given them credit for. 'The Tamil boy will have to wait,' she decided reluctantly. 'Perhaps I'll meet him along the road tomorrow, making his way back to his tea plantation.' She abandoned the idea of returning to the market place, and strolled back into the showroom just as the manager was bidding his only customer goodbye at the door.

'I think I'll take a taxi back to the Consulate,' she began.

'I'll run you back there myself, Miss Isla, just as soon as I've locked up here. It's on my way home,' he brushed aside her protestations.

Locked up . . . home. . . . 'Surely it isn't that time?' Isla glanced at her wrist watch, and her eyes widened. 'I'd no idea it was so late,' she exclaimed. If she was to reach the Consulate before Woolfe, there would be no time to return to the market place in any case.

As it was, Woolfe reached the Consulate just ahead of her.

'Mr Wieland's just pulled up at the steps,' the manager said unnecessarily, and drew to a halt behind Woolfe's taxi. There was no time for Isla to tell her escort to drive on. No time to beg him, 'Go round the block again, and wait until Woolfe's gone in,' as her panic-stricken instinct begged her to do, while her more rational thinking mind told her, 'The manager will think you've got a touch of the sun, if you carry on like this.' Helplessly she watched Woolfe get out of his taxi, reach into his pocket to pay the driver, and glance behind at the car just pulling up.

'He's seen us. He's recognised the manager.' Woolfe's alert look told Isla he had recognised her as well. His taxi pulled away, and she sat on, tautly, in her seat, but instead of walking into the Consulate, Woolfe remained where he stood, waiting.

'I'll help you out.' The manager gripped his own door handle, preparatory to circling the car to come to her aid, misinterpreting her reluctance to move for inability to do so.

'No, please don't, I can manage.' Woolfe's keen eyes would not miss any over-solicitous attention on the manager's part, and he would draw his own conclusions. And doubtless come up with all the answers, Isla told herself resignedly. She looked up, straight at the manager, and she did not need to repeat her earlier plea, 'Don't tell Woolfe.' Her beseeching eyes repeated it for her. The manager looked from Isla to Woolfe, and back again, and his face took on a joyous expression. It was almost possible, she thought pityingly, to watch him dip his lance and pick up her favour, and ride off with it, fluttering triumphantly, like the knights of old. She tried, not altogether successfully, to stifle a prick of conscience for using the manager so badly. 'Just like Woolfe used me, to suit his own purpose.' Bitter experience told her how much it could hurt, but there was nothing she could do about it now, she had to keep up the pretence in front of Woolfe.

'Thank you for bringing me back. It was sweet of you to give me a lift.' Somehow she forced her leaden limbs to climb out of the car and take her round the front of the bonnet to thank her kindly escort with a brilliant smile, that brought a dazed look into his eyes, and made Isla despise herself even more. 'I'll call and see you again before I return to England,' she promised. That would let him down lightly, she gave a sop to her conscience, and perhaps also it would give Woolfe the impression that she had spent the entire afternoon on a duty call to her firm's showrooms, 'showing the flag' while she was in the country, as behoved a member of the management, and a business woman of her standing.

Her legs, she realised uneasily, were not standing as ably as they should. 'If I don't sit down soon, I'm likely to fall down,' she predicted unhappily. 'Goodbye!' She dismissed her escort with another smile, and hoped fervently that she could manage to mount the Consulate steps unaided. 'Oh, hello? How did the question-and-answer session go?' She raised a hand to the departing car, and turned a casual glance on Woolfe as if she had noticed him for the first time.

'I thought you were going to rest in your room this afternoon?' He greeted her abruptly, dismissing her question as the insincerity it was. 'I told you to. . . .'

'Rest in my room until you returned from the Conference,' Isla finished for him tightly. Her cheeks flushed at his accusing tone, and quick resentment acted like an astringent douche on her failing resolve, and her equally failing legs. 'I thought your advice. . . .' she stressed the word 'advice'. He had given her an order. He seemed to make a habit of giving her orders, Isla thought irately, and she was not inclined to make a habit of meekly obeying them. 'I thought your advice was given merely to deceive the policeman, and was not meant out of consideration for me personally,' she bit back at him acidly, and turned to mount the steps beside him with angry energy.

'I won't excuse my afternoon expedition. Why should I?' she asked herself mutinously. She was a free agent, and under no obligation to explain her movements to anyone. Her heart mourned her lack of obligation to explain her movements to Woolfe, and her normal sturdy independence wavered beneath the onslaught of its urgent longing.

'It'll behove you to give some consideration to the after-effects of racing about in the midday heat over here, at this time of the year,' Woolfe retorted critically.

'I thrive on the heat,' Isla lied, borrowing Professor Armstrong's words, 'and I've been in Kaul before,' she reminded him sharply. But never under the same pressure as she was now, her throbbing head reminded her, to ignore the heat in favour of other, more urgent considerations than her own wellbeing. She took in a long breath as the hall of the Consulate welcomed them with its artificially cooled air, a benediction after the burning glare outside.

'Are there any messages for me?' Woolfe paused beside the commissionaire's desk, and Isla paused with him, thankful to stand still and let the coolness wash over her.

'None today, Mr Wieland,' the uniformed man shook his head, and smiled across at Isla. 'Did you enjoy your walk, miss?' he asked, in a tone that said he was surprised to see her return on her own two feet.

'Surely you didn't walk to the showrooms?' Woolfe's brows met in a frown as they turned away from the desk.

She had walked half way round Kaul. At least, that was what it had seemed like by the time she reached the showrooms, and she felt strongly tempted to tell him so. 'And see what he's got to say about that,' Isla thought rebelliously, and only prevented herself with an effort. If she antagonised Woolfe now, it would make him even more watchful of her future movements, and she dared not risk jeopardising her plans for tomorrow, to collect her car at nine-thirty and be away along the road out of Kaul soon afterwards, following the route marked on the manager's map. She felt she could hardly wait to set off.

With stupendous luck, she might meet the Tamil boy going back to his tea plantation. She visualised herself giving him a lift, finding out how he had come by the Kang amulet, and why he had pushed it into her hand, and—wild hope—finding out if he had any inkling of where Robin might be. Her daydream refused to acknowledge the language difficulty. 'I'll cope with that when I come to it,' she told herself sturdily.

'Of all the crazy, irresponsible things to do!' Woolfe trampled ruthlessly across her daydream. 'D'you want to give yourself sunstroke?' he demanded furiously.

'How could I, when I was wearing the hat you gave me?' Isla

countered, and drew in an apprehensive breath as his jaw tightened until it resembled a rock.

'Hats are no protection,' he began harshly, and she rounded on him, goaded into retaliation by the lash of his criticism.

'Perhaps the hat doesn't have the powers of a talisman?' she flashed back heatedly, and had the satisfaction of seeing him pause. 'Which reminds me,' she pressed her vantage, 'you still haven't answered my question as to where. . . .'

'Ah, Miss Barclay . . . Mr Wieland. Dinner's in the main dining room tonight. The Consul's entertaining the gentlemen from the Conference.'

The gargoyle's grin must surely have widened as the messenger rounded the corner of the corridor by the potted palm, and imparted his customary mealtime warning, accompanied by a look of open curiosity that galled Isla's already sensitive temper to breaking point. It was the same messenger who had delivered her parcel, and discovered Woolfe to be in her room.

'You can have your dinner served in your room if you wish, miss,' the messenger added, and paused.

'That's an excellent idea,' Woolfe began.

'I'll come to the dining room,' Isla replied sharply, and glared at the man's retreating back. 'What's he suggesting . . .?' she began furiously as she flung open her bedroom door.

'Take a look at your own face, and it'll tell you why he suggested you might want your meal served in your room. That you might not want the effort of coming to the dining room to eat.' Woolfe caught her by the shoulders and propelled her into her room.

'You can't come in here. What on earth will the messenger think, if he sees you come in a second time?' She tried to shrug herself free, but his grip was like a vice, and he marched her across the room and stood her in front of the mirror, and commanded her sternly,

'Take a good look.' Remorselessly he faced her with her own reflection, forcing her to look at the exhausted face staring back at her from the mirror, the eyes enormous, and ringed by sooty smudges; the skin shining and reddened by the searing rays of the sun promising a painful peeling on the morrow, and the whole grubby as an urchin where rivulets of perspiration—and tears, she remembered with shame—had left telltale streaks of dust in long lines down her cheeks to her chin.

'There's nothing that a shower won't repair.' Taking advantage of Woolfe's momentarily slackened grip, Isla spun round to face him, with her back to the mirror, and her eyes defying him. 'As soon as you're gone, I can start making myself presentable for dinner,' she told him baldly. The very thought of food made her shudder. The prospect of having to eat it, or pretend to eat, and at the same time endure a repeat of the interminable scientifically biased conversations of her first evening at the Consulate, was almost more than she could bear, but the alternative of having to admit her weakness to Woolfe was unthinkable.

'It'll take more than a shower to repair this,' Woolfe predicted, with grim truth. He reached out and tipped her face up to his with a firm finger under her chin. 'Your skin's burned sore.'

It was not half so sore as her heart. At the slight, light touch of his finger it lurched over the edge of the precipice of control, and began to beat with a wild, erratic pain. It made her breast heave and her breath come in shallow gasps, and betrayed her agitation to Woolfe's merciless scrutiny, telling him its cause, and showing him its effect with humiliating clarity.

'I can't even begin to make myself presentable while you're still in the room.' Desperately Isla reached into her almost empty quiver for the few frail arrows she had left with which to defend herself. Desperately she wished Woolfe would loose her, and go, for while his hand still held her, all her strength drained away through his fingers. If he remained a moment longer, she would burst into tears and beg him not to shout at her, promise to obey him. . . .

Promise to love, honour and obey. She closed her eyes against the pain of the promise she would never make, and opened them again quickly, because with them closed she could not see Woolfe, only the bleak, empty future without him. The sight was more than she could bear, and she spoke quickly, changing the subject, shifting her ground from defence to attack, regardless of the consequences.

'You still haven't told me where you've put the Kang amulet.' Despairingly she hurled her last barb, a broken reed of an arrow that, she observed hopelessly, did not even prick its target.

'I've put it in a place of safe keeping.' His expression remained unmoved, inscrutable, but his fingers left her chin and took her momentary defiance with them. Her eyes blurred and she began to tremble, defenceless without her anger to bolster her courage. The uneven thudding of her heart began a slow drumbeat in her ears, and through it she heard Woolfe's voice answer her,

'In a place of safe keeping. Which is where you need to be, if you insist on racing round in the tropical heat.'

'I came to find Robin,' she justified herself fiercely, clinging on to the memory of her search to hold her fast in the wild storm of emotion that blew her off course, and threatened to engulf her.

'I told you to leave finding your brother to the professionals.'

His arms engulfed her. They reached out and drew her to him, to the only place of safe keeping she ever wanted to be, but which she knew bitterly was only a temporary harbour, inside which the storms blew even more fiercely than outside.

'The professionals aren't interested in Robin,' she fought back against the storm, battling to survive its destroying fury, 'they're only interested in looking for the amulet.'

'I've got the amulet.'

'The talisman, then.' Why quibble over details? she asked herself irritably.

'One will lead to the other. Don't obstruct the work of the professionals,' Woolfe warned her sternly.

It was not herself who was the obstruction, it was Woolfe, Isla told herself bitterly. He intruded on her every thought when she most needed to be free to devote her entire mind to her search for Robin. He destroyed her rest at night and her appetite by day, when she most needed the strength given by sleep and food, to redouble her efforts to find her brother. Far from obstructing the work of the International Security Force, she would not even know its members if she saw them, except for the man who had been with Woolfe in the drawing room at Herondale, and try as she might she could not recall what he looked like, only that he had a gold ballpoint pen, and an infuriating habit of clicking the spring up and down with his thumb. It was Woolfe, not herself, who was the obstruction, immovable, inflexible, deliberately blocking every attempt she made to gain

information of her brother's whereabouts, while leaving himself
free to search for the talisman in his own way.

'One will lead to the other.'

His arms led her to him, and she had not the willpower to
struggle against them. She despised herself for not struggling,
but when his lips sought her own she had not the strength left to
resist. She swayed against him, her defiance melted in a burning
tide of passion that rose and drowned her puny defiance, and
washed away her resistance, and even her concern for Robin.
Woolfe's kiss scorched her mouth as the sun had scorched her
cheeks, and her softly pursed lips moved under his, eagerly re-
sponding, welcoming the pain, remaining still upraised in silent
pleading when he put her from him at last and told her roughly,

'Go and get your shower, or you'll be late for dinner.'

CHAPTER SEVEN

'You're just in time,' Woolfe approved.

'I'm early,' Isla snapped back. Since he had come uninvited
into her room and deliberately delayed her from making ready
for dinner, it was a matter of pride that she should be early. She
consulted her watch ostentatiously. 'There's still five minutes
to spare.' Her watch, this time, was correct, she told herself
triumphantly, she had checked it by the Consulate hall clock.
She tilted her chin independently, proudly conscious that she
looked her best, in spite of the lack of time.

It was no mean achievement. First of all, she had to remove
Woolfe from her room. 'I can't even *start* to get showered and
changed until you're gone,' she blamed him angrily for delaying
her. And then, when he had gone, and she shut the door behind
him, and leaned against the unyielding panels to support her
shaking limbs, another five minutes of the brief twenty left before
dinner, passed before she could steady herself sufficiently to push
herself away from the door, and summon up enough energy to
get undressed and into the shower cubicle.

'Ooh!' she exclaimed. The hot water stung her sunburn, as

painful as acid against her tender skin, but it could not compete with the raw, smarting wound to her pride that cringed away from the memory of her eager response to Woolfe's kiss. Bitterly she berated herself for the ease with which he managed, by a casual caress, to override her anger and suspicion, and she felt sick at the humiliation of his lips deserting her own when he pushed her away from him, indifferent to her whimper of protest, and told her roughly.

'Go and get your shower, or you'll be late for dinner.'

She hated him for his casual rejection, she told herself stormily, and hated herself still more for being so gullible as to be once again taken in by his wiles. She did not want dinner. She wanted to scream at him that she would rather starve than endure an-other meal in his company, but to refuse to go down to the dining room would be to admit that she did not feel capable of making the effort, and that Woolfe's accusation of crazy be-haviour in risking the midday heat was justified. So she steeled herself to stand under the shower, and let the running water cleanse her face and arms, because she dared not risk soaping the reddened skin.

Thank goodness her hair was naturally curly. A quick brush was all that was needed to restore it to its customary neat shape. With one arm she reached into the wardrobe and pulled out a dress at random. There were not many to select from, because Isla always travelled light, as do most hardened globe-trotters, but the long evening dress of uncrushable material that she chose was ideal for the occasion. It was softly patterned in shades ranging from palest primrose to deep apricot, on a white back-ground, and it looked daisy-fresh, and cool. With cautious fingers she creamed away the newly acquired redness from her cheeks and shoulders, soothing their soreness, and wished bleakly that she could apply the balm to her heart as well.

'I said a shower would repair the damage,' she told her re-flection with satisfaction a few moments later. Closer inspection showed that her ministrations had only achieved qualified suc-cess. The sooty smudges still shadowed her eyes, hinting at the dragging weariness and lurking headache that only a good night's sleep could cure, but the moment dinner was over, she would say goodnight, and come away, she promised herself. She would need a good night's sleep. She had to be up early the next morning in order to pick up her car from the hire company, and after the traumas of the incident-packed day, she felt weary to the bone, and longed for nothing so much as rest.

'Would you like a sherry?' Woolfe indicated the hovering waiter.

'No, thank you,' Isla refused quickly, before he could take one for her. The sun had done enough damage to her head as it was, she decided ruefully, it still spun in the most disconcerting manner after her hurried dash through shower and change, without risking making it worse by drinking wine on an empty stomach. She felt she needed all her wits about her while she was with Woolfe.

'I wish I'd waited for another two or three minutes, before I came down,' she regretted silently. By that time, Woolfe might have teamed up with another dinner partner, probably Zoe, although the interpreter was being kept occupied by the Consul himself, Isla noticed. But there were other women in the room this evening, still heavily outnumbered by the men, but sufficient to make their dresses stand out in a vivid splash of colour against the magpie black and white of evening dress.

'I hope you'll join us for our small dance this evening?' The Consul left Zoe to cope on her own, and strolled across to join herself and Woolfe. Isla ignored Zoe's glare, and regarded her host with open surprise.

'Dance?' Nobody had told her anything about a dance. 'Nobody told me,' she began, and sent Woolfe an accusing look. Had he known about the dance all along, and deliberately not told her, hoping perhaps to tire her out with dancing and so ensure she would be fit for nothing but to remain in her room and rest on the following day? Shackling her with tiredness, while his Conference duties kept him occupied elsewhere? It was a novel method. And a sinister one, Isla thought grimly. Typical of Woolfe's deviousness.

'We thought a dance would make a pleasant social gathering, half way through the Conference,' the Consul said genially. 'A month's a long time in which to talk shop, without some kind of break,' he smiled.

'I hadn't anticipated. . . .' Isla began. When she came down to dinner, she had not anticipated doing anything after the meal was over, except drop into bed and allow her weary body, and even wearier mind, to sink into the oblivion they craved for.

'Do join us,' the Consul urged. 'We're desperately short of ladies, as you can see.'

'Indeed you are.' Isla looked round her with a sinking heart. The men in the room outnumbered the women by at least a third of the gathering. Too late she saw the trap closing round her. Woolfe's trap? She had no means of proving it, and his expression, as usual, gave nothing away, except ... did she detect a satisfied gleam lurking in the depths of his eyes? If so, it was gone as quickly as it came.

'And I'll make sure, once and for all, it doesn't return,' Isla determined, and turned apologetically to her host, intending to plead a headache as her excuse for not attending the dance. A quick uprush of indignation at this further evidence of Woolfe's attempt to control her movements made what had been a lurking threat a painful reality, and her excuse became a truthful one, and she blamed Woolfe for that, as well.

'I don't think tonight. . . .' she began, but the Consul spoke first, and urged his cause with charming insistence.

'One more lady would be very welcome,' he coaxed, 'and one in such a becoming dress.'

Put in such a gallant manner, how could she refuse?

In a daze of defeat, Isla felt Woolfe take her by the arm. With gritted teeth she suffered his hold, unable to pull away and risk a scene in company, hating the vibrations that tingled through her from his grasp, telling her that he knew all about the dance, and intended to put her in a position where she could not refuse to attend. Was that why he said she should remain in her room, knowing she would refuse because he suggested it? Using the messenger's considerate offer to his own advantage? She remembered telling herself that Woolfe was a master of expediency. He was also, apparently, an adept at psychological warfare, a deadly foil wielded by the hand of an expert fencer.

'Keep the first dance for me.' He leaned down and spoke in her ear, and she jerked away from him, incensed still further by the open amusement in his voice.

'I'll tread on your toes,' she muttered back vindictively,

and relished the thought of doing just that.

'In that case, let's hope it's a light dinner.'

It was a meal of Cordon Bleu quality, but Isla's earlier attempt to double her usual intake of food at the buffet lunch spoiled what appetite the sun had left to her. She picked unappreciatively at her plate, and listened uninterestedly to the conversations being conducted around her, too weary to attempt to join in.

'The Conference has been a most useful one. Most useful.'

The Consul's attempt to steer his scientist guests away from talking shop was singularly unsuccessful, Isla decided sympathetically. The scientist on her righthand side—'her' scientist, as she mentally labelled the Professor who had purchased the Clichy paperweight—was in full verbal spate, and talked enthusiastically to another delegate across the table from him, who from his accent Isla judged to be a German.

'There has been much of value learned at the Conference this year,' the latter replied in careful English. 'We shall take home with us many new ideas to think about. What say you, Armstrong?'

'Indeed, yes,' Isla's neighbour agreed, and deliberately looked across the front of her to catch Woolfe's eye on her other side, as the German turned to answer a question put by someone else. 'I expect to take home something of—inestimable value,' he said softly.

Isla's tiredness fled. The scientist's eyes held a curious glitter, as if from suppressed excitement, and she drew in a quick breath. 'Something of—inestimable value.' The slight pause gave the last two words a peculiar emphasis. She did not doubt it was deliberate. Until now she had found the scientist's pedantic manner of speaking to be extremely irritating. He chose each word with care, weighing its exact meaning almost as if he was measuring chemicals over a Bunsen burner. Now, his irritating mannerism crystallised her attention in a way that his words might not otherwise have done.

Inestimable. Priceless, incalculable. And he was expecting to take whatever it was home with him. A fever of excitement took hold of Isla. She wanted to grab the scientist, and throw questions at him, and demand answers. Such a description could only apply to the Kang amulet. Had Woolfe asked him . . .? No, she corrected herself bitterly, Woolfe did not ask, he ordered.

Had Woolfe ordered the scientist to travel back with the Kang amulet? And if so, where was he to take it when he arrived in England? Was it to Herondale Court? Her mind felt hot with the pressure of unanswered questions, and her hand trembled, making her spoon click against the silver goblet of ice cream on her plate.

The click reminded her of the International Security man, and his gold ballpoint pen, and at the thought of him the fever inside Isla subsided a little, sobering the uprush of excitement. At all costs, she must guard her thoughts from Woolfe. He read them too easily for it to be safe for her to think in his presence. She moved restlessly, and her arm brushed against the sleeve of his jacket next to her. The slight contact tingled a warning through her, and she snatched her arm away, as if the material of the sleeve might act as a conductor to betray her thoughts to its wearer. Hastily, she took a large mouthful of ice cream to divert her thoughts, and the cold of the indiscreet bite froze the roof of her mouth, and the surface of her tongue, and made her teeth ache almost as badly as her head, but she scarcely noticed the protest of her outraged nerves as her mind strove to answer the question.

Were her suspicions of Woolfe correct? And if so, what could she do about them? She was bound to do something, for Robin's sake. He had tried, and failed. It was as if he had handed on the baton to herself. She fumbled with it, uncertain of her hold, daunted by the weight of its responsibility. In the race against time, she was miserably conscious that her opponents had a head start, because now she held the baton she was unsure in which direction she should run. Or, more importantly, to whom she should run.

Should she approach the Consul, and tell him what she suspected? Unconsciously Isla shook her head. The diplomat would be more likely to listen to Woolfe than to herself. Likewise, the local policeman. There was the relief manager at the showrooms, of course, but she dismissed him as soon as the thought occurred to her. He was too young, and inexperienced, the Consul's description of him, which Isla found herself sharing, in spite of her gratitude for his help. Against Woolfe, the manager would appear as a yapping puppy challenging the leader of the pack.

Huw would have been a different proposition, but Huw was not available. In the midst of the convivial gathering, Isla felt herself to be desperately alone.

'Something of—inestimable value.'

'The Professor could have meant the Clichy paperweight,' she told herself doubtfully, and knew that he had not. The paperweight's value was not inestimable, it was a clear nine thousand pounds, she told herself matter-of-factly, and thrust aside the temptation to opt out of the race, and save herself from being torn apart in the emotional tug-of-war between her need to find Robin, and her love for a man who had no love for her. She thrust that thought aside too, hastily, for fear the tears that rode in its train should get the upper hand.

'I must try to talk to the Professor on his own,' she planned. She knitted her brows thoughtfully. It would have to be somewhere where Woolfe could not intervene. Her mind became a millrace of possibilities. One surfaced, like a bright, shiny bubble, and she grasped at it eagerly. 'Of course, the dance after dinner!' She would be out of Woolfe's reach, if she and the Professor danced together. Bless Woolfe for inveigling her into agreeing to go to the dance! His manipulations, this time, had done her an unexpected good turn, she realised jubilantly. While she was dancing with the scientist, she could talk to him, and he to her, and Woolfe would be none the wiser as to what went on between them. Unable to stop herself, Isla glanced up at him, a narrow, triumphant glance, that widened into a startled stare as she saw Woolfe give a slight, almost imperceptible shake of his head.

'What . . .?' Her frown deepened. What was he shaking his head at her for? She had done nothing, said nothing. And then her thoughts stopped, and she caught her breath as she realised that Woolfe was not even looking at her. He was looking past her, to the Professor. And shaking his head. Warning the scientist—of what?

'I *knew* I was right,' Isla breathed. If Woolfe had nothing to hide, why should he try to silence the scientist? Was he afraid that wine might have loosened the other man's tongue? She had not noticed that the Professor drank, either now or at dinner the evening before. Isla cast her thoughts backwards, trying to re-

member if she had seen him drinking. She slid a glance at the
place setting next to her. There was a full glass of dinner wine
beside the Professor's hand, but it might have been topped up
by the hovering waiters, who knew how often? If her dinner
neighbour was an abstemious man, perhaps Woolfe was fearful
that the unaccustomed indulgence might make him indiscreet.

'If the wine doesn't work, I'll see what charm can do,' Isla
promised herself, and deliberately put herself in the Professor's
path when they entered the ballroom after the meal was over.

'This is very pleasant. Very pleasant indeed.' She forgave his
mode of speech when the scientist regarded her with a smile
that said he could appreciate other things than talking shop,
and for the second time that day Isla stifled a pang of conscience
for so shamefully using a member of the opposite sex.

'It's all in a good cause,' she used the universal excuse for
treachery, and pinned on an inviting smile.

'Do you dance, Miss Barclay?'

Isla glowed inside. Success! she congratulated herself, and
answered out loud, trying not to show her eagerness,

'Yes, I. . . .'

'She does, and she's promised the first dance to me.'

With a nod to the Professor, and a mocking, 'My dance, I
believe?' Woolfe swept her into his arms and steered her on to
the floor.

'I didn't promise you anything of the kind!' Isla denied
furiously. Another minute, another few seconds, even, and the
Professor would have asked her to dance with him, and they
would have been circling the floor together, and talking, out of
Woolfe's reach. She might not have such another opportunity
for the whole of the rest of the evening, she realised angrily. She
had hoped for it, planned for it, and just as a tête-à-tête with the
Professor was within her grasp, Woolfe stepped in and snatched
it away from her, foiling her neatly contrived plan as he had
foiled all the others she made since she first wrenched herself
free from his grasp and ran from the drawing room at Herondale,
on the start of her journey to Kaul.

Isla glowered up at him, loathing him for his interference,
and helpless to do anything to prevent it. 'For two pins, I *would*
tread on his toes, just as I threatened to!' she gritted furiously,

anger and frustration combining to tempt her to risk even a fall
on the dance floor, in order to relieve her pent-up feelings, but
insidiously, as Woolfe guided her through the steps of the dance,
the temptation evaporated. The rhythm of the music caught at
her, beckoned her, cooling her anger in spite of herself.

'Music hath charms,' she thought with a wry grimace, and
knew the opportunity to vent her anger against Woolfe was lost.
The sweet, throbbing insistence of the music drew her, claimed
her, calling to an answering chord within her that she was unable
to resist. Isla was a born dancer, and her light, supple body
melted into the arms of her partner who, she discovered with
a thrill of pure pleasure, excelled even her own prowess in the
art.

Woolfe drew her to him with a firmer grip, but instead of
resenting his hold, regarding it as capture and detention, Isla
scarcely noticed it, and automatically adjusted her balance so
that their steps blended together in perfect unison, flowing with
the rhythm of the music that drew them both like Pan-pipes, on
a ribbon of haunting sound into a world of makebelieve. It made
the other, real world of uncertainty and strife, a vague and
shadowy thing, existing only on the outer limits of her consciousness, that exulted in the limits of the world that held her
now, the world within the circle of Woolfe's arms. They circled
the ballroom without speaking, once, twice, and Isla felt as if
she was floating on a cloud.

'Whatever schemes are hatching in that pretty little head of
yours, forget them,' Woolfe advised her curtly.

Isla stepped on his toes then, without even meaning to. Her
feet stumbled and she would have fallen, but Woolfe anticipated
the disaster before it occurred, and with his usual swift reaction
he tightened his grasp upon her still further, and swung her
straight off her feet, and executed two neat turns with her in
mid-air.

'Put me down!' she exclaimed. Her face flamed at the indignity of it, ignoring the fact that he had saved her from the even
greater indignity of a headlong fall. 'Put me down!'

He put her down, lightly, like a piece of thistledown alighting
on the ground, and without conscious directions her feet resumed
the rhythm of the dance, but the cloud she had floated on was

gone, and the hard, unfriendly, dangerous world came back again, more daunting than before.

'What schemes?' she countered quickly. 'I'm not. . . .' But her treacherous colour rose in a guilty flush, and his eagle glance swept her face, noting the burning tide flood her throat and cheeks, betraying the fact that his random probe had touched the spot it aimed for.

'No?' he enquired silkily. 'Then tell me what it was that so absorbed your thoughts that you didn't hear me mention Jim and Mary Donaldson wanted to meet you.'

'Jim and Mary Donaldson?' Her blank look, as well as her incautious tongue, confirmed that she had not heard him, but she refused to allow the latter to give away what her thoughts had really been about. With her chin held high, and her colour rising even higher, she faced him defiantly and lied,

'I was thinking about Robin.'

She had been thinking about Woolfe. Dreaming about him, while the music wove a magic spell that tempted her to believe, if only for a moment, that her dreams might come true.

'I've told you to leave your brother to the professionals,' Woolfe reiterated harshly. 'Let the International Security Force do any negotiating that might be necessary.'

'Negotiating?' He spoke the word baldly, as if it was a foregone conclusion, and Isla ran her tongue over lips that had suddenly become dry. 'Do you mean . . . do you think . . .?' The colour drained from her face, leaving it chalk-white under her tan as the meaning of his words penetrated her protesting mind. Vividly, her grandfather's evaluation of the Kang amulet came back to torment her.

'It's worth a king's ransom.'

'Do you mean, negotiate a ransom?' The word had been said. Her voice came out in a hoarse, broken whisper. 'Do you mean Robin's being held to ransom? Is that what you've been keeping from me? Tell me!' her voice rose when Woolfe did not immediately reply. 'You know where Robin is,' she accused him wildly. 'You've been keeping it from me all along!'

'Keep your voice down,' he growled, and emphasised his order with a slight shake, forcing her back to the realisation that they were in a ballroom crowded with people, each one of whom had two listening ears. 'I don't know where Robin is.'

'You must have some idea, or you wouldn't have said what you did.' What else could the word 'negotiate' imply? 'I'm doing the same as the Professor, now,' she thought hysterically, 'dissecting the meaning of every word.' This one hardly bore dissection. She caught her breath on a sharp note of fear. Its meaning, in the context of Robin's disappearance, was cruel, terrifying. 'You must have some idea,' she insisted, and her voice trembled, even though she kept it low in deference to his order. In deference to the fact that he might shake her again, or what was worse, refuse to say anything more if she disobeyed him.

'I only said, "negotiate *if necessary*",' Woolfe stressed. 'So far as I know, there hasn't been a demand received for a ransom of any kind, but we've got to keep an open mind, and be prepared for any eventuality.'

Nothing had prepared her for the eventuality of falling in love with Woolfe. It was holding her to a ransom she could not hope to pay, and exacting a price that could not be negotiated, because her heart was its currency, and that could not be exchanged.

'But you think there'll be a demand,' she answered him flatly. 'You're expecting one to come.' She made it a statement, not a question. An accusation, not a statement. By one slip of his tongue, Woolfe had opened up a new and horrifying possibility, that for some reason had not occurred to her before, and her eyes were wide and fearful on his face, demanding an answer, and at the same time dreading to hear what news the answer might contain.

Was this what Woolfe had meant when he said, 'leave it to the professionals'? 'What if,' a thought flashed unbidden through her mind, and she froze in horror at its implications, 'what if Woolfe refuses to release the amulet? Even denies having it?' Only he and she knew that it was in his possession, and it would be Woolfe's word against her own. Woolfe Wieland, of Herondale Court, a nationally known and respected collector of antiques, and promoter of the Society for the International Exchange of Knowledge and Trade. 'What hope would I have of making anyone believe me instead of Woolfe?' she asked herself despairingly, and knew that she had none. 'Everyone would assume I was lying, probably regard any accusation I might make against him as personal spite, retaliation from a woman scorned.' Her pride shrivelled at the thought. 'No one would believe me, and Woolfe would get away with the amulet.'

But not with the talisman that belonged inside it, and was still missing. 'Of course, I'd forgotten the talisman,' Isla breathed. 'Woolfe was livid when he discovered it was missing.' That his anger had been genuine, she had no doubt. Remembering the missing talisman gave a lift to her spirits, as if its supposedly magic powers had reached out and touched her from wherever it was now. If only she knew where that was, Isla wished fervently.

'Woolfe can't make a move until he recovers the talisman.' She clutched at the fragile straw. 'And whoever holds the scroll can't do anything until they get the amulet back.' It was stalemate, and Robin was caught in a war of wills between the two. 'Whoever holds Robin will have the scales balanced in their favour,' she realised unhappily, 'and no matter what the odds are against him, Woolfe will never give in.' The collector was determined, inflexible, and had vowed to find the talisman and restore it to its rightful place inside the amulet, and that Isla knew he would do, no matter how long it took to accomplish. 'Nor who suffers as a consequence,' she told herself bitterly. And in the meantime, the unanswered questions remained to torment her.

What of the Professor? What was his connection with Woolfe? And where did the Tamil boy fit in? How had the boy gained possession of the amulet? And *had* Woolfe made a slip of the tongue when he mentioned the possibility of negotiations? Or was it a deliberate ploy on his part, to prevent her from trying to look for Robin? What if it was simply a fabrication, and Robin was in no danger at all? Woolfe did not, in her experience, make slips of the tongue. . . .

'If only Huw were here! If only I'd got someone I could talk to,' she wished desperately. 'I can't handle this alone, it's too big, too complicated.' The computations were too many, and the responsibility was too much for her to bear.

'It's high time you introduced us, Woolfe. Don't keep her to yourself all the evening,' a laughing voice demanded as the music stopped, and a wave of clapping rippled round the room, and perforce Isla had to cease conjecture, or risk Woolfe once again reading her thoughts. 'Come and cool off for a moment at our table, my wife's longing to meet you.' The speaker smiled engagingly at Isla. He was tall and rangy, and in his mid-forties she guessed, and bronzed as only years of exposure to tropical suns could bronze a European. Isla envied him his immunity to sunburn.

'Meet Jim Donaldson,' Woolfe confirmed her guess at his identity, 'and this is Mary.'

Isla liked her on sight. Her skin was as brown as that of her husband, her hair, that had probably once been fair, was bleached almost colourless by the sun, but her merry blue eyes held a friendly twinkle, and her voice was as warm as her handclasp as she exclaimed without envy,

'To think I once owned a complexion like yours!'

'And you risked it all to marry a humble tea planter,' her husband teased, and the look he directed at her said he still could not believe his luck, and her complexion, in his eyes, would always be that of the proverbial peaches and cream.

'She's lucky. They're both lucky.' Isla felt a swift stab of envy as she watched the two together. This was how marriage could be, should be, if only one found the right partner.

'Did you say tea planter?' She tried to make her voice sound only politely interested, but it was impossible to quell the stir of excitement that rose in her at Jim Donaldson's casual description of himself. The Tamil boy was a tea picker, maybe even from his actual plantation.

'Yes, for my sins,' the planter tried unsuccessfully to look as if life behind an office desk might have been an acceptable alternative, 'though luckily for Mary we're not based too far out of Kaul, so she can get dressed up and drag me into town for the occasional spree.'

'You goose!' his wife laughed indulgently. 'Jim's idea of a spree is to buy a couple of whodunnits, and the latest batch of newspapers from England, and settle down to read himself dizzy while I go shopping on my own. But being close to Kaul, we enjoy the best of both worlds,' she admitted contentedly. What was it like, Isla wondered bleakly, to feel content, let alone happiness? Since she had met Woolfe, her peace of mind had deserted her, and left her with neither.

'We enjoy the best of three worlds,' the planter reminded his wife smugly. 'It won't be long before I'll be buying my newspapers from the village shop in Marten Wolden.'

'Are you due to go on leave?' Woolfe enquired, and Mary nodded happily.

'Three whole months of it,' she gloated. 'When the heat out here gets unbearable, I cool myself down by thinking about home leave. Just imagine,' her eyes became dreamy, 'harvest suppers, and riding back from the fields with the last load, under a great big harvest moon.'

'You're giving away your age,' her husband laughed. 'The last time we were home, they were using a combine harvester, so there'll be no last loads to ride back on. Mary's people are farmers,' he explained unnecessarily, and added in a brisk voice, though his eyes as they rested on his wife were kind, dealing gently with her dreams, 'We'll miss the harvest moon as well, this time, Mary love. Three months' leave only stretches from October to the end of December, and you specially wanted to be at home for Christmas,' he reminded her.

'So I did,' his wife acknowledged. 'Oh well,' she shrugged philosophically, 'there'll be the other one, the what d'you-call-it moon, to follow. We'll have to make do with that.'

'You mean the hunter's moon,' Woolfe put in quietly, and Isla glanced up at him sharply, stirred by some strange undertone in his voice that did not speak to Mary, but spoke instead directly to herself. 'The harvest moon comes first, and the hunter's moon follows it.'

Woolfe had followed her across the world, dogging her steps with the persistence of a hunter after his quarry. His eyes met her own, and locked with them, and Isla found herself unable to look away, trapped by his grey stare that bade her contemplate the hunter's moon, the yellow globe that rose above shorn fields, and drew wild skeins of geese to yelp like packs of phantom hounds across the frosted skies.

'First comes the reaper, then the hunter. . . .' The childhood jingle hammered at Isla's mind as if it was trying to tap out a message. A warning? In spite of the warmth of the room, she shivered. Woolfe, the hunter. No, that was wrong, it should be wolf, the hunter. 'I'm getting as bad as the Professor.' She caught herself up sharply. 'Why on earth should I bother about a triviality like spelling? What difference is there between the two?'

'There's a world of difference—and none,' Woolfe's relentless stare told her, and Isla shivered again, and discovered she was shaking, her limbs trembled as if she had been running, fleeing for her life from a pursuer. . . .

'It's lovely to have another woman to join our small circle,' Mary welcomed her enthusiastically, and Isla blinked, and broke the shackles of Woolfe's stare, and the bright chandelier of the ballroom took the place of the golden globe of moon. She drew in a deep, quivering breath, and her limbs steadied, and she turned gratefully to the other couple, grasping at their presence as a creature that is pursued grasps at the nearest sanctuary on offer. 'Will you be staying on here for long?' Mary enquired hopefully.

'I intend to remain in Kaul until I've contacted my brother,' Isla replied evenly, employing Woolfe's own tactics against him, talking to Mary, but speaking to him. Telling him that nothing—and nobody—would move her until Robin was found.

'Is he out here on business?' Jim Donaldson enquired, and Woolfe answered for her, smoothly.

'Something like that, but Isla wanted to contact him, and he hasn't been in touch with their showrooms for a week or two. I'm making some efforts to trace him, if only for the sake of Isla's peace of mind,' he finished easily, as if he considered her peace of mind to be important, even if her search was not.

'*Some* effort just about describes it,' Isla told herself bitterly. 'Some effort, but not enough. And not to trace Robin, only to find the talisman.'

'You hypocrite!' her eyes accused him. She hated him for his hypocrisy, for pretending to be concerned about Robin, when all he cared about was the amulet, and the missing talisman. How dared he insinuate that she was making a fuss about nothing, giving the others the impression that she was raising a furore like a spoiled child, in order to gain attention? Bright flags of temper stained her cheeks, and she choked back the

angry retort that trembled on her lips as Mary leaned forward
and said comfortingly,

'Don't worry too much, I'm sure your brother will be quite
all right.'

'Communications aren't good out here,' Jim Donaldson put
in, reinforcing his wife's attempt to reassure Isla. 'Once you get
away from the towns, life becomes a bit spartan, and if your
brother isn't within easy reach of a radio telephone, he'd have
to rely on a runner to send any messages back, or someone else
travelling in the opposite direction. It might take some time for
his message to eventually get through!'

Some time, but not six weeks. Seven, now, Isla counted up
silently, and the cold feeling that was inside her each time she
thought of Robin clamped on her mind like a dark cloud, but it
was of no use her talking to the Donaldsons about her search in
front of Woolfe, he would merely denigrate her efforts, and make
it look to them like an impulsive escapade.

'While you're here, you'll have to try to see something of the
country,' the tea planter said heartily. 'You'll find it well worth
exploring.'

'Before we go on leave, you and I must have a chat about the
latest fashions in the Old Country,' determinedly Mary brought
the conversation down to a more mundane level, and her husband relapsed into silence with a resigned grin as his wife
regarded Isla's simple ensemble with frank admiration. 'Bring
me up to date on what are the latest things to wear,' she begged
earnestly, 'then I shan't be completely at a loss when we arrive
home. There'll be plenty of time, we don't go until. . . .'

'I'm going to steal Mary from you, Jim, for this one dance.'
Mary broke off as the Consul joined them, and she rose with a
smile to take the diplomat's outstretched hand.

'That's the nicest thing about the ladies being in the minority,'
she quipped, 'it gives you such a cosy feeling of being wanted.'
She twinkled at Isla wickedly. 'You have to work very hard for
the privilege, though,' she warned humorously, 'the men don't
allow you to sit out even one dance.'

'Not even one,' Woolfe agreed, and gathered Isla into his
arms even as the tea planter held out his hands towards her, to
appeal for the dance for himself. 'Better luck next time, Jim,'

Woolfe wished the luckless planter, and steered Isla expertly away from him and on to the floor.

'You might have had the courtesy to ask me first!' she fumed, and wondered uneasily if Woolfe guessed how much she wanted to dance with Jim Donaldson, to have the opportunity to talk alone with the tea planter, just as she had wanted to talk to the scientist, and Woolfe had whisked her off under the very noses of both of them without even deigning to ask her permission first. 'I wanted to sit this one out,' she lied angrily.

'Like Mary said, there's no chance of a lady sitting out any dance tonight,' he retorted, unmoved.

Mary had also said that it gave her a nice, cosy feeling of being wanted, but Isla could not remind Woolfe of that, and her heart mourned, 'If only I could share the feeling as well,' because although Woolfe's arms held her, they did not want her, except to keep her from the arms of another man, and that only to prevent her from being able to talk with him un-interrupted. Stung by the success of the manoeuvre, Isla tilted her head back and demanded stormily,

'Do you *have* to dance at twice the speed of the music?' Woolfe was putting as much energy into the quickstep as if it was a barn dance, she thought breathlessly. Her own expertise made it possible for her to follow him without difficulty, but his totally unnecessary enthusiasm, she discovered angrily, was making her both hot and weary.

'If you keep up this pace, I'll be tired out by the end of this one dance,' she protested furiously.

'In that case, you'll have all day tomorrow in which to rest,' Woolfe retorted, and accelerated his pace still further.

'He's doing it deliberately. He means to tire me out, so that I won't be fit to do anything tomorrow, except lie down and rest.' The glint in Woolfe's eyes as he glanced fleetingly down at her, the slight uptilting of his lips as he took in her wrathful expression, confirmed that her guess was right on target, and Isla seethed in helpless fury as he spun her in a succession of neatly executed turns that brought a wave of congratulatory clapping from the assembled company, and a wave of dizziness to her beleaguered head. At any other time she would have enjoyed the challenge of the fast pace, but now it left her hot and weary. 'As

Woolfe intends it should,' she knew resentfully, and closed her eyes against the dizziness that threatened to overwhelm her if he did not slow down soon.

'You're doing this deliberately,' she choked, and to her dismay felt her throat close with urgent tears, that cut off her accusation, and blinded her eyes, and made Woolfe's face swim mistily above her. She had to call on every ounce of willpower she possessed to prevent the tears from falling. Pride would not allow her to cry in front of Woolfe, and instead her feet danced on, like the feet of the unfortunate wearer of the red shoes in the fairy tale, until she longed to lean her aching head on Woolfe's white starched shirt front, and forget the heat and the tiredness, and the never-ending steps of the dance, forget everything except that for the moment Woolfe's arms were round her, and Woolfe's hands clasped her close against him.

Even in the fairy tale, the dancing had to stop some time. With a last dizzy spin Woolfe drew her to a halt, and she leaned limply back against him, too exhausted to wonder why, although they had stopped dancing, the music still played on.

'That was a beastly trick to play!' she flung at him, and her ire rose at the easy manner in which it had succeeded. No one, looking on, would realise what it was Woolfe had done to her. 'His own halo's still shining brightly in front of his friends,' she thought bitingly, and knew that, no matter if she shouted his infamy aloud to the assembled company, as she would have dearly liked to do, no one would believe a word against him.

'It was mean, despicable. . . .' Her voice hammered at him. Her small, balled fists urged to reinforce it, but in a crowded ballroom the ethics of good behaviour demanded that you did not hammer at your partner's shirt front with your fists, even though he had just nearly destroyed you with exhaustion, and that deliberately, cruelly, to further his own ends.

'He shan't get away with it,' Isla vowed, and pushed herself away from him and stood proudly on her own two feet, which ached so badly that she feared they might refuse to hold her for much longer. 'I'll collect the hire car tomorrow morning and follow Robin's route out of Kaul, in spite of Woolfe,' she promised herself resolutely, and somehow managed to hold herself upright when Woolfe dropped his arm from round her and turned away, and Zoe's voice said spitefully,

'You can't hold on to one partner for the entire evening. This
is a ladies' tag dance, so you'll have to let him go,' and she put
her hand on Woolfe's arm in a possessive gesture, pushing Isla
aside. Claiming Woolfe in public, her green eyes declaring, 'He's
mine. Even if he did come to your room, he still belongs to me.'

'I don't want to keep him.' Isla coloured furiously and pulled
her hand away from Woolfe's sleeve, scarlet with humiliation at
the accusation that she was deliberately holding on to him, and
keeping him to herself. The malice in Zoe's green eyes stung
strength back into Isla's aching limbs, and fire back into her
voice, and with her head held high she lied valiantly, 'I don't
want to keep him,' when all the time her heart wept within her
at the need to let him go, and lamented bitterly that it wanted
to hold on to him, and keep him, for ever.

'You can have him, with pleasure,' Isla rejected him fiercely,
and faced the two of them, her eyes flashing. 'You're welcome
to one another,' she cried, and fled before the scalding tears
could overflow, and burn her cheeks more cruelly than the sun
could hope to do.

CHAPTER EIGHT

THERE was a package on Isla's breakfast tray the next morning.

'Mr Wieland asked me to give it to you, miss.'

'Woolfe sent it?' Isla fingered the envelope curiously.
Whatever it contained was hard, and knobbly, and more or less
round.

'Surely he hasn't sent me the. . . .' She checked herself just in
time, and her teeth closed on her lip, biting back the words she
must not speak.

'Mr Wieland asked me to give you a message, as well, miss.
He said to tell you he wanted a word with you after you'd
finished your breakfast.'

'He does, does he?' Isla gritted silently. 'Well, I don't want a
word with him. After last night, I don't want to see him, ever again.'

'I heard Mr Wieland tell the commissionaire he'd be back about nine o'clock, miss,' the trim maid offered helpfully when Isla remained silent, and she recollected herself with a jerk.

'In that case, there's plenty of time,' she smiled at the maid, and wished privately that the girl would stop fiddling with the curtains and the coffee pot, and would go away and leave her in peace to open the package Woolfe had sent to her. It burned a hole in her fingers, and sent a chain of questions seething through her mind.

'There'll be nice time just to eat your breakfast,' the maid agreed doubtfully, 'though it isn't far off nine o'clock now.'

'It isn't—what?' Isla stared at her watch in shocked disbelief. 'Twenty-five to nine!' she exclaimed. 'It can't be that time yet! The breakfast tray comes up at eight o'clock.'

'Not this morning, miss,' the young maid shook her head, 'Mr Wieland asked me specially to delay your tray for half an hour or so. He said you'd be tired after the dance last night.' She smiled wistfully at the evidence of such gentlemanly consideration.

If only she knew! Isla thought wrathfully. Once again Woolfe had managed to appear to outside eyes as the perfect gentleman. No doubt the girl envied her the attention of so good-looking a swain, and wished she was in Isla's shoes. 'She'd be welcome to my feet!' Isla winced ruefully as she swung her weary appendages out of bed. Woolfe could not know how she intended to spend the day, but that he had tried deliberately to exhaust her at the dance last night was proof enough that he suspected she might be planning to go in search of Robin, and if further evidence of his suspicions was needed, he had purposely delayed her breakfast tray. 'He must have guessed I was relying on it as an alarm call at eight o'clock,' she fulminated. And because it had not arrived on time, she had slept on, as Woolfe intended she should.

'Whatever words Woolfe wants with me will have to wait,' she decided mutinously. By nine o'clock she would have to be gone, or she would miss picking up her hire car at nine-thirty. A plan had been forming in her mind during the endless, restless hours of the night, and it crystallised into a decision by the time she finally fell into a troubled sleep.

'I'll go and see Mary Donaldson tomorrow.' Instinctively Isla felt she could trust the planter's wife. And from the security of an obviously happy marriage, Mary would not be so liable to be swayed by a blind faith in Woolfe as the Consulate staff seemed to be. 'Jim Donaldson said their base wasn't far away from Kaul, and if they can run into town easily, it must mean their home's somewhere along the main route sketched on the manager's map.' There were tea plantations marked on the one printed map sheet, not far from where the mountain pass joined the road. 'It must be one of those,' Isla decided, and with that comforting thought she had turned over and slept at last. And overslept.

'Thank you, I'll cope with my own coffee.' The young girl was lingering, her eyes on the unopened package, wasting the speeding minutes. 'She's probably got all sorts of romantic notions about it being a love token,' Isla thought impatiently as the girl departed at last, and Isla's fingers trembled so that they nearly dropped the packet as she tore open the wrapping and revealed, not the Kang amulet, but a jar of sun-tan cream! 'Of all the beastly, sarcastic. . . .' She could almost hear Woolfe's low laugh mocking her as she stared down at the heavily embossed glass jar, oval in shape, and knobbly with the embossing in a way that he must have known would suggest the amulet when her fingers probed the wrapping.

'I hate him! I hate him. . . .' she choked furiously, and raised her hand to hurl the jar at the door. She wanted to spill it, smash it. . . . She remembered just in time that it was the maid who was departing through the door, and not Woolfe. Shaking all over, Isla drew her hand back and sank down again on to the bed.

'Coffee. . . .' The aroma penetrated the mist of her anger, and she groped blindly for its source, drinking the liquid black in a desperate attempt to steady her demoralised nerves.

'I won't have time to eat anything.' She looked longingly at the daintily laid tray—the boiled eggs, bread and butter, two thin slices of wholemeal toast, and fresh fruit tucked into a paper napkin. The latter gave her an idea. 'I'll drink the coffee, and take the food with me.'

Hastily Isla stuffed the maps and the guide book inside her

shoulder bag, and gulped down her third cup of coffee. 'If I start off with plenty of liquid inside me, I shan't feel quite so dehydrated,' she thought. The lessons of the previous day were still unpleasantly sharp in her mind. 'I can eat the food on the way.' She rolled it into the paper napkin. 'The fruit will serve me instead of a drink.'

It was one thing to put the food ready to carry, she discovered, and quite another to fit it into her already overloaded shoulder bag. 'Bother!' Stubbornly the fastening on the flap refused to fasten. 'If someone sees the food, they'll guess,' she panicked. 'They'll know I'm going out for the day, and tell Woolfe.' Her brow furrowed. 'The food wouldn't show if I put it in the bottom of the bag, and the maps on top, and the guide book on top of the maps. It won't matter if the guide book shows.' It was a piece of necessary equipment for any tourist intent on 'doing' the sights. 'And I've broadcast widely enough that I mean to do just that,' she remembered thankfully. She checked her watch. 'Ten minutes to nine. I'll just make it, if I hurry.'

Without ado she tipped her bag upside down on the bed cover and started to repack it. 'Food first.' Haphazardly she threw in the next thing her fingers came in contact with. 'Bother, I didn't mean to pack Woolfe's suntan lotion. Oh well,' she shrugged, 'it'll have to stay packed now, there's no time to sort it all out again. Now for the fruit. It's a good job it's a banana and an orange, a peach would have turned into a squashy mess.' Briefly her thoughts ran wistfully on the peach she had shared with Woolfe. The sunny, carefree moments that ended almost as soon as the peach was finished. 'Now the maps on top. Oh, go in!' she exclaimed impatiently, as the stiff paper covers sprang back against her pushing fingers, resisting her efforts to make them inconspicuous. 'Got you!' With a final thrust, the covers capitulated, and she tugged the flap across the top.

'It still won't shut,' she discovered in disgust. 'Oh well, it won't matter. If anyone looks, they'll only see the guide book.' She gave another, nervous glance at her watch, and drew in an apprehensive breath. 'It's five to nine already. I'll have to fly if I'm going to miss bumping into Woolfe.'

She flew. The flap of her bag bobbed up and down as she ran, and the maps and the guide book bobbed with it, and with a click of annoyance Isla slapped her hand down on top of them to keep them still. 'It'll be the limit if they give the game away, now, after all the trouble I've been to,' she muttered.

'To Barclays showrooms, please.' Luck was with her. The entrance hall was empty except for the commissionaire, and she slid into a cruising taxi and gave directions in a clear voice to the driver. 'If anyone heard, it'll put them off the scent,' she thought with satisfaction.

'I've changed my mind, I want to go to the Kaul Car Hire instead.' The moment they were out of sight of the Consulate, Isla leaned forward and countermanded her previous instructions, and felt like a conspirator as the taxi began to weave and dodge among side streets, and finally deposited her on the forecourt of what appeared to be a small garage business.

'I ordered a car for nine-thirty,' she told the attendant.

'It's being made ready for you now.' To her relief the man spoke good English. Her relief faded into annoyance when ten slow minutes passed without any sign of her car appearing.

'I ordered a car for. . . .'

'It's being made ready for you now.'

'Please make sure the petrol tank's full.'

'It's being filled up now.'

'Now' in Burmese means something different from 'now' in English, Isla discovered irately when another quarter of an hour passed, and her sorely tried patience snapped when the car finally made its appearance, and drew to a triumphant halt on the forecourt beside her.

'I *deal* in antiques, I don't drive them,' she gasped, appalled by the venerable appearance of the piece of machinery presented as her hire car. 'It must be at least twice my own age.' Back home, it would practically qualify for the annual old crocks' race, she thought witheringly. Back home. . . . Her thoughts flew longingly to her own Mini, bright red and cheerful, and as easy to drive as a child's pedal car. This one had knobs and levers, the purpose of which she could not even begin to guess.

'I need an up-to-date car,' she expostulated. 'Something reliable.'

'This one goes.'

'So shall I, when I'm in my dotage,' Isla retorted disparagingly, 'but not at the speed I need to travel today. What other makes have you got available?'

'There is only this one.'

Slowly the unpalatable truth penetrated her stunned mind. The Kaul Car Hire meant precisely what it said. One car for hire, and no more. It was either take this one, or go without.

'If only I'd known, I could have kept the taxi!' she wailed. Or even borrowed the showroom manager's car. Or taken any one of half a dozen alternatives that, too late, presented themselves as feasible means of achieving her objective.

'It goes,' the man insisted. 'See. . . .' He pulled the engine to life again with a mighty swing of the starting handle.

'I wonder it doesn't go into orbit, making that noise,' Isla snapped crossly, and jumped violently as the engine backfired, and continued to run to the accompaniment of the most disconcerting rattles from somewhere beneath the battered bonnet.

'It goes.'

Isla began to tire of the man repeating the obvious. It was like listening to a long-playing gramophone record.

'And so must I.' It was pointless to waste further time in argument, so she took her courage in both hands, and climbed up into the driving seat. 'I won't dare to let the engine stop until I get to the Donaldsons' place,' she frowned worriedly. 'If I do, I'll never be able to start it again with that handle thing.' Cautiously she released the brake, and her confidence began to return as her out-of-date transport moved obediently across the forecourt and into the road, and her spirits rose as she successfully negotiated the corner, and pointed the bonnet in what she judged was the direction of the main road.

This must be the highway, just ahead. The stream of traffic slowed down and joined a queue to turn into the thoroughfare, making a T end to the road she was traversing. 'My bump of direction's accurate, it must be a good omen,' she decided, encouraged, and delved into her bag on the seat beside her. 'If this is the main road, I should turn left here. I'll check with the map just in case. The pen and ink sketch will do.' With her eyes on the road ahead in case the traffic should begin to move on, she searched blindly for the manager's sketch. 'Oh well,' she shrugged as her fingers failed in their attempt to locate the piece of paper, 'the printed map will have to do. The sketch has probably worked its way down to the bottom of the bag, and I can't park up and look for it in this traffic.' She cast a hasty glance at the printed map to confirm her position. 'With luck, I should be on the outskirts of Kaul in under ten minutes.'

It took considerably longer before she finally left the town behind her. 'They've probably built a lot more houses, and extended the town since the map was printed,' she muttered, and settled down to nursing the little car over a road that grew considerably rougher as she left the town behind.

Whatever the road surface was like, travelling over it couldn't be so bad as the waiting. The awful, fear-filled hours of waiting, with frustration, and worry about Robin as her constant companions. At last she was going somewhere, and doing something positive, and because of it the load seemed to fall away from her shoulders.

'An ancient car's got some advantages,' she discovered reluctantly. The vehicle had an antiquated, creaking sunroof, that nevertheless, when she managed to push it back, let in a delightful breeze, as refreshing as the knowledge that Woolfe was probably still waiting for her to finish my breakfast and come down to see him, as per his orders. The thought of keeping Woolfe waiting gave her unrepentant glee, and added to her feeling of freedom, and enjoyment of the sight of yellow green, terraced fields of rice flowing ahead of her. The colour reminded Isla of the bags of sticky peardrops she and Robin had consumed with such relish when they were children, and she screwed up her face at the memory of the sharp, acid taste of the sweets, that used to send pleasurable shooting pains up the sides of her childish, bulging cheeks.

'I wish I could join the women for a paddle.' She looked enviously at the groups of straw-hatted women, with their sarongs hitched up to their waists, working up to their knees in water among the rice. They looked up and stared as she approached. 'My feet could do with a cool dip, it might stop them from aching.' She would not easily forgive Woolfe for making them ache so badly, but there was no time to stop for a paddle now, half the morning was gone already, so she waved a hand to the women instead, and felt immensely cheered when the workers waved back.

Surely the rice fields should be coming to an end by now? Even allowing that the roughness of the road made each mile seem like two, she must have travelled a considerable distance, and still the light acid green seemed to stretch on and on, and the distant rise of hills, darkened by their miniature forest of tea bushes, seemed to remain as distant as when she first started out. And the farther she progressed, the worse the surface of the road became.

The manager had said it was quite a passable road. She frowned at the increasingly frequent, spine-shattering jolts, that were not helped by the age of the car, whose date of production had yet to see the dawn of modern, spring-borne comfort.

He must have meant it was passable by local standards. The standards did not coincide with her own, Isla decided critically. 'I hope the car's able to withstand the shaking it's getting,' she muttered worriedly. The garage man's repeated boast that, 'It goes,' might apply when the car was running over the well made roads in Kaul, but for how long it would continue to apply if the vehicle was subjected to much more of the awful surface it was travelling over now, was not something she cared to contemplate.

'I daren't slow down much more, even to save the car. There simply isn't time.' She looked at her watch, and her eyes widened with dismay. 'It's almost midday already!' Nearly lunchtime, and still she had not even reached the outer edges of the first tea plantation. For all she knew, the plantation that Jim Donaldson managed might be the second or even the third one marked on the map. 'I'd reckoned on being there by lunchtime.' She viewed her miscalculation with growing discontent, the while her stomach reminded her that her breakfast was still packed in her shoulder bag.

'I'll stop and eat now,' she decided, 'and study the map at the same time, and if it's too late to turn back when I get to the Donaldsons', I can always stay there for the night and get them to telephone the Consulate to say where I am, and that I shan't be back until the morning.' Even Woolfe could not accuse her of lack of consideration, so long as she made her whereabouts known. 'Anyway, I'm not obliged to report to him where I'm going, or for how long I intend to stay,' she declared independently, and took out an egg and cracked it with unnecessary vigour against the innocent steering wheel. 'I'm glad they don't serve Continental breakfasts on the early morning trays.' The substantial offering quelled the complaints from her stomach, but it could not silence the uneasiness that was beginning to grow in her mind. She shook out the map on the seat beside her, and consulted the legend at the bottom of the page.

'The bright green bits are the rice fields, and the little bushy pieces are the tea plantations.' She had not mistaken the pictorial message of the map. Slowly an unpleasant suspicion began to form in her mind.

'I compared the map with the manager's sketch, but I don't remember checking what scale it was drawn to.' She had looked at the map, compared it with the manager's sketch, and rushed off before Woolfe could question her as to where she was going. Rushed off impulsively. . . . She scowled bleakly as his earlier taunt came back to jeer at her.

'Check the scale of the map, and prove him wong, if you can.'

She checked the scale, and a cold feeling seeped through her as the thin line with its tiny black figures marked off along its length proved his taunt to be only too accurate.

'Thirteen and a bit kilometres, that's roughly seven and a bit miles to the inch, say eight miles for good measure.' Her knowledge of the conversion tables was sketchy to say the least, but she was in no mood to quibble about decimal points or percentages. She stared at the message of the figures in horrified disbelief. 'I'd only reckoned about two miles to the inch. That makes the journey nearly four times as long as I'd allowed for,' she calculated with dismay.

Four times as far, along a road that was rapidly disintegrating into little more than a track, with a vehicle that was almost a museum piece.

'Why didn't I think to check the scale before I started out?' Her cheerful optimism vanished, and black depression seeped through her like a dark cloud. 'All this time I've been hoping, deluding myself.' And now stark reality stared her in the face, and it was already too late for her to turn back.

'Why didn't I stay in the ballroom last night?' she wailed. 'If only I'd waited, I'd have had the chance later on to talk to Mary and Jim, and to find out how far it was to their plantation.' Mary had already pressed her to another meeting very soon. 'I could have made an opportunity then to talk to her alone.' Once again half a dozen possibilities presented themselves, and once again it was too late to take advantage of any of them. She had rushed off impulsively, as no doubt Woolfe would have accused her, and her own lack of thought was her undoing.

'No wonder the rice fields seemed to go on for ever. According to this there must be at least another five miles of them yet, before the tea plantations even begin. I'll have no option but to stay with the Donaldsons overnight, it's too late to go back now.' To return to Kaul, and admit defeat to Woolfe. . . . Just to think about it left a bitter taste in her mouth, that spoiled the prospect of further food, and with a gesture of impatience Isla rolled up the rest of the bread and butter and fruit, and thrust them back into the depths of her shoulder bag.

'I don't suppose the manager put a scale on his map, either.' She refused to accept all the blame on herself, and riffled through the rest of the papers for the sketch to back up her supposition. 'Oh well, it's not important, I can look at it later.' The sketch remained stubbornly hidden, and she had no time to mount a search for it now. 'The sooner I reach the Donaldsons' house, the better. I don't relish travelling in this bone-shaker through the worst heat of the day.' Memories of her experience of the previous day were still unpleasantly strong, and without the cooling breeze made by the motion of the car, the heat inside it was becoming unbearable.

'I should have kept going while I ate.' It was too late for that, as well, she had been stopped for only ten minutes or so, but it was long enough to become a target for the scorching rays. A lot of things were too late, Isla thought wearily, but this one at least could be remedied. If she simply kept on travelling, she was bound to reach the tea plantation some time. At least she had remembered to keep the car engine running while she ate.

'Woolfe can shout as much as he wants to, I shan't be there to hear him.' She dredged what consolation she could from the situation, even while her expression darkened at the thought of

Woolfe shouting at her at all. Even here, his image pursued her relentlessly, invading her thoughts, destroying her concentration on what she was doing. Resentment boiled up inside her, and spilled over at his merciless pursuit.

'Leave me alone, can't you? Just leave me alone!' she shouted out loud, and was not aware that she had shouted until the sound of her own voice mocked her.

'Alone, alone. . . .' it echoed across the vast, empty landscape, emphasising her aloneness, emphasising the growing fears that nagged at her like the raw edges of an exposed nerve, flaring into pain at the slightest touch.

'For goodness' sake stop thinking about Woolfe, and get going.' Angrily she shook her thoughts back to the task in hand, and gave a quick upwards glance through the open sunroof as she eased off the brake and set the car rolling again. The brassy glare of the sky had darkened. It still remained the same cloudless dome as before, but the colour of it was subtly changed. It had a pecular, coppery tinge. 'It's probably just the usual midday heat haze,' Isla told herself reassuringly. One did not notice such things in the town. It was only out here, where there was nothing else to look at except the endless expanse of paddy fields, with now not even a woman worker in sight, that one began to notice things that were always there in the background, like the sky, and so were always taken for granted, and more or less ignored.

'I expect the women have knocked off work to get away from the midday heat, the same as the people in the market place yesterday.' She missed the company of the women, and felt relieved when at last the monotonous acid green gave way to more broken country, and the road began to rise up into the first of the foothills. It wound as it rose, becoming progressively more difficult to traverse, until it demanded her complete concentration to nurse the car through the potholes and bumps and hairpin bends that, if they took a toll of her nerves, at least kept at bay the eerie feeling of isolation engendered by the deserted paddy fields behind her, and the first dark fringe of tea bushes clothing the slopes ahead.

'I might come upon the Tamil boy at any time now,' she thought. The possibility honed her mind to a fresh alertness, and slowed her pace almost to a crawl. She dared not miss the chance of seeing the Tamil boy, and she dared not risk hitting one of the large and increasingly frequent rocks that scattered haphazardly across the road at every turn. Her arms and shoulders ached with the strain of holding the bucking steering wheel, and her eyes ached with the impossible task of looking ahead and to each side and searching for a sight of the boy at the same time.

'If only it wasn't so hot!'

Wearily Isla wiped the back of her hand across her eyes, brushing aside the perspiration that dropped from her forehead, and formed a haze in front of her vision that she feared might be caused as much by exhaustion as by perspiration. She blinked urgently, frightened by the haze, but when she opened her eyes again it was still there, worse than before. It enveloped the windscreen, blew streamers out of the side of the car bonnet, and snorted steam from the front like a miniature dragon.

'The radiator's boiling. It's only the radiator, not my eyes.' Isla began to giggle weakly, laughter that faltered on the edge of tears. 'I told them to fill up the petrol tank. I never thought to check if there was plenty of water in the radiator.' The sun could be partly responsible for it boiling, by evaporating what coolant there was. And she had left the paddy fields, and the easy access to a refill, several miles behind her.

'There's always a stream somewhere close by, in the hills.' Burma abounded in water, she told herself robustly, but now she needed some urgently, none appeared to make itself available.

'I can't see a thing through the screen,' she muttered. The car did not boast windscreen wipers, and she reached round the windscreen pillar and wiped a space clear with the palm of her hand.

'Help!' With desperate feet, Isla stabbed for the brake, and the car shuddered to a halt on the very brim of a deep depression, that cut straight across the road only inches in front of her wheels. 'Why in the world don't they erect a warning sign, or something?' She stuck her head out of the window indignantly. The depression must be a permanent feature of the road, it snaked up the hillside on the one side of the car, and down the hillside on the other, a natural watercourse draining the hills from the higher slopes above.

'It must be an absolute torrent when the snows melt on the high tops.' Isla regarded the depression with awe. Now, the watercourse held a mere trickle, glinting at her from the bottom with the mocking invitation,

'Refill your radiator from me if you can. Cross me if you dare.'

'I've *got* to get across,' Isla realised fearfully, 'there's no way round it.' The road continued tantalisingly on the other side of the depression. The bank on her side was hair-raisingly steep, but there was a longer, gentler incline on the other side running out of the depression to join the road. A Land Rover would negotiate it easily enough. 'But I don't know if the car will manage it,' she scanned it anxiously.

There was only one way to find out.

'I've either got to go on, or go back, and it's too late to turn back.' There was no choice. She was already a mile or two into the first tea plantation, so Jim Donaldson's house must be closer than Kaul. 'In any case, there's nowhere I can turn round.' The road was narrow, and unfenced, and one false move would precipitate herself and the car down the side of the nearby slope.

'That settles it,' Isla made up her mind determinedly. 'I'll stop at the bottom of the watercourse and fill the radiator, then go on and find Mary and Jim.' She drew in a deep breath, wiped a patch of the windscreen clear again, and inched the car forward towards the lip of the depression.

'Please let the brakes hold,' she prayed fervently. She wanted to shut her eyes. She did not dare to look, and she did not dare not to look. The engine rattled, the bodywork shook as if it was about to disintegrate, and the bonnet dipped at an alarming angle, but the car remained upright, the brakes held firm, and the vehicle half slid and half rolled down the slope towards the narrow, shining ribbon of water at the bottom.

'The stream's not very deep, thank goodness.' Isla let out her breath in a puff of relief, and allowed the front wheels to roll slowly through the water, and out on the other side of the narrow trickle, then braked with the car neatly straddling the water. 'I suppose this must be the radiator cap?' She regarded the shiny chrome cap doubtfully as a thought struck her. 'I've got nothing to scoop up the water in.' She frowned, then brightened. 'I'll use my hat.' The straw would make a leaky receptacle, but it would be quicker than using her cupped hands. 'First of all I'll have to prise the radiator cap off.' She grasped it with a firm hold.

'Ouch! It's boiling hot.' Scalding water underneath, and scorching sun on top, combined to turn the chrome cap into a lethal weapon, and Isla drew her hand away with an exclamation of pain, and sucked her scorched fingers. 'I think I remember seeing a piece of rag inside the car.' It was oily, and unclean, but it made an effective pad against the heat, and cautiously Isla wrapped it round the radiator cap and began to twist.

'Isla! Leave the cap on. *Leave the cap on!*'

'What. . .?' She looked up, startled. The urgent shout echoed from the top of the depression, bouncing back at her from off the surrounding hillsides, like the voice of conscience. 'Leave the cap on . . . leave the cap on. . . .' Isla shielded her eyes and squinted against the sun. Another vehicle loomed above the watercourse, in the place where her own had recently stood. She was in time to see it dip over the edge and come hurtling down towards her.

'*Leave the cap on!*' A face stuck out of the driver's window, shouting at her. The glare of the sun prevented her from recognising the face, but there was no mistaking the voice.

'Woolfe! What's he doing here? How on earth did he find out . . .?' Once again he had pursued her, and the moment he found her, he started to shout at her. He drove the Land Rover straight towards her, still shouting, and something inside Isla seemed to snap. Frightened by the unexpected shout, in pain from her scorched fingers, driven by her need to speak to the Donaldsons, and to find Robin, and torn apart by frustration and nervous tension, to say nothing of being perpetually worn out by the almost unendurable heat, her sorely tried temper gave way.

'If Woolfe says, "Leave the cap on", that's all I need to give me the strength to get it off!' she cried mutinously. 'How dare he charge down on me like this, bellowing at me like some old-fashioned sergeant-major?' With an upsurge of strength she did not know she still possessed, she gave a mighty wrench at the radiator cap, and felt it begin to turn beneath her hand. 'One more turn, and it'll be off,' she gloated triumphantly.

'*Leave the cap on*, I said.' Woolfe jerked the Land Rover to a halt and catapulted out of the driving door. With one bound he vaulted the stream. He was almost upon her. Desperately Isla tightened her grip on the radiator cap. She had to remove it before he could prevent her. She craned her head over the bonnet the better to see how much water was still left inside the radiator the moment she freed the chrome stopper. 'One more turn,' she muttered through set teeth. She managed to give it half a turn when Woolfe grabbed her.

'Let me go!' She struggled frantically to make him loose her.

'Are you crazy?' He snatched her clear of the front of the car, and held on to her grimly.

'Go away, and leave me alone. . . .'

Ping!

With a whine like a ricocheting bullet, the last thread of the cap screw gave way, and the radiator cap flew high into the air, the bright chrome of it winking in the sunlight, until it turned over and descended with a loud hiss into the watercourse. The sound registered at the very back of Isla's consciousness, but she did not turn round to see where the cap landed. Her eyes were riveted on the jet of scalding steam that erupted from the radiator opening like a miniature boiling spring. She stared at it in horror. Another minute, another second even, and her face would have been right over the jet.

'If you'd been peering into the radiator to see how much water was still left,' Woolfe seemed to have second sight where her actions were concerned, Isla thought wildly, 'you might well have been blinded by the steam!'

He flung the awful consequences of her actions full in her face, his words scalding her pride almost as much as the steam would have wounded her skin, brutally laying out before her the thing he had saved her from. Condemning her, because if she had done as he ordered her to, it would not have happened. His face had gone grey beneath its tan, a pallor that might result from anger, and might not, and his eyes were black with an expression she did not try to judge, her own were still fixed on the erupting radiator opening.

'You might have been blinded!'

There was nothing she could say, no excuse she could give. Isla gulped and remained silent, speechless at the awful possibility of what might have been. What *would* have been, if it had not been for Woolfe.

'What are you doing, careering along this road in that contraption, anyway?' Woolfe had no such difficulty with his voice. He made a gesture of contempt towards the car which still straddled the stream, and whose engine, Isla realised with rising panic, was coughing to a halt even as she listened.

'Don't let the engine stop. Loose me, I mustn't let it stop!' Frantically she wrenched herself free from Woolfe's hold, and ran back towards the car, reaching it just as it gave a final asthmatic wheeze and lapsed into ominous silence. 'Now look what you've done!' she shouted at him furiously. 'I'll never get it to go again.'

'That I can well believe,' Woolfe agreed, and Isla could have slain him for the quick uptilt at the corners of his mouth. 'The thing's probably expired from sheer old age,' he grinned disparagingly. 'Where on earth did you get it from?'

'I hired it,' Isla flared, with what dignity she could muster. 'I wanted to visit Mary Donaldson. She asked me to talk with her about fashions, before they went on leave.' Even to her ears, the excuse sounded puerile.

'Fashions!' Woolfe exploded. 'You've come all this way, on your own, in that thing,' he gave an expressive gesture to the silent car, 'merely to talk about fashions?' he shouted disbelievingly.

'I did, and I have.' The scorn in his voice flicked at her pride like a whip, and Isla rounded on him stormily, goaded into retaliation. 'And since I've come this far, I intend to complete the journey.'

'How?' He cast a sarcastic glance at her immobile transport.

'I'll start the engine somehow.'

She had never swung a starting handle in her life before. She had never even seen one before today, except in a museum. Bright flags of temper stained her cheeks at his sarcasm, and impulsively she spun round, and stooped to grasp the starting handle.

'Don't pull that. . . .'

She pulled. With every ounce of anger-born strength, she gripped the starting handle as tightly as her fingers could hold it, and gave a mighty tug.

Bang!

The car backfired like a pistol shot, and the starting handle kicked like a mule.

'My wrist. . . .' she wailed.

'I told you not to pull the thing!' Woolfe caught her as she staggered off balance, nursing a wrist that felt as if it was broken in a dozen pieces.

'How was I to know the handle would kick back like that?' She jerked away from his touch, which hurt even more than her wrist.

'You shouldn't have gripped it so tightly. If you'd just curled your fingers loosely under the handle, and let go the moment you pulled, it wouldn't have happened.'

But like the radiator cap, she hadn't been aware of the consequences, and it had happened, and the pain in her wrist sent streaks of agony shooting like fire from her fingertips to her shoulder.

'You'll never start an old car like that.'

'The man at the garage did.' Isla groaned under her breath with the pain. She felt in no mood to listen to a lecture from Woolfe on how to start an ancient roadster.

'A quick yank on the handle with a cool engine is a very different proposition from trying to set that machine running now,' grimly he educated her unwilling ears. 'The thing looks so hot, it's more likely to burst into flames than start running.'

'It'll cool down as soon as I've refilled the radiator.'

'It'll have to cool down *before* you fill the radiator, if you want to preserve what little life it's got left,' Woolfe contradicted her again, and Isla bit her lip angrily, but perforce remained silent because she did not possess sufficient mechanical knowledge to argue with him.

'This'll cool it down. And maybe it'll fill the radiator at the same time.' She turned her face up to the sky jubilantly, and in spite of the excruciating pain from her wrist, she could have laughed out loud at the sudden onslaught of the rain.

In Burma, it doesn't start to rain. Rain happens. One minute the only water in sight was the rivulet flowing peacefully beneath the car. The next, long stair-rods of water descended from the sky in a mighty deluge that sent clouds of steam hissing skywards from the bonnet of the car. Within minutes it had plastered Isla's skirt and blouse in a clinging wet bandage round her slender body, and told her the reason for the peculiar tinge in the sky that she had assumed to be a heat haze.

'Run for the Land Rover!' Woolfe shouted.

'I can't—I've left the sun-roof of the car open.' The only time Woolfe shouted anything sensible at her, was the one time she couldn't take advantage of his orders, Isla thought grittily, and ducked her head against the battering force of the rain, and groped for the handle of the car door.

'Even Manchester can't compete with this,' she gasped. The inside of the car was already saturated, and water poured through the open sun-roof as if someone was tipping a bucket of it upside down on top of her.

'Come and help me,' she yelled urgently to Woolfe. 'I can't manage to move the sun-roof with only one hand.' How did he imagine she could cope on her own, when her right wrist hung limp and useless? It was already swelling at an alarming rate, but there was no time to attend to it now, no time, indeed, to even heed the pain. 'Come and help me!' There was a strange excitement in the violence of the elements, almost akin to the excitement she had felt when she first walked up the Consulate steps beside Woolfe. A meeting with an irresistible force. It was a feeling alike, and yet unlike, Isla could not decide which, and there was no time to ponder on that, either, if she was to rescue the car before she drowned in the driving seat.

'Come and help me.' What on earth's he waiting for? she asked herself furiously, and pulled one-handed, ineffectually, at the sun-roof, which baulked and jammed with maddening lack of co-operation, while the rain poured through the open gap like a waterfall.

'Where are you going? Woolfe! Don't go. Don't leave me here!' Unbelievably, he was getting into the Land Rover, starting the engine, and beginning to move away. 'Woolfe!' Her voice rose to a shriek.

'I'll have to winch you out.' He pulled round her car and stopped, then stuck his head through the side window of the Land Rover, and shouted back above the roar of the rain.

'I don't want to be winched out.' Presumably he meant tow her out, she translated irritably. 'I want to close the sun-roof. The water's ruining the inside of the car.'

'It'll ruin more than the inside, if you remain here for much longer.' Callously he slammed his window shut on her impassioned plea for assistance, and set the Land Rover rolling towards the bank in front of them. The sturdy vehicle climbed the rough incline with the agility of a cat, driven with a skill that drew Isla's eyes in reluctant admiration to its progress.

'He could have stayed to help me. It wouldn't have taken a minute. He could have winched the car out afterwards, if he'd wanted to.' Isla stamped her foot on the floor of the car, in sheer frustration at Woolfe's deliberate unhelpfullness.

'Good heavens! The car's beginning to fill with water already.' Her angry stamp shot a splash of water up to her knees, and sent it streaming down her already wet legs.

'For goodness' sake, come and help me to shut the sun-roof.' Woolfe was back, running down the slope from where he had parked the Land Rover on the road beyond the opposite bank. He trailed a long something behind him that gave out a metallic rattle as he ran, but instead of coming to her aid, he ignored Isla's shouts and dropped to his knees in front of the car, and began to feel about underneath it. 'The upholstery will be ruined if you don't do something soon,' she shouted at him desperately. 'The car hire people will want compensation.'

'They'll want compensation for the entire car, let alone the upholstery, if I leave you here for much longer.' Woolfe looked up briefly from what he was doing, his eyes narrowed to slits against the rain, and his hair plastered flat against his head with the streaming wetness, the dark line of it emphasising the clean, chiselled outlines of his face.

'He looks like a Greek god. . . .' What a time to start studying someone's bone structure! Isla thought wildly, and raised her voice, and yelled despairingly, 'The rain's filling the car!' The fact that it was also filling both her shoes effectively took her mind off the subject of bone structure.

'More likely the stream's flowing through the car. Look below you!' Woolfe yelled back, and pointed downwards with his thumb.

'What are you doing, standing in the stream?' Isla stuck her head out of the window, and stared. Woolfe was standing in water almost up to his knees. 'When I came, the water wasn't that high. . . .' She stopped, appalled. When she first came, the car straddled the water. Now, all four wheels stood up above their hub-caps, and water poured upwards through the floor of the car even more swiftly than it came down through the sun-roof. Regardless of the rain, Isla leaned out of the door and stared fascinated at the erstwhile narrow rivulet, which grew deeper and wider even as she watched.

'Grab your bag and come with me.' Woolfe finished fixing whatever it was to the car's front axle, and rounded the bonnet to her door.

'I'll stay in the car and steer.' She settled herself behind the wheel, and left her bag where it was on the passenger seat.

'You'll come with me,' Woolfe stated flatly, 'with or without your bag.' With a quick twist he wrenched open the driving door and reached inside. One lean whipcord arm grasped her under the knees, the other room her waist.

'I said I'll. . . .'

'And I said, you'll come with me.' Effortlessly, he lifted her clear of the seat.

'My bag. . . .' She just had time to grab the end of the shoulder strap as he swung her high in his arms, and without waiting to check whether she had collected her belongings or not, he waded out into the water, that widened her eyes by its fast pace as she looked down.

'Now, run!' He dropped her unceremoniously on to her feet on the other side, and grasped her round the waist and pulled her with him, away from the foaming, frightening turbulence of what a few minutes before had been a mere trickle of water, up the bank towards the Land Rover on the top. Loose shale slipped under her feet, and sliding rocks tripped her up, but Woolfe gave her no respite until, spent and breathless, he loosed her to lean against the side of the Land Rover while he opened the passenger door. 'Get in.' Without waiting to see whether or not she was willing to obey him, he boosted her up into the high seat and joined her on the driver's side.

'What on earth's that?' A high-pitched whine brought her eyes in startled questioning to his face.

'The winch. We might be in time, if the car isn't too bogged down already.'

'You mean . . .?' Isla swallowed hard, but Woolfe did not answer, and the whine rose to a crescendo that set her teeth on edge, and drove her nerves to screaming point, and just as she was beginning to think, 'I can't bear this a moment longer,' the whine settled down to a steady drone, and Woolfe remarked laconically,

'She's coming,' and Isla glanced back, and went limp with relief as she caught sight of the car, rising out of the water like a hippopotamus out of its wallow, and creeping up the bank towards them at the end of the hawser, as meekly as if it was on a lead.

'What a blessing we were in time!' Isla could not bring herself to say, 'Thank you.'

'Count your blessings when we get back to Kaul,' Woolfe advised her curtly, and effectively silenced her conscience on the score of thanks. 'From the spate of water that's going down the gulley now, the storm must have broken higher up in the hills first. It could take hours to clear the gulley, before it becomes fordable again.'

'So?' Isla's eyes snapped at the accusation in his tone. 'The storm wasn't my fault.' He blamed her for most things, but he could not blame her for the rain. 'We can leave the car here,' she pointed out sharply, 'and go back to Kaul by a roundabout route.' With a Land Rover for transport, the roughest road should present no problem, she told herself impatiently.

'There isn't a roundabout route,' he disabused her shortly. 'This road doesn't go anywhere, any more. It peters out at the border, where it's cut off by a landslip.' No wonder she had not met any other vehicles along the way. No wonder the women in the paddy fields had stared to see her pass.

'Until the water spate subsides,' Woolfe went on remorselessly, 'we can't get back across the gulley, and since the road doesn't lead anywhere, it's no use trying to go on. Thanks to your latest madcap escapade,' he shouted at her angrily, 'we might be stranded here all night!'

CHAPTER NINE

'IT's your fault, for winching the car out on this side of the watercourse!' Fierily Isla thrust the blame back on to Woolfe's shoulders. 'If you'd pulled it out on the other side, we could simply have turned round and gone back to Kaul. Now, we might be stranded here all night.' She borrowed his own words and hurled them back in his face, piqued in spite of herself by his attitude. Most men would not have regarded it as a penalty, to be stranded with her. Most men—but not Woolfe. Her pride smarted under his ungallant bluntness, and because of the hurt she lashed back, wanting to hurt in return. Perhaps being stranded here would prevent him from keeping an evening engagement with Zoe. 'If it does, I'm glad,' she fumed unrepentantly.

'If I'd waited to pull the car up the other bank, you'd probably have lost it for good,' Woolfe retorted, shrugging off her blame as one would brush away an irritating fly, of nuisance value, but unimportant. 'Look behind you,' he bade her grimly.

His command took her unawares, and before she could check herself she turned round to look. And stare. She caught her breath in horrified disbelief.

'In case you hadn't noticed,' Woolfe pointed out grimly, 'the bank's on the bend of the watercourse, as well as half way down a steep hillside, and it takes the full force of the downward thrust from the water. We'd never have managed to winch out the car in time, if we'd waited. At the pace the water was rising, the shallower run out on this side was our only chance.'

The water itself made his logic unarguable. So long as she lived, Isla would see again in nightmares the swirling brown flood, bearing all sorts of unidentifiable debris along with it, hurling itself to the very tip of the first bank. She closed her eyes. If Woolfe had not arrived when he did, both she and the car might have become a part of the debris. She supposed she ought to thank him, but the words stuck in her throat, refusing to be uttered, and instead she blurted out,

'How did you know where to find me?' He seemed to possess a sixth sense as to her intentions, she thought resentfully.

'If you want to avoid detection, you shouldn't drop maps drawn up on your firm's notepaper,' he retorted, and reaching into his pocket he pulled out a sodden piece of paper, on which the inked lines were already blurring with the wet, and a large blot was forming from what had once been an asterisk, to show the point from where Robin had sent his last message to Huw Morgan.

'The manager's map!' It must have fallen from her bag when she ran from her room. She remembered the flap bobbing up and down because the bag was too full for it to close properly.

'So the relief manager at the showrooms drew it up for you?' Woolfe's eyebrows drew together in a black scowl. 'He should have had more sense than to encourage you.' His expression boded ill for the manager when the two next met, and Isla spoke hastily in the man's defence.

'The manager didn't do anything of the sort. I asked him for some maps, and he sent them to me, that's all. He'd no idea what I wanted them for.' She stopped, and bit her lip. She had not meant to betray to Woolfe the thoroughness of her own preparations. It would have been better to allow him to assume that she had acted on impulse, as he had accused her of earlier. 'Now you've ruined the map, the water's completely spoiled it, and I wanted it as a souvenir for Robin.' She hurled the accusation at him as a red herring, hoping he would not notice her ill-considered comment, hoping he would not draw from it the implication behind it, and knew with a sinking heart that she hoped in vain. Woolfe's keen ears missed nothing, his even keener mind sifted everything he heard, and placed his own accurate construction upon it.

'From now on, you won't require maps.' Coolly he reached across her, and removed the other two from her bag.

'You can't take those, they're mine!' Quick as a flash Isla grabbed at the maps to prevent him from taking them, but she was hampered by not being able to use her right hand. The swelling wrist made the whole of the bottom half of her hand and arm stiff and clumsy, rendering it useless as well as painful, and she had to reach across with her left hand instead, and the few seconds' delay lost her the maps. Her fingers closed on empty air, and Woolfe turned away and tucked the maps down the side of his seat, and Isla spat at him in impotent fury,

'You've no right to confiscate my property!' She had said that to him, how often before? she remembered furiously. It had had no effect upon him then, and it had no effect upon him now. 'The maps belong to me!' she hammered at him, and anger choked her utterance when he did not deign to reply, but instead cast her an oblique glance and continued to dispose of the maps down the side of his seat, and with an upsurge of uncontrollable anger Isla threw discretion to the winds, and leaned right across him, and snatched at the edge of the maps that she could see still protruding from beside the seat.'

'I've already confiscated them, and they belong to the relief manager at the showrooms, not to you. I'll return them to him personally, when we get back to Kaul.'

If he meant her to be grateful for his offer, it had the opposite effect. 'I'll return them myself,' she cried, her eyes blazing, and with a final desperate effort she managed to grab a corner of the one map.

Woolfe was stronger than she was. Effortlessly, he fielded her hand, removed the map from her fingers, and thrust it back beside its fellow, under the seat, and then put Isla back on to hers, but not so far back that he had to loose his hold upon her.

'Don't defy me, Isla,' he warned her harshly. He held her to face him, and burning grey eyes locked with angry brown as their glances met in an almost audible clash of wills. 'I've told you before to leave finding Robin to the professionals. If you attempt to meddle in this, you tread on dangerous ground.'

Woolfe looked infinitely more dangerous than any ground. His black brows met in a thunderous scowl that sent a shiver tingling the length of Isla's spine, and his hands held her with a force as if for two pins he would shake her into submission.

'You're hurting me!' she gasped, and her eyes faltered away, unable to withstand the relentless magnetism of his stare.

'If you weren't so stubborn, you'd realise I'm trying to *prevent* you from getting hurt. You'd listen to me. . . .' Instead of shaking her, he pulled her roughly towards him. She struggled and tried to pull away, but she was no match for the muscular strength of his arms, which pinioned her own to her sides. She tried to twist her face away, but he pressed one spread hand against the back of her head, tilting her face up to meet his. 'If you won't listen to what I say, perhaps you'll heed this,' he gritted, and pressed his lips down upon her own with an abrasive force that demanded, if her ears refused to listen to his words, that her lips must comprehend the clarion warning of his kiss. It devoured the parted fullness of her lips, commanding her compliance, robbing her of her breath, making her heart beat with slow, heavy thuds that aroused a wild clamour in her senses, and made the world grow dark in front of her eyes.

'Now will you do as I say, and leave well alone?' An eternity later Woolfe raised his head, and Isla swayed away from him, and drew in deep, sobbing gasps of air. The cold metal of the vehicle door struck chill against her back as she leaned against it for support, and a tremble shuddered through her as the cold spread through the clinging wetness of her clothes. It dispersed the darkness from her eyes, and brought Woolfe's face back into focus, and brought her anger back to save her pride, that a mere second before was ready to abase itself, and shame her for ever by promising to obey whatever it was Woolfe might order her to do, and to abandon everything, including Robin, if only his lips would remain pressed against her own, his arms continue to hold her.

'That was a despicable thing to do!' Anger forced the words through her clenched teeth, while her heart protested passionately, 'Kisses aren't meant to be used as a lash. Kisses are a sweetness, and a promise. Kisses are for always.' She raised her uninjured hand to brush away the feel of his kiss, and knew even as she drew it insultingly across her mouth that the action was useless, because his lips had branded their print upon her own with an indelible mark that no amount of rubbing could erase. 'You can't force me that way, to do as you say.' Her hand slid across her lips, and as if it realised its task was hopeless it carried on uncertainly upwards, and brushed away the drips of water that still streamed from her wet hair.

'You're soaking wet!'

'So are you,' Isla retorted shortly. His shirt stuck to him, the fine material clinging to the hard muscles of his shoulders, and water dripped on to it from his hair, running down the strong tanned column of his neck from the neatly barbered outline that made Isla's fingers urge to stroke it dry. She clenched them tightly in her lap to subdue the urge, and opened her eyes wide as he said brusquely,

'You'll have to change out of those wet clothes, or you'll end up with pneumonia.'

'Change here? In the Land Rover?' Was he mad? 'Who does he think I am?' she asked herself indignantly. 'Eve?' Furiously she felt her cheeks blush scarlet, knew that he watched her, gauging her reaction. She stole a glance at his face, and her lips compressed as she saw his teeth gleam in a dawning grin, latching on to her thoughts with ease. Mocking her for them, daring her to put them into words.

'Change into what?' she asked sarcastically. 'There aren't any fig-leaves handy.'

'And tea-leaves aren't an adequate substitute?' he taunted, his eyes glinting to the serried rows of tea-bushes outside, and returning to rest on her burning face.

'We can go on to the Donaldsons' place and borrow some clothes there,' she countered desperately, and sat tight on her seat, wishing it was covered in some material that would soak up the water, instead of holding it, and leaving her sitting in a rapidly growing pool that seemed to get wetter and colder with every passing minute.

'The Donaldsons don't live along this road any more. None of the tea planters do, now.'

'But the map said ... I came specially to see Mary,' Isla stammered, shaken by his casual pronouncement. 'Do you mean I've come all this way for nothing?' All the long, lonely, spine-shattering miles of potholes and rocks and empty desolation, only to find that Mary did not live along this road any longer! The discovery was almost more than Isla could bear. She blinked against a sudden uprush of tears, and Woolfe said,

'The map marks the tea plantations, but the tea planters'

bungalows are sited on a new road going out of Kaul at right angles to this one. It isn't marked on the official maps yet, because they were printed before the road was built. The old sites of the planters' bungalows were abandoned after the landslip diverted the watercourse about two years ago. It cut off the road a few miles farther on from here, and since the new watercourse becomes unfordable every time there's heavy rain, it was uneconomic to continue to transport the tea along this route. Even you must have noticed that the road hasn't been maintained.'

She did not need to notice, Isla thought ruefully, the state of the surface had made itself abundantly plain in the poorly sprung car.

'There's nothing farther along the road from here, except a few villages,' Woolfe went on remorselessly, 'and the inhabitants use the nearest river as their highway.'

'And I came all this way, to talk to Mary about ... about fashions,' she finished hastily. About other things too, but Woolfe must not know about the other things. A bubble of hysterical laughter rose inside her at the irony of it all.

'So you said before.' Woolfe's hard eyes said he disbelieved her, and the laughter inside Isla subsided, and the desire to cry returned, and she thrust that down to join the laughter, and flung at him angrily, perversely resenting the fact that he did not believe the unbelievable.

'You heard Mary invite me.'

'If you'd waited to see me after you'd had your breakfast this morning, you'd have received Mary's message to meet you in Kaul for an hour or two before she and Jim left for the airport. Didn't you get the message I sent for you?' he questioned her abruptly.

'I got your order, to see you the moment I'd finished my breakfast,' Isla contradicted him bitterly. 'If you'd got a message for me from Mary, why didn't you scribble it down and send it along with my breakfast tray?' He had sent her the jar of suntan cream instead. She writhed at the memory of his unwanted gift.

'There wasn't time to write messages, and if you'd done as you were asked, for once. . . .' he condemned her.

'How was I to know there'd been a change of plan?' Isla

defended herself hotly. 'Jim said last night that their leave didn't begin until October, and Mary said there was plenty of time. . . '

'She meant plenty of time for your talk, before they caught the morning plane to Rangoon. They're flying down to meet Jim's relief manager, and attend to various matters at the plantation head office there, before they start their leave, which is how I came to acquire their Land Rover. I'm to hand it over to Jim's relief manager when he flies into Kaul tomorrow morning. Supposing, that is, that I'm back by then,' he blamed her for the possibility that he might not be.

'I couldn't know there'd be a storm.' Isla fought back, denying responsibility. 'You needn't have followed me, just because you'd got Jim's Land Rover for the day.' She made it sound as if he had come out for an illicit joyride, abusing his stewardship of the vehicle, and saw his face tighten, but she felt beyond caring. If she did not fight back in the battle of words between them, she would burst into tears, and it was better to fight back.

'It's a good job I did follow you.' Abruptly Woolfe twisted round in his seat, and Isla braced herself at his sudden movement, and went tense, while for a split second he paused and raked her face with a hooded glance that concealed the expression in his eyes. She held her breath, waiting for she knew not what, and then with a slight shrug Woolfe completed his movement, reaching right over the back of his seat and fumbling behind him in the rear of the vehicle, and she swallowed on a dry throat and went limp, lashing herself with scorn for the surge of longing that ached to feel his hands hold her again, his lips press down upon her own.

'If Jim and Mary run true to form, there should be some sort of emergency kit stowed away in the back of the vehicle. This feels like it.' He straightened up and turned round to face her again, and pulled a long, slim, padlocked box over on to his lap. 'One of these keys should fit.' He removed the ignition key and tried the other keys that dangled from the same ring, one by one in the padlock. The last one gave a satisfying click.

'Just as I thought.' He lifted the lid on to what looked like neatly folded cloth. 'You're about Mary's size.' His glance flicked over her as he shook out the cloth, and it became a brown tunic in a warm-looking material, with a pair of slacks to match. He delved deeper, and produced a similar outfit in black, in a much larger size, and discovered two pairs of canvas shoes at the bottom of the box. He thrust the brown outfit and the smaller pair of shoes into Isla's lap.

'It's stopped raining.' She had not noticed. The storm inside the Land Rover waged with a ferocity that made the weather on the other side of the windows pale by comparison. 'If we both get out, you can change on one side of the vehicle, while I change on the other. Yodel when you're ready.' And without a backward glance, he was gone. With a quick wrench he flung open the driving door and swung out on to the road. Isla heard the light smack of his shoes as they hit the ground, then he disappeared from her view. For a moment she sat still, torn between an urge to defy Woolfe and her need to get out of her wet clothes, and into something warm and dry.

'If I don't go now, he might come back to see what I'm doing.' The possibility galvanised her into action, tipping the scale on the side of the dry clothes. 'It's a good job the door handle's on my left-hand side,' she thought thankfully. She tucked the clothes and shoes under her right arm, and used her good hand on the door handle. It was a long drop to the ground. She had not the advantage of Woolfe's height, and handicapped by the bundle of clothes, and only one good hand, she shuffled awkwardly to the end of the seat, and half wriggled, half slid over the edge. She landed on the road with a jolt that jarred her teeth, and pain shot through her frozen feet, but the movement warmed them, and the pain began to subside into pins and needles as the blood ran freely again down to her toes.

'The last thing I need now is a ricked ankle, as well as a damaged wrist.' The latter posed more of a problem than she anticipated, when she came to divest herself of her blouse and skirt. The wet cotton clung to her, wrapping itself round her, and resisted her efforts to tug it off one-handed. Delicate as the embroidered blouse looked, her numb fingers found it a formidable adversary, and in an agony of nervous haste she gripped the bottom of it with both hands to try to pull it over her head. The blouse came off, but agony shot through her swollen wrist, and she leaned back against the side of the Land Rover and closed her eyes against a wave of faintness.

'Aren't you ready yet?'

Woolfe's impatient call ripped through the mists of faintness. 'Nearly, not quite. Don't come round yet.' Panic pushed Isla off the side of the Land Rover and back on to her own feet, and she began to tug at her skirt. It had no fastening, only the elastic shirring at the waist, and it proved easier to remove than the blouse. With a lopsided wriggle, she dropped it round her feet and toed it aside. Thank goodness Mary's clothes hadn't got any fastenings. The slacks were elastic-waisted, and the tunic was a loose pop-over, and in seconds she was cosily inside them both. They felt warm and comforting after the clammy chill of her own wet garments, and in spite of herself, her spirits began to rise. With a double kick she divested herself of her shoes and slipped her feet into the canvas pumps.

'I can't tie the laces, with only one hand.' The laces presented an unexpected problem. If she left them flopping loose. Woolfe was bound to notice, and question why she did not tie them up, and she felt reluctant to disclose the extent of the injury to her wrist. She surveyed it worriedly. The swelling was spreading across her hand, making her fingers and thumb stiff.

'It's probably only a bad sprain,' she consoled herself. If Woolfe noticed it, he was bound to say, 'I told you so,' which would not improve either her wrist or her temper, she decided forcefully, and tucked the laces inside the pumps, impatiently pushing them out of the way. One of the end tags stuck into her foot, and she wriggled it uncomfortably, and turned to call to Woolfe, 'I'm ready,' and did not notice that her wriggle had made the tag drop out of the side of her shoe again, taking the lace with it, and presenting an immediate threat if she was to take an unwary step. 'I'm ready!' she called. It was the nearest she could manage to a yodel, she thought, her humour restored by the comfort of warm, dry clothes.

'Give me your wet things, I'll put them in the back of the Land Rover along with mine.' She handed them over to him, and had time to feel a heartfelt thankfulness that she had only removed her outer garments, when he added, 'And tie up your shoe laces before you trip over them.'

'They won't hurt as they are. I shan't be walking anywhere,' she responded indifferently, and turned away from him to get back into her seat in the Land Rover before he could argue. Too late she remembered that when she got into it before, Woolfe had given her a boost up. The passenger seat looked even farther away from the ground than when she slid out of it.

'Do you want a hand?'

'I can manage,' she retorted independently, and grabbed at the door with her left hand. If Woolfe helped her up he might grip her other arm, and that she could not bear. She lifted her foot.

'Oh!'

The loose lace caught under the sole of her other shoe and tipped her off balance. Desperately she clung on to the Land Rover door, leaning her full weight upon it, but the vehicle was well maintained, and the door swung easily, on oiled hinges, and her own weight added to its momentum, and carried her along with it.

'Woolfe!'

Her arms flailed at empty air as she scrabbled to regain her feet. She staggered backwards, and the lace caught under her other foot again and tossed her helplessly towards the hard, unyielding surface of the road.

'Woolfe!'

He caught her as she fell. 'I told you to tie up your shoe laces.' With his usual quicksilver reaction, his arms reached out and caught her even as she cried out, and he swung her upwards and cradled her high, as easily as if she was no heavier than a child. The sky swung in a dizzy arc above her, and she noticed hazily that it was blue again. The dark tinge was gone, and so was the thunderous cloud that brought the rain. It seemed to have settled on Woolfe's face instead. The blackness of it glowered from his frowning black brows, and flashed sparks of lightning from the angry grey glare that he fixed on her upturned face.

'I told you to tie up your shoe laces!'

Her own eyes threatened to provide the rain. She had been drenched, frozen, frightened and hurt, and Woolfe's curt impatience was the last straw. She blinked frantically to clear her vision, but another wave of faintness washed over her again, and the blink was not a success, and another one was too much of an effort in a world that the faintness made hazy, leaving only the bronzed outline of Woolfe's face silhouetted above her against the sky, the strong feel of his arms underneath her, and the steady beat of his heart demoralisingly close to her ear through the black stuff of his tunic. Isla wanted to close her eyes and remain in the hazy, blissful world of Woolfe's arms, but his voice dragged her back, relentlessly demanding that she open them again on a world she did not want to look at, and listen to words of blame she did not want to hear.

'Do you *have* to risk injuring yourself, as well as stranding us here?' he thundered exasperatedly. 'I told you to tie. . . .'

'I c-can't.'

'Why not? Surely you can manage to tie a simple knot in a pair of shoe laces?' His tone accused her of deliberate perversity.

'It's my wrist. . . .' She meant it to sound matter-of-fact, dignified even, but the road and the surrounding tea-bushes began to waver about in the most disconcerting manner, and her voice came out wobbly and uncertain, with a whimper in it like that of a puppy with a hurt paw.

'Let me see.' He lifted the toe of his shoe and pushed open the Land Rover door to its fullest extent, and slid into the passenger seat with Isla still cradled in his arms. For a moment he rested her across his lap, and it was all she could do not to beg him, 'Leave me here. Don't set me aside,' when he lifted her up again off his lap, and set her aside, and a low moan broke from her lips, that brought his eyes sharply on to her face as he put her down on to the passenger seat and rested her against its inhospitable back, that felt cold and hard and alien after the warm shelter of his arms.

'Why didn't you tell me your wrist still hurt?' He misunderstood the moan, that was dredged from an anguish such as no physical pain could produce, and made worse by each gentle touch of his probing fingers as he carefully picked up her arm and pushed aside the tunic sleeve, investigating the injury with a light touch that turned a dagger in the unseen wound that drained her heart of its lifeblood, and sent the slow tears escaping from under her closed lids, to wash down her ashen cheeks, and taste salt against her lips that still trembled from the bruising imprint of his kiss.

After an aeon of time Woolfe pronounced, 'It's a bad sprain, but I don't think it's broken.' Strangely, he forbore to remind her that it was her own fault that her wrist was damaged, that he had warned her against trying to crank the starting handle of the car. His voice became as gentle as his touch when he bade her, 'Don't move your arm. I'll get the first-aid-kit, and bind it for you. It'll feel more comfortable then.'

Once more he reached into the back of the vehicle, and once more turned back gripping a box, unlocked this time, which yielded in turn a splint, bandages, and a large arm sling. He fixed them expertly, immobilising her wrist, then resting her arm in the copious sling, and tying the knot, knowledgeably, in the hollow made by the delicate ridge of her collarbone, so that she could lie back against the seat in comfort, untroubled by the hard lump of the knot. She lay back exhaustedly when he finished, and closed her eyes.

'My old nurse always kissed it better.'

This time his lips were as gentle as his hands had been on her wrist. Her eyes flew open and fixed with startled wonderment on his face. Instead of being on his side of the seat, above the steering wheel, it hovered close above her own, blotting out the windscreen light, blotting out everything except the hint of a smile that played about the corners of his well cut lips, and the strange, unreadable expression that lurked deep in the enigmatic mystery of his eyes. She stared upwards into them, hardly daring to breathe, searching for an answer to the mystery, striving to read the expression, drowning in the depths of the cool grey pools.

'It feels better already.' She heard her voice utter prosaic words, while her heart did silly things inside her breast, that made it flutter like a bird under the practical brown stuff of Mary's tunic, and made it hate her voice with a fierce hatred when he replied,

'In that case, we'll be on our way.' He removed his fingers from beneath her chin and gripped the steering wheel with them instead, and his other hand left its hold on her shoulder and felt for the gear lever, and all the passionate longing of a heart bereft pleaded with him from the luminous depths of her pansy eyes, not to heed her traitorous voice, that only uttered foolish words to mask her heart's desire, and was not its spokesman. Pleaded with him to prolong the precious moment, until the mystery was solved, and the expression was an enigma no longer. Begged mutely for just one more kiss, as tender as the last.

'We can't go back yet,' she heard herself protest, 'the flood's still in full spate.' Her heart embraced the wild flood water, that trapped them on its other side. She did not want to return to Kaul, to people, and to Zoe. Passionately she longed to remain here, alone in the wilderness with Woolfe. But the world intruded, even here, with work to be done, and appointments to be kept.

'The spate won't go down for several hours,' Woolfe bent a calculating eye on the watercourse behind them, 'but it should be fordable by tomorrow morning. We ought to be able to get across in time to return to Kaul, for when Jim's relief manager flies in, and hand over the Land Rover to him without any delay. In the meantime,' he went on purposefully, 'there used to be a village about a mile or so ahead of us along this road, and if my memory serves me correctly, there should be one of the old government resthouses there. I know it was in use until the landslip blocked the road and stopped the through traffic across the border. With a bit of luck the resthouse will still be standing, and if so, we can camp there for the night.'

Which would not be very long in coming now, Isla realised with a sense of shock. Imperceptibly the sun had lost its strength, and the chill which she blamed on the storm and her wet clothes, she realised now was a harbinger of the coming darkness. She remained silent as Woolfe freed the winch and keyed the engine into life.

'We'll come back for the car on our return journey. It'll be safe enough here until then.' It looked singularly forlorn, stood by itself on the edge of the watercourse, and Isla felt a sympathetic pang as the next bend of the road hid it from her sight.

'At least the village is still here.' Grass-thatched huts came into view, raised high on stilts. A babble of brown-eyed children appeared from nowhere and swarmed round the Land Rover as Woolfe braked to a halt.

'Stay here, I'll come back for you in a minute or two.'

The children followed him. Woolfe spoke to them in their own tongue, and they chattered back to him, confident and unafraid. Pain pierced Isla as she watched them walk away together.

'He likes them. And they like him.' He was unselfconsciously at ease, and happy in the company of the children. Agonisingly her mind flew to Herondale, to the high, spacious rooms of his lovely home, to the cool, inviting greensward of the parkland. A paradise in which to bring up children. The woman who married Woolfe would be blessedly fulfilled.

With a breaking heart she visualised Woolfe's children, clustered about him as the village children clustered now, their faces and his merry with laughter at something he was saying to them. She could visualise Woolfe and his children, but it was more difficult to visualise them with Zoe. The hard sophistication of the red-haired interpreter did not fit into the domestic scene. But what if Woolfe thought the prospects of having a family well lost for the sake of Zoe?

'I prefer to collect miniatures. . . .'

What if he was prepared to fall back upon his miniatures, and substitute his collection for a family? The picture it conjured up made Woolfe's future look as bleak as her own would be without him, but he would be capable, Isla knew, of sacrificing much for the sake of the woman he loved. Daringly she thrust the unacceptable picture aside, and recalled her vision instead, placing herself in the picture beside Woolfe and his children; knowing it was madness, knowing that it would tear her apart, but the temptation was too great, even though she knew the price would be high for her brief flight of imagination. She closed her eyes and tasted for a sweet, dangerous moment, the happy fulfilment of her secret dreams.

'It's a shame to disturb your nap, but you'll sleep easier in the resthouse.' Woolfe's voice shattered her vision, tearing aside the flimsy fabric of her dreams. She opened her eyes and stared at him for a blank, uncomprehending moment, unable to make the adjustment from an ancient, stone-built ancestral home, to bamboo huts clothed with grass thatch.

'Wake up!' She had not been asleep. She had been dreaming,

but she could not share her dreams with Woolfe. 'Let me help you out.' She slid stiffly out of the Land Rover, supported by his arm, and walked woodenly beside him. The children danced about them, a parody of her dreaming, and led the way among the thatched huts until they came to one standing slightly apart from the others. They stopped and crowded round the bottom of the short flight of wooden steps that led up on to its verandah, and watched wide-eyed as Woolfe steered Isla towards them.

'This is the old government resthouse. The rooms aren't habitable any longer, the thatch has given way and let the storm water through, but the roof above the verandah seems sound enough, we can camp on it until the watercourse is low enough to ford again.'

The verandah looked dry. Isla's dubious glance told her that someone had just swept the boards clean, and two rush mats were spread side by side across the floor.

'We can use the two sleeping bags from Jim's emergency kit,' Woolfe offered when she did not speak. 'It's hardly five-star accommodation, but we'll be warm and dry. What more could we want?' he teased away the doubt in her face.

'What more, indeed?' Idiotically Isla's heart started to sing inside her. The bare, wooden verandah in the crumbling resthouse suddenly became a castle to her shining eyes, the grass thatched huts of the village, nestling on the edge of the tea plantation, with the dark mysterious backdrop of the forest crowding behind, a fairy landscape.

'It's even got a moat!' she gasped. Her eyes caught the gleam of water between the huts.

'It happens to be the local river, but it'll do nicely for a moat.' Woolfe laughed down into her face, joining easily in her happy imagery, shedding the stern, disciplined face of the Woolfe she knew for the joyous, carefree, boyish face of one who suddenly finds the moment good, and grasps its sweetness while he can. With a smiling word that scattered the children laughing in the direction of their homes, he stooped suddenly and scooped Isla up into his arms, then ran up the wooden steps and placed her gently on her feet on the verandah.

'Like a bridegroom carries his bride into their new home.' But she could afford to ignore the pain of the comparison, be-

cause his arms were still round her, and he held her to him and
quipped gaily,

'Welcome to the Hotel de Luxe!'

His lips smiled, his teeth gleamed whitely in the deep mahogany tan of his face to prove it, but his eyes that looked deep into
her own remained curiously grave, and held again that fleeting
mystery that she longed with all her heart to grasp, and each
time she reached up to catch at it, it eluded her fingers and
danced away, as elusive as a will-o'-the-wisp.

'Welcome to the Hotel de Luxe.'

He was careful not to hurt her wrist. He folded her to him
gently, so that it might not be crushed between them, and his
mouth sought the tremulous softness of her lips, and lingered on
their responsive fullness as eagerly Isla lifted her face to his, and
sought with her lips for an answer to the mystery that her eyes
denied her.

'Woolfe. . . .'

His kiss deepened, hungrily demanding that she cease to
search, and give herself up to the magic of the moment, and
heedless of her wrist Isla melted against him, returning kiss for
kiss, while the passionate longing of her heart cried out that,
whatever the future might hold, this moment, this magic
moment, belonged to them alone.

'Food. . . .'

Swift darkness fell, and the spicy smell of cooking permeated
the air, coming from the bamboo huts, and a young girl
appeared from the one nearest to the resthouse, scuffing her
bare feet tactfully on the steps, and bearing a bowl of richly
smelling something towards them. She bent and laid her offering
down beside the rush mats, and retreated with a shy smile.

They shared it between them, eating the bread and butter
with the curried rice-and-vegetable stew that tasted as good as it
smelled, and finished off the meal with the banana and orange
left over from Isla's breakfast, leaning back against the bamboo
walls of their crumbling castle while the orchestra of night sounds
started to tune up in the forest behind them, and the moon rose,
and cast its silver witchery to light the darkened world.

A hunter's moon.. . . .

The magic fled for Isla, and she stirred restlessly beside

Woolfe, gripped by a strange sense of foreboding as she watched the silver light rise above the road that brought her to this spot, conscious of guilt that even for a moment she had allowed herself to forget the reason why she came along the road in the first place. Remembering that she had still not found the Tamil boy.

'I thought you said this was a *rest*house.' She wriggled into Mary's sleeping bag, and Woolfe reached out and zipped it up for her before he performed a similar service for himself.

'So it used to be. Why?' he asked quizzically.

'It might be a house, but where does the rest come in?' she grumbled. Weary though she was, she felt far from sleep. The light of the moon brought reality back to torment her, and the knowledge that even a magic castle cannot keep the world and its problems at bay for ever. Could not keep her own tumultuous thoughts at bay. As if to emphasise them, her wrist started to throb again, a nagging accompaniment to the forest orchestra that was by now in full, unmusical swing.

'How anyone can sleep through this racket is beyond me!'

Something rustled in the thatch overhead, and something else scuttled over the edge of the rush matting, making urgent little scratching noises as it ran.

'Ugh! I hate creepy-crawlies!' Isla hunched herself into a tight ball inside her sleeping bag, keeping well away from the bamboo wall.

'Lean back and relax,' Woolfe grinned at her through the moonlight, 'it's probably only a cockroach.'

'I can't,' she snapped back, incensed by his own amusement. 'Something else might crawl down the wall.'

'Then lean back against me—I'll defend you.'

She did not return his sally. He might defend her from creepy-crawlies, but he could not defend her from the peril of her own feelings. She flinched away as he reached out to draw her to him, but her arms were pinioned inside the sleeping bag, trapping her in its soft folds, and he leaned her against him, sleeping bag and all, bent his dark head above her, and trapped her lips in a kiss from which there was no escape. From which she did not want to escape, she thought despairingly, only hungered to remain enchained, bound by the spell of their magic castle, and the silver witchery of the moon. Bound by her love for Woolfe that ran like quicksilver through her veins, leaping to meet his exploring lips as they trailed downwards to touch their impress on the wildly pulsing hollow of her throat, lingering there until she arched her neck to draw his kiss back to her lips, which uttered a low moan of sensuous pleasure at his touch.

From somewhere overhead a mechanical rattle sounded through the darkness, the twentieth century intruding on their magic castle as a helicopter passed over them, and went on its way, and through the drugged sweetness of his lips once more covering her own, Isla scarcely noticed its passing, only that they were alone once more in the silence and the moonlight, and life could offer no greater gift than to leave her where she lay, cradled by sleep, and protected in Woolfe's arms.

They could not protect her from her dreams.

Through sleep closed eyes she saw, once again, the Tamil boy race towards her. He held out something in his hand, but when she reached out to grasp it he was gone, and it was she herself who was running, and not the Tamil boy, and in her hand she held, not the Kang amulet, but the knobbly, oval shape of the glass bottle of suntan lotion. Frantically she flung up her arm to try to throw it away, but it stuck to her hand, refusing to let go, and all the while her pursuer gained on her.

She cast a terrified glance over her shoulder, to try to glimpse who it was who pursued her so relentlessly, but the road that lay behind her was as bleakly empty as the lonely road that lay ahead, and the face that looked back into her frightened eyes was not of human form, but the bland, round face of the hunter's moon.

CHAPTER TEN

'STOP fighting, and let me unzip you.'

Woolfe's voice reached her through a haze of trapped terror, and Isla's eyes flew open. 'You were battling with the sleeping bag as if it was a boa-constrictor that had got hold of you!'

'I was dreaming,' she managed to gasp. She panted still from the terror of her dreams. She leaned against him weakly as

Woolfe's fingers slid open the zip of her sleeping bag, freeing her from its confinement, while his other hand supported her. Woolfe's hand, not the hand of some faceless pursuer.

'It looked more like a nightmare to me,' he responded cheerfully, and helped her to step out of the bag. 'Stay here and eat some breakfast before we set off. I'll fold up the sleeping bags, and put them back in the Land Rover.' He loosed her and folded up the sleeping bags, and Isla's cheeks whitened. He made no attempt to kiss her upturned face, he did not even seem to notice how close it was to his, the mute appeal in her eyes. With quick, practical strokes he folded the sleeping bags, and made no reference by word or look that he remembered his kisses of the night before. When the bags were folded to his satisfaction, he turned to Isla and raised his hand, and she flinched away as if he would strike her, but he only gave a casual wave towards a platter of what looked like pancakes, and a small bowl of some thin golden substance, standing invitingly beside her rush mat.

'Wild honey,' he explained nonchalantly. 'Try it, it's good,' and as she hesitated, 'I've already had mine, so make a good meal, it's a long way back to Kaul. Oh, by the way,' he added casually, 'your blouse and skirt are dry. I've hung them over the end of the verandah for you. You'll find them cooler than Mary's track suit, on the way back.' It was already hot, the sun shone with undiminished brightness as if the storm of yesterday had never been.

'Is the watercourse . . .?' She had to ask, even though she did not want to know. Fervently she wished the watercourse could remain at full flood for ever.

'It's back to a trickle this morning. We'll start as soon as you've eaten,' Woolfe replied briskly, and picking up the sleeping bags he descended the verandah steps, and left her to eat her honey and pancakes alone.

'He might have waited, and eaten his breakfast with me!' she thought. She hated him for not waiting, for treating the magic moments when she had lain in his arms last night as if they had never been. The mists of her nightmare clung like wraiths around her still, and she longed for the feel of Woolfe's arms to dispel them. Listlessly she picked up her skirt and blouse. The dull brown of Mary's track suit matched her mood. Perhaps the bright colours of her own clothes would act as an antidote to her depression. Achingly she longed to bring back the magic of the evening before, to recapture it, and let it transport her, before she left the village behind her for ever. Part of her heart would always remain here, she thought wistfully, haunting a magic castle that was lit by a silver moon, and lapped by a gleaming moat.

The village was already astir. A woman ladled rice into the begging bowl of a saffron-robed monk, gaining merit by donating food. The monk moved on, his shaven head as bare as his feet, and Isla winced at the thought of walking the rough mountain road without the protection of shoes. A young novice, little more than a child, walked behind him, and he, too, carried a begging bowl. Isla watched the boy interestedly, but in spite of his tender years he made no attempt to join the group of youths who besported themselves in the swift-running waters of the river.

'I wonder . . .?' A sudden thought sharpened Isla's attention on the youths. 'I wonder if the Tamil boy's among them?' Hope rose in her that she might, even now, manage to accomplish one of the objects of her ill-fated journey. 'I must go and find out, before Woolfe comes back.' He would try to prevent her, she felt sure. She called it finding out. Woolfe called it meddling. Isla's lips tightened as she glanced cautiously over the verandah rail towards the Land Rover. Woolfe leaned inside the back of it. He had removed his track suit, and his white shirt gleamed against the dull khaki of the vehicle top.

'He won't see me, if I go now.' Quickly Isla stooped and drooled honey on to the pancakes, and rolled them into a thick spill the better to eat them one handed as she walked. 'Mmm, these are good!' Buoyed up by new hope, she hurried down the verandah steps, and in between the huts towards the river, relishing the sharp sweetness of the wild honey, licking it off her fingers where it oozed from out of the end of the pancakes.

'The boys aren't old enough!' She gulped down sick disappointment with her pancakes as she halted on the river bank, and her eyes searched the line of lads strung out across the width of the river. They were little boys, not youths. The young peach stealer in the market place had been, she judged, in his late teens. The laughing lads splashing in the river would be, at most, nine or ten years of age.

They looked up at her approach, and Isla smiled at them, but although they smiled back they did not come crowding round her, as the children did when Woolfe spoke to them, and her smile faded, and she felt rebuffed by their aloofness, until one of the boys, his eyes intently watching the current flowing towards him, suddenly bent to grab at something in the water. Another of his fellows followed suit, and suddenly the whole line of boys was grabbing at the water, picking up something from it, Isla could not see what, and stowing it under thin arms while they energetically bent to grab again.

'Surely they're not fishing with their bare hands?' she ejaculated, and stepped closer to the edge of the bank, intrigued by their antics.

'They're not fishing, they're collecting rice plants.'

Isla spun round with a startled gasp. She had not heard Woolfe approach, soft-footed across the dusty earth, silent as a hunter approaches his prey.

'One more step backwards, and they'll be collecting you,' Woolfe warned her humorously, and reached out and grabbed her, and pulled her back from the brink. 'You'd be a bit heavier for them to carry than a rice plant,' he teased, and his eyes glinted down at her softly rounded form.

'Don't be sarcastic!' Isla snapped, flushing. 'In any case, rice plants don't grow in rivers. Even I know that.' Fiercely she thrust down the tingling excitement that surged through her at his touch, determined not to humiliate herself again by baring her heart to his gaze, still raw from the wound of his earlier rebuff.

'Look for yourself,' he replied indifferently, and gestured towards the boys, some of whom were by now splashing towards the bank, their arms already full to overflowing with young, green plants.

'Someone from the next village upstream will be sending them down by arrangement, for the boys to pick up at the most convenient spot,' Woolfe commented. 'It's a common method of delivery by the people who live beside the river. If a man promises to supply something to another, and that something floats, he uses the river as a conveyor belt to save himself the trouble of delivering the goods by hand.'

'What a novel idea!' Isla was so intrigued that she forgot her anger for the moment. She wished it was as easy to forget her acute awareness of Woolfe's slim brown fingers, still holding her by the arm.

'It's a practical idea,' Woolfe replied casually, 'the people simply harness the natural resources to serve a human need. The river's here, so they use it,' he said simply.

Would that all of life was so simple! Isla sighed to herself, and depression descended again like a dark blanket on her spirits. 'What do they want all those rice plants for?' She tried to keep the bleakness at bay by talking. 'This is a tea plantation. The paddy fields are some miles away.' The children had already disappeared with their plants beyond the huts, to where she could not see.

'Each family in the village has its own rice patch, just the same as we have a patch of garden at home,' Woolfe answered her equably. 'Before we've gone far along the road, they'll have their plants dibbed in and starting to grow.' In spite of his earlier protestations of urgency to get the Land Rover back in time to hand it over to Jim Donaldson's relief manager, he did not seem to be in any hurry to depart, Isla thought. He paused, and idly watched a small boy lead a water buffalo along the river bank; smiled down into Isla's widened eyes as she took in the tiny child, dwarfed by the animal's huge head and wide-spreading horns.

'Don't worry, their fierce looks bely a gentle nature,' he reassured her.

'I wish I could paint,' she breathed rapturously.

'Paint it on your memory,' he advised her softly. 'That way, you can take it out and look at it at any time you want.'

Was Woolfe doing the same thing? Isla asked herself bleakly. Was he, too, storing the scene in his memory, to treasure it, because it was something they two had shared together? Or was he merely tucking it away in his mind as an interesting sight that, one day, he might tell his children about, when he regaled them with stories round the fire on a winter afternoon? His children, and Zoe's. . . .

'The Nats must surely favour this spot.' He turned to walk back towards the Land Rover, and Isla turned with him, dragging leaden feet that did not want to leave the spot behind.

'Nats?' Whatever they were, she envied them if they could remain here.

'Spirits that live in the natural things,' Woolfe explained, his face serious with respectful acceptance of others' beliefs, 'in the trees, and the rivers. . . .'

When they went away, her spirit would remain here, Isla acknowledged bleakly, the bright, shining hopefulness of it clinging to the fragile hours of happiness she had spent in Woolfe's arms, that were all she would ever know. When they went away, she would take with her a travesty of her former self, as empty as a shell from which her yearning heart would strain to catch the echo of Woolfe's voice, that must grow faint with the passing of the years.

Her spirit fainted now at the bleak prospect of those years, and her feet stumbled as she walked beside him, her eyes misting so that she could not see clearly where she walked, only the road her inner vision showed her, that was rougher and lonelier than the road she had travelled along the day before.

'Aren't your laces done up?' Woolfe questioned her sharply when she stumbled, and his brows met in a quick frown.

'There aren't any laces. I've put my sandals back on this morning, they're slip-ons,' Isla retorted defensively. She and Woolfe had slipped back into their old relationship, she thought bleakly, his frown was as quick as his hand that fielded her stumble.

'Does your wrist need rebandaging?' He misinterpreted her quick avoidance as she flinched away from his hand, and she winced again at his indifferent enquiry. He did not ask her how her wrist felt, whether or not it still hurt her, only, 'Does it need rebandaging?' as if he grudged the time he had already spent with her at the river bank, and was reluctant to waste any more on attending to her injured wrist.

'The worst of the swelling's gone this morning.' The worst of the pain was in her heart, but valiantly she kept her voice casual, determined not to let it show. 'I left the bandage on for support, that's all. I've put the splint and the arm sling with Mary's track suit, to go back into the Land Rover.' The bandage she had left on was loose, and it offered no support, but she was too proud to beg Woolfe to retie the ends that she had managed to untie with the aid of her teeth, and like the shoe laces, discovered she could not do them up again. As before, she compromised by tucking in the ends. 'At least the bandage on my wrist can't catch in my feet and tip me off balance,' she told herself ruefully.

Her heart lurched off balance without any aid as Woolfe helped her up into the Land Rover, grasping her round the waist and giving her a boost up into the high seat to start the journey she did not want to travel, away from a place she did not want to leave. He did not speak as he keyed the engine into life, and Isla could not, her throat was too choked with tears her pride would not allow her to shed. Agonisingly, she longed to cling with one hand to their magic castle, and cling with the other to Woolfe, while it seemed as if the spinning wheels were tearing her apart between the two, until she could have cried aloud at the pain of the separation. With a fainting heart she stared stonily in front of her, through eyes that could not bear to look behind, and which were too misted to immediately recognise the dark something looming in front of them until they were right up to it, and then, in seconds, gone past.

'The car . . . we can't go without the car!' She blinked her eyes clear and twisted round to face Woolfe, and demanded, 'Stop the Land Rover. 'We've got to take the car back with us.'

'How?' Woolfe asked her laconically, and kept on going, and Isla's temper erupted at his casual ignoring of her demand, her overwrought nerves eroding her normal self control.

'Tow it, of course,' she flashed indignantly. 'Or if you don't want to be bothered,' her tone lashed him for not wanting to be bothered, 'I'll drive it back to Kaul myself. I won't trouble you,' she thrust at him proudly. She had driven it here, so she could take it back. 'I drove it here. . . .'

'I don't need reminding,' Woolfe observed drily, and Isla's cheeks flamed, but before she could retort he went on forcefully, 'Even if it could be started again, you can't possibly drive it back with a damaged wrist. On a surface like this,' he gestured expressively towards the road ahead of them, 'you need both hands to hold the wheel, so how do you think you'd manage with only one?' As logic it was unanswerable, but Isla felt in no mood to listen to logic.

'I've *got* to get the car back to Kaul,' she insisted angrily. 'The hire company will want it back.'

'Jim Donaldson's relief manager will want this Land Rover, the moment he lands in Kaul,' Woolfe retorted dismissively, as if, Isla thought furiously, his promise to return the Land Rover was of paramount importance, and her own agreement to return the hired car to its owner was a triviality that did not even warrant thinking about. 'If I stop to winch the car over the water course, it'll take at least an hour, which I can't spare,' Woolfe went on, 'and the same applies if I try to tow the car back behind the Land Rover, it'll slow us down too much to be able to get to Kaul in time to give the manager his vehicle. As it is, I only hope I manage to get it back to him in one piece,' he added significantly, and Isla caught her breath as he changed gear and crawled towards the run-in to the watercourse.

'It's not very deep,' she countered, and tried not to let her relief show in her voice.

'The water's gone down,' Woolfe acknowledged. 'I wish I could say the same for the opposite bank.'

'We can't go up that!' Isla's eyes widened in a horrified stare. Had she really come down that awful bank, the day before? 'I must have been mad,' she whispered.

'Is your seat-belt fastened?' Woolfe did not seem to hear her. He braked, and without waiting for her to answer his question, he turned and checked the seat-belt for himself.

'We can't possibly climb a bank as steep as that!' She raised her voice and shouted at him, to make sure that he heard her. 'We'll tip over. No vehicle can climb an incline as steep as that, it's almost vertical!' What was it Woolfe himself had said about the bank?

'It takes the full force of the downward thrust from the water.'

And that downward thrust, she saw shrinkingly, had undercut the lower part of the bank, making the slope terrifyingly steeper now than it had been the day before. 'We'll tip over,' she cried shrilly. 'We'll be killed!' And it'll all be my fault, her heart cried in silent anguish. She clung to Woolfe's arm with both hands, no matter that her wrist screamed in agony at the force of her grip, while her eyes pleaded with him, begged of him, to go back before it was too late. He had warned her.

'You're treading on dangerous ground,' he said, and followed her to snatch her back from the unknown peril, and now he was going to drive into a deathtrap, that she had drawn him into, and there was nothing she could do to pull him back.

'Woolfe, please . . .!' Her voice cracked with terror, but her fear was for him, not for herself, for what did her own life matter, if she could not share it with him?

'Woolfe, please. . . .' she begged with hoarse words, while her heart pleaded in silence through the desperate brightness of her fear-wide, pansy eyes.

'Woolfe, I love you. I love you,' they told him as they searched his face in an agony of fear. Surely he must hear their silent plea, even if he did not heed her words?

'Shut your eyes if you're frightened.' Incredibly he heard, and did not heed her. With a firm hand he removed her clinging fingers from his arm.

'Woolfe. . . .' she choked, but the tyres crunched on debris and shingle as he loosed the brake and the Land Rover moved forward, and drowned her pleading. Woolfe's hands gripped the steering wheel, his knuckles white under the pressure of his hold, and the strong, uncompromising lines of his face tensed with concentration as he drove the vehicle forward at the slope. The bonnet rose in front of them at an almost unbelievable angle.

'No!' With a quick, convulsive movement, Isla covered her face with her hands, but not seeing was worse than seeing, she discovered. With her eyes closed, she saw again the wild, swirling water, carrying with it the mass of tangled debris. Pictured a khaki-coloured Land Rover, caught among the debris. She gave an inarticulate cry and her eyes flew open, and the rocky bank rose above the windscreen, so close that it seemed as if she could reach out and touch it, looming above them so steeply that it blotted out the sky.

'We'll never make it. It's all my fault. Oh, Woolfe! Wollfe! I love you.' Her fingernails dug ridges into the palms of her clenched hands. 'Why didn't I listen to him? Why didn't I do as he said?' The wide tyres clawed upwards, catlike, seeking the firmer patches, avoiding the loose shale that might slip under the wheels, and send them hurtling down to the bottom again.

Drops of perspiration beaded Woolfe's forehead, betraying the intense strain he laboured under. Isla longed to brush her fingers across his face, to wipe them off. Her hand began to rise, but with an effort of will she pulled it back again. Even for a minute, a second, she dared not risk cutting across his vision, destroying his concentration. A pulse beat at the corner of his jaw, throbbing an accompaniment to the anguished throb of her heart.

'Now we can get a move on at last.'

Unbelievably, they were on the road. With a final Herculean effort, the Land Rover scrabbled over the top of the bank, slipped, righted itself, and pulled up on to terra firma. A wave of faintness passed over Isla, and she leaned limply back against her seat.

'I didn't think we'd make it.' She felt too relieved for the moment to care that she bared her fears to Woolfe.

'This vehicle's built to take obstacles like that in its stride,' he commented practically, as if such obstacles were, alike, a matter of small moment to him. His unemotional acceptance of the vehicle's achievement, and his own, stung Isla's pride, reducing her own very natural fear to craven cowardice by comparison.

'The car isn't built that way. It'll have to be winched across the bank.' Rawly she flung round to face him, using her concern for the car as a sop to her injured pride. 'While we're here, it wouldn't delay us all that much to bring it across to this side of the watercourse, even if we have to come back to collect it later. Surely an hour wouldn't make all that much difference?'

'It'll make the difference between giving the manager his Land Rover, and stranding him without a vehicle,' Woolfe retorted unco-operatively. 'I promised to hand over the vehicle on time, and I intend to do just that. And besides, I need to get back to Kaul myself.'

His need mattered, and hers did not, Isla thought furiously. She felt abrasively certain that it was Woolfe's own need, and not the manager's for the Land Rover, that drove him to ignore the car standing forlornly on the other side of the watercourse. He did not say so out loud, he did not need to, she thought angrily, he underscored his meaning by driving on in indifferent silence, and at a speed she herself would not have dared along such a surface, but with a skill that eliminated most of the jolting she had endured on her outward journey.

Angrily Isla flung round in her seat and looked out of the window, seething in helpless frustration as the miles rolled behind them, separating her inexorably from the car, and from the transient hours of happiness that would never come again. Through blurred eyes she saw that the women were back in the paddy fields again. They waved, and Isla returned their greeting, but halfheartedly, too incensed by Woolfe's attitude to take pleasure in the hail-fellow-well-met salute, made rawly conscious by his uncompromising demeanour that, so far as he was concerned, he was bringing her back to Kaul under a cloud, like a naughty child being returned to school after a silly scrape. No one, absolutely no one, took her search for Robin seriously, she fumed resentfully.

Thank goodness for a decent road surface! Scattered buildings lined the road, the rocks gave way to luxurious smoothness, and traffic appeared. The main street produced hotels, shops, and Barclays showrooms.

'I'll get out at the showrooms, the manager might have heard from Robin.' Isla was sure he had not heard, but she did not want to continue all the way to the Consulate with Woolfe. Like a jailer, delivering a prisoner! she thought resentfully.

'You can find out about Robin later.' Woolfe ignored her request to be put down, and drove on.

'But I must. . . .' she protested angrily.

'There's a job you must do at the Consulate first.' He ignored her protest as well.

'A job? What job?' she demanded furiously. If Woolfe wanted a job done, he could do it himself! Or give it to Zoe. She was not a servant to do his bidding, she told herself proudly.

'To make your peace with Zoe.' Baldly he told her what job, and his tone said she was welcome to it.

'Zoe?' Isla's patience gave way. 'I'll make no peace, or anything else, with Zoe,' she refused forthrightly. 'What has Zoe got to do with . . . ?'

'You took off without letting anyone at the Consulate know

where you were going.' Grimly, Woolfe enumerated her transgressions. 'You stayed away overnight, without notifying the Consulate. . . .'

'How on earth *could* I notify the Consulate?' Isla snapped back. 'In case you hadn't noticed, remote Burmese villages don't possess telephones, and the car wasn't fitted with Citizens Band radio,' she pointed out sarcastically. 'And may I remind you,' she added forcefully, 'I'm a guest at the Consulate, not a prisoner. I'm not obliged to report my every movement to anyone, and that includes Zoe.' And you, her angry expression added, and Woolfe's face tightened.

'Except as a matter of courtesy.' He jerked the Land Rover to a halt at the bottom of the Consulate steps. 'For all anyone here knew, you might have had an accident and been lying injured somewhere, and no one would have known in which direction to search for you.' He spelled out the possible consequences of her own thoughtlessness with remorseless vigour. 'If it hadn't been for the fact that I found the map you dropped, and told the people at the Consulate I was going to follow you, they might well have mounted an expensive and time-wasting search for nothing,' he accused her.

'Well, I haven't, and they didn't,' she thrust back unrepentantly. She spurned his hand that reached out to help her, and jumped down from the Land Rover unaided, and ran ahead of Woolfe up the Consulate steps. 'So all's well that ends well,' she added tritely, from the top.

'Indeed it is, Miss Barclay, I'm glad to say,'

'Consul! I—I'm sorry.' She had not meant to apologise. She would not have done, to Zoe, but the courtly diplomat made her feel unaccountably guilty, as if remaining out all night had indeed been her fault, and not the fault of the storm, and she blurted out an apology in spite of herself, and could have bitten her tongue that spoke it because Woolfe was within earshot, and heard the words she declared she would not speak.

'Think no more of it, my dear,' her host urged her kindly, 'we knew you'd be perfectly safe while Woolfe was with you.'

She did not want to be safe with Woolfe. She wanted. . . . With a burning face she thrust down what she wanted, and lashed herself with scorn for wasting time dreaming of her own wants, when Robin was still missing. 'Woolfe can do no wrong in the eyes of these people,' she told herself angrily. 'What hope have I got of making them see he's got feet of clay? They're besotted by the man.' So was she, but. . . .

'If only Huw were here!' Unconsciously she spoke out loud, and a lilting voice answered her,

'Huw is here. And glad he is to see you.'

'Huw!' A wonderfully fit-looking, if slightly less bow-fronted Welshman than before, who enveloped her in a fatherly hug, and kissed her firmly on both cheeks, then held her at arm's length for inspection.

'You need coddling,' he announced critically, his eyes taking in the dark rings underneath her own, the telltale hollows in her cheeks that had been rounded when she saw him last. 'Some of Bethan's good home cooking, and. . . .'

'Oh, Huw, it's good to see you!' Isla clung to him like an anchor, torn between laughter, and tears of relief. 'Is Bethan here? I so need to talk to you both.' Huw and Bethan would listen. They would understand.

'Bethan's at home preparing the most stupendous lunch, which you're going to help us to eat.' Huw's searching glance saw through the laughter, and guessed at the tears, but he could never guess at the reason for them, Isla told herself wildly. 'So cut along upstairs and put on your prettiest dress. I'll give you exactly half an hour.'

She did not mind taking orders from Huw. She fled upstairs on light feet, sang her way through a shower, and put on a gaily patterned print sun-dress with a crisp cotton bolero to match, and hurried downstairs again. Everything would be all right now Huw was back.

'Huw's gone on ahead. He asked me to give you a lift.'

Woolfe was waiting for her by the commissionaire's desk, tall, and debonair, and dressed in fresh whites, and looking as if he had spent the morning in leisurely debate round a conference table, instead of a night camping out on a leaking verandah, followed by a hair-raising trek back to Kaul that was a feat of endurance rather than a journey. Isla looked up at him dumbly. 'I've been invited to lunch, too,' he told her gravely.

Woolfe was coming, too. She was not to spend the meal alone

with Huw and Bethan, after all. The eager greeting died on her lips, and the brightness faded from her face. 'He hunts me down, no matter where I go,' she told herself despairingly, 'even when I'm invited to lunch with Huw and Bethan.' Making sure that, during the lunchtime, she would have no opportunity to pour out her fears and suspicions to the only two people who were likely to listen to her. Countering this move, as he had so successfully countered all the others she had made.

'Huw's right, you need coddling,' Woolfe misunderstood her dazed groping as she felt rather than stepped her way into the chauffeur-driven Consulate car. Isla watched frozenly as the collector got in beside her, and the driver closed the door, shutting them in together. She did not need that kind of coddling, she told herself wearily. At least, not from Huw and Bethan. She needed. . . .

'Sherry? Sweet or dry?'

Sherry was a poor substitute for what she really needed, but she took one anyway. Holding the glass against her lips served to disguise their tremble, and the sharp warmth of the wine flowing down her aching throat helped to armour her against the black disappointment of what she had supposed was to be a quiet luncheon party. There would be no opportunity of a tête-à-tête with Bethan and Huw, that much was clear from the moment Woolfe steered her through the door.

'As if he knows Huw's house as well as I do!'

Isla scarcely had time to register surprise at the discovery before she received another. Huw's relief manager was there. That was to be expected, she thought. She had not expected Professor Armstrong to be one of the gathering, as well. She stared at the scientist in shocked surprise. He seemed to pop up like a bad penny, and always with Woolfe, like a satellite circling round the sun.

'Who is this man?' she asked herself uneasily, for the hundredth time. 'And what is his connection with Woolfe?' Even more worrying, what was he doing here, in Huw's house? Surely Woolfe had not managed to hoodwink Huw and Bethan as well? They were the only people she had left whom she could trust.

'Sorry to keep you all waiting,' Bethan apologised gaily, 'the cutlets aren't quite cooked yet.'

Bethan's cutlets were always cooked perfectly, and on time. She never kept her guests waiting. Isla cast her friend a puzzled look. Bethan was an excellent cook, and an accomplished hostess, whose meals never went wrong. Out of the corner of her eye she caught a small movement beside her. Woolfe glanced surreptitiously at his watch—for the second time, she realised, in ten minutes. The small movement irritated her out of all proportion to its importance. It rasped her nerves like the clicking of the forgettable man's ballpoint pen, in the drawing room at Herondale. She frowned. Woolfe did not forget so easily that he had to check his watch twice in ten minutes, any more than Bethan ever mistimed her cooking. Both were suddenly, and unaccountably, acting out of character.

A sense of foreboding assailed Isla. Something about the luncheon party was not as it should be. On the surface, everyone was gay and friendly and at ease. Below the surface a brittle undercurrent crackled like an electric probe, tensing the atmosphere. Only the young relief manager seemed to be unaffected. Covertly Isla watched her companions. Huw was being altogether too hearty, and Bethan too bright, she decided worriedly. Woolfe. . . . Her glance at him gave her no information whatsoever. His face was as expressionless as his eyes were unreadable. If she had not noticed him repeatedly glancing at his watch, she would not have noticed anything was amiss. Which was doubtless what he intended, she thought restlessly.

'More sherry?' She did not want any more. If Woolfe had topped up her glass she would have refused to drink it, but Huw wielded the bottle, and she sipped and tried to look as if she was enjoying it, while her raw nerves screamed at the pressure of the tension around her, pummelled by unspoken thoughts, wild conjectures, and questions to which she could find no answer. A tense air of waiting hung over the gathering. But for what? It could not be for food, because no one was bothering to nibble the crisps and nuts on offer with the wine, but she was not mistaken, Isla felt certain. An almost tangible air of expectancy pervaded the gathering like a brooding electric storm, and fear of she knew not what tingled along her spine. It was like waiting for a bolt of lightning, and not knowing where, or at whom, it would strike.

This time it was the Professor who looked at his watch.

Instead of irritating her, the gesture sent an unexpected flood of relief through Isla. 'Perhaps Bethan's keeping us waiting, and the Professor and Woolfe are afraid of being late for one of the Conference sessions.' Perhaps it was as simple as that, and her fears were totally unfounded. 'Perhaps. . . .' Another hope rose to join the first. 'Perhaps, after all, Woolfe and the Professor will excuse themselves, and go, and I'll be able to talk to Huw and Bethan alone.' She would not mind the relief manager being present while she talked, he was on her side, not Woolfe's.

'Is it too early to congratulate you, Armstrong? Or must we keep your secret until tomorrow?'

Huw spoke, making conversation, ostensibly filling in time until the cutlets were cooked. In reality, filling in time until—what? Isla's relief vanished, and her fear returned.

'Secret? What secret?' She tried to make herself sound interested, and join in the surface small talk, while her mind screamed, 'What are you all waiting for?' and her fingers gripped the stem of her wine glass until she feared the delicate crystal might snap. It was brittle, like jade. . . . With an effort she released her fingers, and put the glass down on the table, clenching her hands together instead, bruising herself with the ferocity of her hold, and unaware of the pain.

'I think among friends it needn't remain a secret any longer,' Woolfe put in easily, 'after all, the inauguration ceremony is tomorrow.'

'We'll all be there,' Huw beamed.

'Be where?' Isla felt as if she was acting in some peculiar kind of play for which she had not properly learned the lines. 'At what ceremony?' Was this like the dance at the Consulate? she asked herself furiously. Something else that Woolfe had taken for granted she would attend, and had not bothered to mention it to her beforehand?

'The Professor's going to take over from Woolfe as President of the Society,' Huw looked surprised. 'I thought you knew?'

She had not known. She burned with resentment that Woolfe had not told her. There was no reason why he should tell her, but she did not feel in a reasonable frame of mind. Through a daze of anger she heard the Professor speak.

'It's a great honour. A great honour indeed.' His eyes glittered with excited anticipation of the morrow. 'When I came to the Conference this year, I had no idea that I'd be travelling home with the badge of office of President of the Society.' He fairly purred with gratification.

The President's badge of office. Something of inestimable value. Vividly Isla recalled the scientist's own words at the dinner table two evenings ago. An honour bestowed by his peers as a mark of their respect, something of inestimable value, incalculable, priceless. Something that, to a man of science, would rank supreme above mere worldly wealth. This, then, was the Professor's connection with Woolfe. Isla felt her head begin to spin.

'It's the sherry.' She knew that it was not. A glass of Huw's good wine, sipped for the sake of appearances, had not the potency to make her senses reel in this disconcerting manner.

'It's like a crazy jigsaw puzzle,' she told herself bemusedly. A puzzle that lay tidily in its box until Robin's letter scattered the pieces, and sent her racing half across the world to collect them together again, and fit them into a picture, one slow piece at a time. The Professor had just slotted several pieces together to fill in one corner of the puzzle, but there were still some missing to complete the whole. Robin was one, and the talisman another. If only she could find them all, and complete the picture, then put it back in its box and never look at it again, she wished fiercely. She could almost visualise herself fitting in the final pieces. Click, click. Like the clicking of the top of the gold ballpoint pen.

It was so real in her mind, she could actually hear it. Click, click. She spun round. The sound *was* real. The owner of the gold ballpoint pen was real. Isla stared at him in stunned disbelief. He wore the same nondescript mackintosh that he had worn in the drawing room at Herondale. He held the same gold ballpoint pen. And he was indulging in the same infuriating habit of clicking the top of it up and down with his thumb. Isla caught her breath hysterically. The man in the mackintosh stood just inside the doorway, and behind him stood. . . .

'Robin!'

The man in the mackintosh must have moved aside. Isla did

not see him go. With a choking cry that was half a sob, she fled across the room and flung her arms round her brother.

'I thought you were being held hostage!' she sobbed.

'Steady on, Sis, I'm not too used to balancing on this thing yet.'

'Your leg's in plaster!' she realised, horrified.

'There was a bit of a rough-house, but I managed to escape across the border, and bring the amulet back with me,' Robin announced cheerfully, 'and thanks to the monks at Tan Gwe, my leg's healing nicely now. My Tamil guide took me to the monastery when I became lightheaded, and it wasn't until two days later, when I eventually came round, that I realised he'd gone on to deliver the amulet himself. He knew how important it was to me to get it into safe custody, although the gang who stole it are in the hands of the authorities now, but even so he still took a considerable personal risk by going on alone.'

'He gave it to me, in the market place. Woolfe took it from me.' Tensely Isla waited for Woolfe to deny that he had it. Her eyes were hard on his as she dared him to deny it, but to her surprise he merely remarked in a mild voice,

'The amulet's in the safe at the Consulate.'

So he had not lied to her, after all. The evening was providing the final pieces of the jigsaw puzzle, one after the other, and at such a speed that Isla scarcely knew where to fit them in.

'Dan told me how you came by it,' Robin nodded. So the forgettable man had a name. It made him seem more human, somehow. 'As I understand it,' her brother grinned, 'the lad helped himself to a peach from the market when he was on his way to the showrooms with the amulet, then when he got chased he rid himself of the jade for fear he might be accused of stealing that as well.'

'The talisman's still missing.' Woolfe pinpointed the last remaining piece of the puzzle.

'I've got it here.' Robin clicked it into place to complete the picture himself. He fumbled at his belt, and unhooked a small carved wooden receptacle with which Isla was very familiar.

'You've been carrying the talisman in your Japanese *inro*, all along?' The antique medicine box would make an ideal receptacle to keep the fragile scroll safe from harm. 'What a good thing you always carry the *inro* with you.' Robin never travelled far without it, and used it for the same purpose as that for which it was originally made, to carry necessary medicaments when he travelled in out-of-the-way places.

'I'd explained to my Tamil guide what the talisman was intended for,' Robin smiled, 'so when he decided to bring the amulet on to the showrooms himself, he left the talisman with me in the hope that it would cure my fever. I found it in my *inro* when I woke up in the monastery. You'd better take care of it, Woolfe,' he held out the container for the collector to take.

'Leave it with Dan,' Woolfe refused it, and Isla stared at him in disbelief. 'It's better left in the hands of a member of the International Security Force,' he excused his reluctance to accept responsibility, and added frankly, 'I must admit I'll be glad to see the back of the thing. The sooner the amulet and the talisman are put together again, and in the hands of their home museum, the better I'll be pleased. I can give them my opinion in writing, later on, as to which dynasty the jade and the scroll each belong.'

'I've arranged for them to be taken back under armed guard,' the security man spoke in the quiet voice Isla remembered.

'Then it only needs to reward the Tamil guide,' Woolfe began, and Robin laughed.

'I've already rewarded him beyond his wildest dreams. When I last saw him, he was wondering if he'd got enough to start his own tea plantation,' he grinned cheerfully, and added, 'Though I think the thing he valued more than the reward money was the lift Dan gave him back to his plantation, in the helicopter which you sent to ferry me from the monastery back to Kaul hospital yesterday. Oh, by the way, the 'copter's on its way now, to air-lift Isla's hire car from the other side of the water-course, as we arranged on the telephone when you got back to the Consulate today.'

'Come and eat,' Bethan interrupted cheerfully, 'the cutlets are done to a turn.' She shooed her guests towards the dining room, but Isla did not follow them. She stood staring at Woolfe, as if she had been turned to stone.

'You sent a helicopter *yesterday*, to fetch Robin back?' She faced him with blazing eyes. 'You knew Robin was safe, and you didn't let me know?' She had heard the helicopter overhead when she lay in Woolfe's arms last night. He must have heard it, too, and even then he had not told her. 'How *could* you keep me in suspense, when you knew that Robin was safe?' She would never forgive him for the sheer mental cruelty of not telling her, and putting her mind at rest.

'I only knew a report had come in, that Robin was at the monastery, and was injured. I didn't know for certain that the report was true, or if so, how badly he was hurt. It would have been cruel to raise your hopes unnecessarily.'

'You should have told me.' Nothing could excuse his silence, she told herself passionately.

'What was the point?' Woolfe demanded impatiently. 'There was no way we could get back across the watercourse until the spate had subsided, so. . . .'

'I'd have swum across, if necessary,' Isla declared heatedly, and Woolfe's face tightened.

'Which is exactly what I feared, and the reason why I kept silent,' he countered her accusation harshly. 'You're far too prone to put your life at risk on the impulse of the moment, and having rescued you once yesterday, I felt in no mood to repeat the process unnecessarily,' he told her forcefully, and added, as Isla opened her mouth to retort, 'and in case you're planning to go back for the car you hired, forget it. You've just heard Robin say the helicopter will airlift it back to Kaul, and I've arranged for a Consulate chauffeur to return it to the car hire people, and reimburse them for any damage it's suffered.'

'I'll pay the full cost of the damage myself.' She would not be beholden to Woolfe for anything, Isla told herself furiously. 'I'll pay every penny of the cost myself,' she declared, with an independent toss of her head.

'The price is high,' Woolfe warned, and there was a strange light in his eyes that should have warned her, but Isla was too incensed to notice, let alone to care.

'Name it,' she cried recklessly. She would pay it, if it cost her everything she possessed.

'Marry me.'

He named his price, spelling out the warning she had failed to heed. She gulped, and stammered,

'M-marry you?'

The hot blaze died from her eyes, eclipsed by the glow that warmed the grey of his. She gazed up at him, transfixed, unable to believe what her ears assured her they had heard. She felt her mouth drop open. She shut it, and swallowed, hard.

'M-marry you?'

'That's what I said. I warned you the price would be high.' Woolfe's look challenged her to accept his price, dared her to refuse it, and pay the even greater price of lack of courage. She did not dare. Her heart beat with a long, slow beat, echoing his demand, 'Marry me—marry me.' Isla hesitated only for the brief space of half a second, listening to its message, and then with a small, muffled sound she ran to the shelter of Woolfe's waiting arms.

'I'll pay every penny of your price.'

Quivering, she lifted softly parted lips to his, to meet the intimate demands of his mouth with a passionate longing equal to his own. Eagerly she raised her arms to clasp his dark head even closer, and through the open windows the light chiming of pagoda bells fell sweetly through the hot air, like distant wedding bells.

'Marry me soon, the moment we get back home,' Woolfe begged her huskily. 'I can't bear to be parted from you any longer. I love you ... I love you. ...' He crushed her to him, fiercely protective. 'I've been mad with fear in case you should come to harm.' His eyes burned with the remembered depths of his fear.

'Is that why ...?' Remorse choked her. She had been so afraid for Robin, it had not occurred to her that Woolfe had suffered, too.

'Why else would I track you across the width of the world?' he demanded hoarsely. 'What else would bring me to Kaul?'

'The Kang amulet,' she started, wonderingly.

'I cared nothing for the amulet.' He shrugged away its total unimportance to him. 'Robin was more than capable of dealing with the amulet, without my interference. I cared only for you.' He drew her to him tenderly, his lips brushing her hair, her cheeks, her eyes, telling her how much he cared. 'From the very moment I first saw you, in the drawing room at Herondale, nothing else mattered to me but you. Nothing ever will.' Hungrily his lips pressed his vow indelibly upon her own.

'The Conference . . .?' Isla knew it was not the Conference, but she wanted to hear him tell her so. So long as she lived, she would never tire of hearing him declare, 'I love you.'

'The Conference was already half over before I started on my journey. I arranged it, but I wasn't due to attend. I wired my resignation as President of the Society when I set off to follow you to Kaul.'

'You resigned, because of me?' Isla had not known of his sacrifice. 'But you founded the Society,' she protested.

'We'll found something even better, together.' His ardent gaze asked a question, and begged an answer, and brought a soft, shy rose to warm her throat and cheeks, but bravely, confidently, Isla met his eyes, her own bright with the promise of her dream come true.

'I love you, I can't live without you.' Urgently Woolfe strained her to him, and buried his face in the soft brown of her curls.

'Only for a little while longer, until we reach home.' Home for Isla now meant Herondale, and Woolfe.

'We'll wait until Christmas to get married, if you really want to? I know brides like time to plan.' Desperately he tried to be patient, while his eyes grew dark with the agony of his longing.

'We've got all the rest of our lives together, to make plans.' Sweetly her lips brushed aside the darkness, and took away the agony. 'Autumn's a lovely time for a wedding—our wedding,' she whispered happily.

ROMANCE

Mills & Boon Reader Film Service

See your pictures before you pay

Our confidence in the quality of our colour prints is such that we send the developed film to you without asking for payment in advance. We bill you for only the prints that you receive, which means that if your prints don't come out, you won't just be sent an annoying credit note as with the 'cash with order' film services.

Free Kodacolor Film

We replace each film sent for processing with a fresh Kodacolor film to fit the customer's camera without further charge. Kodak's suggested prices in the shops are:

110/24 exp. £1.79
126/24 exp. £1.88
135/24 exp. £1.88
135/36 exp. £2.39

Top Quality Colour Prints

We have arranged for your films to be developed by the largest and longest established firm of mail order film processors in Britain. We are confident that you will be delighted with the quality they produce. Our commitment, and their technical expertise ensures that we stay ahead.

How long does it take?

Your film will be in their laboratory for a maximum of 48 hours. We won't deny that problems can occasionally arise or that the odd film requires

Mills & Boon Reader Film Service

special attention resulting in a short delay.
Obviously the postal time must be added and we
cannot eliminate the possibility of an occasional
delay here but your film should take no longer than
7 days door-to-door.

What you get

Superprints giving 30% more picture area than the
old style standard enprint. Print sizes as follows:

Print Size	from 35mm	from 110	from 126
Superprints	$4'' \times 5\frac{3}{4}''$	$4'' \times 5\frac{1}{8}''$	$4'' \times 4''$

All sizes approximate.
All prints are borderless, have round corners and a
sheen surface.

Prices

No developing charge, you only pay for each
successful print:
Superprints   22p each.
This includes VAT at the current rate and applies to
100 ASA film only. Prices apply to UK only. There is
no minimum charge.
We handle colour negative film for prints only and
Superprints can only be made from 35mm, 126 and
110 film which is for C41 process.

If you have any queries 'phone 0734 597332 or
write to: Customer Service, Mills & Boon Reader
Film Service, P.O. Box 180, Reading RG1 3PF.

FREE-an exclusive Anne Mather title, MELTING FIRE

At Mills & Boon we value very highly the opinion of our readers. What <u>you</u> tell us about what you like in romantic reading is important to us.

So if you will tell us which Mills & Boon romance you have most enjoyed reading lately, we will send you a copy of MELTING FIRE by Anne Mather – absolutely FREE.

There are no snags, no hidden charges. It's absolutely FREE.

Just send us your answer to our question, and help us to bring you the best in romantic reading.

CLAIM YOUR FREE BOOK NOW

Simply fill in details below, cut out and post to: Mills & Boon Reader Service, FREEPOST, P.O. Box 236, Croydon, Surrey CR9 9EL.

The Mills & Boon story I have most enjoyed during the past 6 months is:

TITLE _____

AUTHOR_____ BLOCK LETTERS, PLEASE

NAME (Mrs/Miss) _____ EP4

ADDRESS _____

_____

_____ POST CODE _____

Offer restricted to ONE Free Book a year per household. Applies only in U.K. and Eire.
CUT OUT AND POST TODAY – NO STAMP NEEDED

Mills & Boon
the rose of romance